Totally Bou

MW00513237

Wild Flowers
Most Wanted
Heart of the Storm

The Sinclair Seven
Home Run Cowboy

The Sinclair Seven

HOME RUN COWBOY

GEMMA SNOW

Home Run Cowboy
ISBN # 978-1-83943-976-6
©Copyright Gemma Snow 2021
Cover Art by Erin Dameron-Hill ©Copyright May 2021
Interior text design by Claire Siemaszkiewicz
Totally Bound Publishing

HOME RUN COWBOY

Dedication

To the family who shares places worth writing about.

Chapter One

Oh, they were high up now.

Ev had brought Skylar to Open Air Skydiving to get her mind off things, just as she had taken her white-water rafting, dancing and drinking, hiking, and movie binging, but it turned out that *things* had taken Skylar's mind off skydiving and she was very suddenly hit with the realization that she was about to jump out of a plane.

Sweat ran down the cotton shirt pressed to Skylar's back by the bulk of her diving gear and the attached diving instructor. She leaned over to hear what her best friend was saying.

"Of course you miss her." Ev had to shout to be heard over the roar of the small plane's engine and the whirling wind that beat against metal. This wasn't a good idea. Why had she thought it was a good idea? "You know that's okay, right? You're allowed to miss her."

It was just the rush of air coming from the open door that had Skylar's eyes watering behind the plastic goggles they'd been given when they checked into Open Air Skydiving Center just outside of DC earlier that afternoon. Just the air pressure and not the pressure behind her eyes, or anything ridiculous like that.

"I know," Skylar shouted with more conviction than she felt. How was it she could be more than ten thousand feet above the ground and still feel this sense of malaise? "I was just hoping that sunshine and hot men would make me forget about it for a while."

That had been the plan. A jaunt around Greece — exploring the coasts and the beaches, visiting some of the world's most beautiful historic sites, getting tan and drinking local wine until the day she returned to the city — all with the hope that their home wouldn't feel quite so quiet when she got back.

"You know that Callie is totally going to take on the world, right? Don't think of it as your little girl going off to college. Think of it as...as the next step toward her Nobel Peace Prize." Ev raised her voice even more to be heard. She leaned close and put her hand on Skylar's, and goodness if Skylar didn't need the kind of comforting touch Ev brought, even if it was slightly inhibited by the two diving instructors strapped to their backs, diving instructors who were now communicating that their jump point was coming up.

Oh...boy.

"Maybe this isn't such a good idea..." The words were swallowed by the sound of the instructors moving about the cabin of the plane. Then Skylar was *right there*, standing over the world, her stomach somewhere at her feet, and the sweat she had been feeling a moment ago cooling into a panic that made her shiver.

"Are you ready?" her instructor asked, but the words were swallowed up on the wind and he didn't give her a chance to respond before her feet were no longer anchored to the floor of the plane, before *none* of her body was anchored to the plane, but out in the open air, nearly three miles above the ground, a dizzying display of city and farmland and highway spreading out around them like the rug Callie had had in her room when she'd been a child.

Wait until she told Callie...

Callie would think this was the coolest thing Skylar had ever done.

With that thought in mind, Skylar spread her arms and relaxed her body enough to let the wind buoy her. Her heart pounded faster than the whirling plane propeller above them and her mouth was open in an eternal scream. This was terrifying, this was stupid, this was....

Amazing.

Her instructor pulled the cord and the parachute yanked them back, pressing hard against Skylar's body and knocking the air from her chest for a moment. In a moment they were floating above the Virginia farmlands, a million tiny barns and homes and buildings coming into focus as they followed the natural course of the air. This was peace, somehow, in a tumult of chaos. In a whirlwind of everything that had happened these past weeks, she somehow felt at peace miles above the solid ground and wished, fleetingly, stupidly, that she never had to touch down again.

When her feet hit the ground, she stumbled but didn't lose her balance and a rush of adrenaline coursed through her body. She wanted to dance, to swim across a river, to go back to Greece and figure out exactly what she had run away from by coming back from her Mediterranean adventures nearly a week earlier than she had planned and allowing Ev and her partners to toss her into every available adventure within three hours of the city.

As if she could hear her thoughts, Ev touched down a few hundred yards from Skylar, whooping and hollering with the same delight that raced through Skylar's body right now. Soon they were disentangled from their chutes and Skylar was running over to Ev, wrapping her in a hug and swinging her around. Adrenaline made picking up her friend easier than expected and she could almost see how mothers could lift cars off their children in emergencies.

"That was wild!" She was definitely shouting but Ev didn't seem to realize. "Let's go again!" Ev laughed, wrapped her arm around Skylar's waist and half-pulled her to the facility to drop their diving suits off and grab their bags. When they returned to the parking lot, it was to find Ev's partners, Lucas and Quinn, waiting for them against a large black SUV.

Quinn Langston and Lucas Vallejo were Ev's husbands and friends from back when they had trained at Quantico together. It had been nothing more than a momentary blip for Skylar to accustom herself to their relationship. Not only had the three been thick as thieves for a decade and the transition an easy and natural one, but Skylar's own love for Ev went back even further, and she was never going to begrudge her happiness, no matter what form it took.

Ev had been there since the beginning, since Skylar had been pregnant and alone and desperate for a job, any job. Ev had just moved to DC the summer after graduating from Columbia University, before her training at Quantico, and they'd shared night shifts, and morning shifts and lazy afternoon shifts all summer long, sweating their asses off and working their calves to hell in the City Street Diner, across the street from George Washington University Hospital.

It had formed an impenetrable bond between the two of them, two young women trying to make it in a world not designed for them, and though Ev had gone on to save the world from evil at the FBI and Skylar had created her own successful business from the ground up, they had never lost touch.

Ev had been there the day Callie was born, been the one Skylar had put on her emergency forms, the one Skylar had called when the going had gotten really rough. It shouldn't have come as a shock that Ev the grown-up, now in her late thirties and balancing two relationships and an incredibly successful career, would be able to see exactly what was bothering Skylar without skipping a beat. Well, almost everything that was bothering her.

"I've never seen you look more gorgeous in my life," Lucas teased as the two neared the SUV. He was pretty gorgeous himself, all honey words and thick dark hair that Ev had disclosed one drunken night he very much liked pulled. Beside him, Quinn's stoic expression cracked slightly, and he leaned down to kiss Ev before wrapping Skylar in a hug. It felt like having a brother back and some of the adrenaline of their trip through time and space faded slightly.

"Did you enjoy yourself?" he asked. Quinn was the most reserved of the three, and while they'd been waging a war against Skylar's demons since she had returned from Greece early without an explanation, he'd given her the most space to process things, to be herself. She knew he had secrets of his own and appreciated his methods and gentleness as much as she did Lucas' flirtatious humor and Ev's open warmth.

"It was amazing," she said honestly. For five minutes, she'd been able to stop thinking about Callie, about her empty apartment, about the *what if* of what she had run away from in Greece.

"Night's just getting started!" Lucas chimed in, wrapping his arm around Ev's waist and leaning in very, very close. "We have reservations at Little Cuba in" — he made a show of checking his watch — "ten minutes." Little Cuba had the kind of festive atmosphere that was just perfect for a night out after jumping from a plane and Skylar had to appreciate the extent to which her friends were going to help her feel good.

It might help if I explained what the problem is.

Because she hadn't exactly told Ev that it wasn't so much the sense of being lost at sea with Callie in her first year of school on the other coast that had her in a funk. That had been why she'd left for Greece in the first place. But what she had found there...

* * * *

"I wish I knew what I wanted." Skylar knew her voice was a little too smooth and the Cuban ginger cocktails probably wouldn't feel as good coming up as they went down, but in the haze of the downtown DC restaurant, against the backdrop of live Cuban music, golden bistro lights and alcoholic ginger ale, she didn't much care.

"It's not just the skydiving, you know? I went paddle boarding. And I scuba-dived in Crete, which was completely terrifying, by the way." She took a deep breath. "I was hoping a whirlwind trip would make it easier, but I came home early, so I guess that says something."

"I don't know why you're shocked here, Sky," Ev said. She sat up in her chair, then immediately slid back down. "It's been you and Callie against the world since you were younger than she is. And now she's off on her own adventure and you get to decide who you want to be for the first time in nearly twenty years."

Beside them, Lucas raised his beer in a toast, but Skylar just shook her head.

"Don't play behavioral analyst on me," she said, pursing her lips around the straw in her drink. They were starting to tingle, but the knot she'd had in the back of her shoulder didn't ache nearly as much as it had a few minutes ago.

"I'm not," Ev said, her voice gentle and drink-smooth too. "I'm playing friend."

"I know." Skylar leaned back and looked up at the ceiling of the restaurant, which was strung with even more lights. It was technically still late summer, and the patio doors were open, so a fresh night breeze rippled through the air.

"Now, Special Agents, what do I need? Since Greece didn't work, scuba diving didn't work and having a one-night stand didn't work."

That caught everyone's attention.

"Secrets, secrets," Lucas teased from the far side of the table. Even Quinn had one eyebrow quirked in question. "Tell us everything."

"No."

"Yes."

"His name was Adonis…"

"His name definitely was not Adonis, unless you've secretly been the Greek goddess of love the whole time." This from Ev, who was leaning on her elbows way too close.

Skylar furrowed her brow. "Kostos?"

"Are you asking me or telling me?" Ev ate the cherry from whatever sweet drink she had ordered and licked her fingers. "Was he cute?"

"Eh."

"*Eh?*"

Skylar caught Ev's eye and the two of them burst into laughter until Skylar's abs clenched and tears formed at the corners of her eyes.

"No, I mean, he was fine. I think. I haven't done this in a while. I don't think I remember what it's supposed to be like."

"If you don't remember after doing it, he wasn't doing a very good job," Lucas pointed out. "So, you had a bad lay, but that's not necessarily cause to discount having your fun."

"It's not that." Oh, she was truly and deeply drunk now, if she was even considering bringing this up. It wasn't something Skylar had planned to tell anyone...ever. But Ev was married — if in name, only — to two men and Skylar knew that she had her fair share of dirty secrets. Chances were that this was tame compared to whatever she got up to. Plus, the guys had spent the whole week trying to make her feel better just because they were friends. If there was anyone who wouldn't judge...

Yes, sweet girl, down on your knees. Eyes on the ground. So beautiful in your submission.

His name had been Kostas and he had been every bit the gorgeous Greek hero, olive-skinned, dark-haired and muscled built from a life keeping the land. And he had brought to life something Skylar hadn't even known existed, given her a stage to realize desires she'd never, ever explored before.

And it had scared the ever-loving hell out of her.

"Did he hurt you?" Ev's voice was all business now, and it pulled Skylar from memories of golden sands and brilliant blue skies and ties binding her wrists while Kostas had taught her things about herself she hadn't realized she didn't know.

"No, nothing like that," she assured her oldest friend. "He was gentle and handsome and..." She finished her drink. "He dominated me." This was a whisper, so quiet that Skylar wasn't even sure if she was speaking aloud. "And I *liked* it."

There was no judgment on any of their faces, and for that Skylar was incredibly grateful. She had been raking herself over the coals for days, waking up with her thighs slick and memories of decadence racing through her mind. She could have stayed. She knew Kostos would have had her a second night, but she'd been so terrified of what that meant that she'd booked it home — only to be faced with the same, lonely reasons for why she had gone adventuring in the first place.

"As long as you're safe and comfortable," Ev said, after the pause between them stretched out, "you should enjoy whatever brings you pleasure. There's no shame in going after the things you like, Sky."

"But...." She bit her lip, tasting ginger and mint. "People don't...*do* that."

"People definitely do." This from Quinn who, to be totally honest, she had forgotten was sitting beside her. "In fact..." He looked over at Ev who was already pulling her phone from her purse.

Ev reassured her. "In fact...I think I might have an idea as to how we're going to help you find yourself."

"I love that Skylar isn't quite the innocent we all think she is," Lucas said, his voice full of gentle teasing.

"I had a kid at sixteen," she replied, over the rim of her drink. "I'm definitely not *innocent*."

His laugh was rich and rum-soaked. "Just to be safe, you should take another drink first."

Skylar didn't ask why. A happy, hazy glow had settled around her shoulders and the memories of things she had been trying to forget were closer than she had allowed them to get in days, but they didn't seem quite so scary now, not with the knowledge that her best friend didn't think she was totally out of her mind. Several ginger cocktails didn't hurt either.

"There's a place" — Ev started, dropping her voice like the popular kid at a campfire about to tell a scary story — "only the people who know about it know about it…and I'm going to tell you about it."

She held up her phone. It wobbled in her hands and Skylar took it and held it steady. The website looked like an ad for the Wild West, all dark woods and wrangling ropes. There was even a pair of boots with spurs next to the menu.

"What is this?"

"The answer to your problems," Ev said. "The Ranch." She waved her finger with far less dexterity than she might usually. "You want a safe place to figure whatever the hell happened in Greece, The Ranch is it. And it's in Montana, so you won't have to worry about running into anyone you know."

Skylar scrolled the webpage. Then it wasn't like an ad for the Wild West at all, but closer to something she might find on the nights when she had been home alone and looking for something she hadn't ever wanted to put into words. She nearly dropped the phone into her drink.

"I can't… I'm not going…"

Funny, how her voice didn't sound nearly as confident as she expected it to.

"Are you sure?" Ev asked, her voice not unkind. "Because I think it might just be what you need."

Skylar bit her lip, looked back at the phone, then turned it upside down on the table so she couldn't see the screen. There were reasons not to go, she was sure of it.

"Would you rather go home, go back to worrying about Callie and waiting for work to start back up?" Ev pointed out. "Or would you rather go on an adventure — the wildest adventure you've ever taken?"

"This is absurd." It also wasn't her saying no.

"Maybe that means it'll do the trick?"

Ev's face was hopeful and when Skylar turned to Lucas and Quinn, hoping for some reason from the two brilliant FBI agents, Lucas just shrugged.

"My wife has another husband," he said. "Letting go of judgment and other people's perceptions was one of the best things I've ever done." And, because Lucas Vallejo couldn't leave well-enough alone, he waggled one eyebrow. "Plus, you'll have a hell of a time. I know we di — *ooph*."

That had been Ev smacking him in the gut. Beside her, Quinn just chuckled. His voice was low and just for her when he spoke.

"The place checks out," he told her. "If you don't like it, walk away. But if you walk away now, are you going to spend your life regretting that you didn't go?"

For most of her life, Skylar had felt like things were out of her control. She'd been an unwed teenage mother cut off from her family and trying to make it on her own without any help. She'd built her business from the ground up, waited tables, took online classes, always feeling like the rug could be pulled out from under her at any moment. And now, for the first time in what felt like forever, she had money in the bank,

Callie was safely and happily off at school, and Skylar was in control.

"I guess I'm going to Montana." She said it softly at first, but the words felt so right that she repeated them. Her friends smiled, kind, supportive, and Ev wrapped her in a hug.

"I guess that means we're going shopping."

Chapter Two

"The answer's no, Rhylee."

He turned away from her and heaved several two-by-fours into the truck bed to avoid continuing the conversation...until the familiar twinge in his left shoulder reminded him to slow the hell down. It was a twinge that would turn into an ache that would turn into three sleepless nights of pain and discomfort if he wasn't careful, so while he was slower to pick up the next stack, he kept his back firmly turned to his sister.

"Why, Caleb?" She wedged herself between him and the open bed of the truck, forcing Caleb to take a step back. Where she was standing meant he could only lift the next stack of wood if he clocked her on the back of the head — which was a decidedly enticing option at the moment.

For the sake of needing something to do with his hands that wasn't resorting to childhood horseplay, he grabbed the worn kerchief from his back pocket to wipe the sweat from his brow. His fingers tingled for the pain medication that he often carried, but he stilled and, after forcing her to wait it out, turned back to his sister.

"Why do you think?" he asked. "First two guesses don't count."

She sighed and took a step away from the truck, but that only made it easier to pointedly meet his eye.

"The high school needs a coach or they can't offer baseball for the spring semester and you know those kids are relying on the scouts who come out for scholarships. You're the best in the state. And…" She paused for emphasis. "You're restless."

"I'm not restless." He was plenty busy, thank you very much, and he definitely didn't need to take on any more responsibilities, *especially* not coaching the high school baseball team.

"Hey, Donnie, c'mon here a second," Rhylee called.

Caleb could practically hear Donavan Hunts raise his eyebrow from the entrance to the hardwood store several yards away, but then came the sound of boots and the long shadow of one of his oldest friends standing behind him.

"I told you not to call me that," Van said. His voice was rough and irritated, the way it always sounded when Rhylee engaged him in a conversation he didn't want to be engaged in — which was every conversation.

"It's like having my very own New Kid on the Block," she said, sighing dramatically. Caleb didn't point out that, at just twenty-six, Rhylee had never existed in the same world as New Kids on the Block. The last thing he wanted to do was prolong this conversation any more than was strictly necessary. Already her ambush in town had slowed down his and Van's progress with loading the truck, and it was causing an itchy, irritated sensation to crawl down his back.

"Did you want something?" Van asked. Most men would have been cowed by that voice, but Caleb had to give his sister credit—she wasn't most *anything. Well, beside most-pain-in-my-ass.*

"Tell Caleb he's restless," she said. She had an iced coffee drink in her hand and took a deliberately lazy sip, her eyes trained on him.

Van turned his way and Caleb got the sense that the one friend he could rely on to not stir up any more shit was about to stir up more shit. Which was not a great sign.

"You're not sleeping," Van said, instead.

"How do you know?" Going on the defensive usually meant one was guilty, but Caleb was already over this conversation and his irritation with the day was reaching an all-time high.

"Because I'm not sleeping."
And plateauing again.

Caleb wasn't sleeping because of the pain that kept his adrenaline running high all night long, because of the empty space beside him in the bed he had built for two. Van wasn't sleeping because he was haunted by visions of his years abroad, by gunfire and flashbangs and echoing screams he could never shake. It made for a humbling comparison.

"Listen, Caleb, the papers were finalized a year ago. It's over. You can't live your life like nothing has changed." Rhylee wasn't one of the youngest hydrogeologists working in the field because she was an idiot.

"Nothing has changed." Now he was just being an asshole for asshole's sake, which Rhylee only sort of deserved for trying to care about him, but things had been just fine as far as Caleb was concerned. He really didn't need his sister pointing out the obvious flaws in pretending that the woman he had loved since he was eighteen walking off wasn't a problem.

"You took too many foul balls to the head," Rhylee said. She sighed and turned to Van. "The high school needs a new baseball coach and this lugnut doesn't want to entertain the idea." Her voice got all high-pitched and squeaky and she waved her arms around, supposedly in an attempt to imitate him. After a moment, she pursed her lips. "See if you can't talk some sense into him. I have to get back to the lab."

She was gone with one more swish of her dark brown ponytail and a sisterly huff. Caleb tried not to notice the way Van watched her for a beat too long as she headed back toward her car.

He didn't have a moment to think about it, however, because a man in a dark brown suit had stepped out of the café next to the hardware store and was making fast strides toward him, strides Caleb could recognize a ballfield away.

"Caleb Cash, Caleb Cash…" He wasn't alone. A bald man with a camera and a young woman in heels that had no place in a ranching town were at his back, then all three were crowding his space.

"Caleb Cash…" the man just kept repeating his name and Caleb heard Van let out the curse he was thinking. "Kyle Williams, *Chicago Sports Chronicle*. We've been talking to your ex-wife and we want to hear what you have to say about the divorce."

Of course Becca had talked to the paps. She had felt cheated out of a superstar's lifestyle and gotten her kicks—and her kickbacks—by going to whatever paper would listen to her. He'd thought it would have stopped, a year later, as Rhylee had so lovingly pointed out, but the occasional eel would slither in from Los

Angeles or Detroit or New York to find out the dirt on a story that was *none of their damned business.*

"There's nothing to say." He stepped around the man and checked that the wood was secure before shutting the truck bed. Back when he'd had the support of a PR team, he'd learned his favorite turn of phrase. "No comment."

"She implied that something sordid was going on behind the scenes and that's why she filed. Can you speak to that?"

There was *nothing* he wanted to say to Kyle Williams from the *Chicago Sports Chronicle*, except for a handful of words that weren't allowed in church.

"Becca can say whatever she wants," he said, trying to step around the small group. They didn't make it easy, so he turned and took the long way around to the driver's seat.

"Do you feel like less of man now that you have no career and no wife?" Oh, this guy was scum, bottom of the barrel, bloodsucker if he was going after questions that were meant to get a rise out of him like that. But even knowing that to be the case, Caleb felt the gut punch of those words in the pit of his stomach, just as he had when Becca had hurled them at him a year ago. She wouldn't have mentioned *that* to the sleezy journalist in the two-bit suit, he knew. It painted her in a terrible light and Becca knew her best angles, if she knew anything. But the familiar turn of phrase made his stomach sour and took his frustration with the day, with the conversation and with his past to eleven.

"Can I see that?" Caleb indicated to the recorder that Kyle Williams was holding way too close to him. A slimy grin cut the man's face and made him look like a city rodent. Or maybe Caleb was just projecting. Kyle handed over the phone, recording app opened, and

Caleb grinned. Then he pulled back, old twinge be damned, and hurled the phone across the street, to where Sammy, an old golden retriever in a red bandana, dozed outside the café. The phone landed with a satisfying splash in his doggy water bowl.

"On the record," Caleb said, opening the truck door and climbing in, "there's no story here."

Van joined him, then Caleb was starting the engine and backing up. The small crew scattered, but Caleb was sure he heard the cameraman mutter, "Well, he can still throw like hell."

They were halfway back up to Sinclair Ranch and Caleb really thought he was going to get away without a heart to heart, when Van cut the mountain silence with a gentle tone that made Caleb's hackles rise like a dog in a lightning storm.

"Caleb…"

Caleb shook his head "I don't want to talk about it."

Beside him, Van gave a tight nod. "I know. I didn't want to talk about it either until someone found my ass living in my buddy's basement and gambling my savings away." It had been a dark day for both of them, made better only through years of stilted emotional conversations and too much drinking. The other guys were around more than less, but Caleb took point on Sinclair Ranch and when Van had been looking for a distraction from his distractions, keeping the land and farm happy had worked wonders.

"It's not the same thing."

"You don't need to go to war to have demons, man."

Before Caleb could respond to that, could explain how paltry he felt for complaining about an ancient injury and a broken heart compared to a man who had thrown himself into the line of fire for kin and country, he caught sight of a white crossover making its way up the hill ahead of them from the opposite entrance. It must have been the last-minute booking his email had pinged with when he was ringing up at the hardware store.

"I have to check this one in," he said, pulling into the empty parking spot in front of the lodge. "Do you want to come with?"

Van shook his head. "I'll get this wood unloaded."

And avoid human interaction if at all possible, not that Caleb was going to point it out. Van was part of the Sinclair Ranch and of the business, and if he wanted to keep his distance from the visitors for a while, Caleb more than got it. He wasn't about to start pushing the topic — unlike *some* people.

"Also, that real estate firm called again, the one that bought up the deli and the gas station off Third."

Caleb sighed. He could have set his summer calendar by those calls, each one a little more persistent and a little less patient than the last. Their little town of Duchess has been cut up by the company so much already, sliver by sliver, and even if he hadn't had every intention of living and dying by the land, he wouldn't have given them a square foot of soil if his life depended upon it.

"What'd they offer this time?" he asked.

"Another ten percent," Van replied. "Apparently city slickers don't too much like those seven words you can't say on TV."

Caleb grinned despite himself. Van certainly had learned colorful phrases while in his personal hell, and the company trying to buy up their small farming and ranching town deserved to hear at least a few.

"I'm going to ask Gabe what he thinks about all this." He made a mental note. "The whole thing smells like bad fish."

Van agreed with a tight nod. It wasn't the first time they'd discussed the rapid development of their small town, especially as the calls became more frequent, and each occasion had left Caleb with a greater sense of unease. But what else was new?

"Let me know if you need help with the fence later," Caleb added, with one more tilt of his chin, before tossing Van his keys and heading into the main lodge.

The Sinclair Ranch was just over five thousand acres, with ample room for growing both wheat and apples and for successfully breeding cattle, sheep and horses. What wasn't taken up with livestock and barrels of fruit was left for The Ranch.

Caleb had been back home in Duchess, quite literally nursing his wounds, for about six weeks after the injury when the call had come through, when the man he'd learned how to be a man from had passed, and the men he'd considered nothing less than brothers had returned. When the Sinclair Seven, as they had been called that rowdy summer and had taken to calling themselves in the years since, had been informed of Beau's passing — and the subsequent bequeathal of the Sinclair Ranch and its holdings to each of them, split evenly, it had been like walking a decade back in time.

One night, not long after inheriting Beau and Mary's legacy and land, the seven of them had gotten far too drunk and far too honest — and The Ranch had been born. It had been a conversation within a conversation, until seven close friends — friends who hadn't seen each other in nearly a decade — had all come to realize that their lifestyles, their passions and predispositions, the carnal needs that couldn't be denied, weren't all that different. Their slice of Montana needed a safe, discreet place where people like them could find partners and pleasure.

That had been a little more than two years ago, and with his life at a crossroads and his career at an end, Caleb had taken on many of the responsibilities of both the lodge and management of the club. The others came and went, but he was grateful for the challenge and distraction of good, hard work, and the fresh, open air of the mountain provided a sense of peace and belonging that made the Sinclair Ranch home.

Waking up at the ass crack of dawn to sling hay and round up bovine flesh had a hell of a way of keeping a man humble. Becca had done the rest. For a time.

Caleb scrubbed his boots on the scraper before heading in through the back door. The lodge, the main structure around which the entire Sinclair Ranch was situated, was a deeply masculine and all together striking building, with two dozen guest rooms and a large dining room beyond the lobby that served as both a meal space and activity space. Given that Dante had been mostly responsible for the design, with Reese and Gabriel sticking their noses in whenever they could, Caleb could say that. He was brute strength and steer-herding, and the one place he got creative had nothing to do with design.

It was a three-story building, but the main lobby opened up to balconies and rooms above, all carved from rich, locally sourced wood. The decor was simple, plaid blankets actually designed to keep a man warm on a cold winter night, several large fireplaces that could go up against a Montana snowstorm and photographs of the landscape over the years. A large newspaper article of Beau winning a ranch riding contest had been framed and hung on the wall near the front desk, with a small plaque explaining how they had come to inherit his land.

To anyone who didn't know, and that was most people because the Sinclair Seven had set clear cut rules about discretion — once they had all sobered up — the Sinclair Ranch was just that. It was a wilderness destination for city folks who only thought they wanted a real rancher's experience, with beautiful log cabins for rent for those who didn't want to stay in the main building, horseback riding classes and nature hikes. It was luxury and beauty and adventure in an expensive, stylish package, and it brought in an incredible amount of revenue. More than they could have ever expected, given that the lodge's original purpose was to serve as a front for what they were actually using the land for.

Caleb took a wistful look around the lobby, the place that had truly become home to him after the injury that had derailed his career, after the only woman he had ever loved had walked out of his life. Sometimes it was the simple things that got a man through his day, hard work, a good sweat, calloused hands — forget whatever else their meddling sisters and well-intentioned best friends tried to get into their heads. And forget bad journalists who though there was a story in a man's private business.

"Excuse me, I think I'm in the right place."

Caleb turned to the source of the voice, startled by his own wayward thoughts, then startled even more by the woman standing in the doorway. She was tall with a slender build that was highlighted by long, toned legs. She wore a pair of dark jeans and boots that looked like they were made more for an Instagram feed than trekking through a park, let alone the great Montana wilderness. Higher up was a loose cotton tank top that flowed over her waist and a chunky pink sweater that had fallen down over one arm to reveal a deep-golden-tan shoulder.

Not from around here.

Not that it should be any of my interest.

"I can help you at the desk," he said, striding over to meet her by the door. "Can I grab your bags?"

Getting closer was a mistake.

Getting closer meant he had a much better view of her — a heart-shaped face, the curve of a full smile. Her hair was cut short, dark brown with streaks of honey-gold and rich red that something told Caleb didn't come from a bottle.

He clenched his fist, and not for painkillers this time. No, his baser carnal instincts at this moment had nothing to do with pain and everything to do with the way she called to something within him, with the ache in his groin, the drive to pull her soft hair and whisper promises into the curve of her neck while he took her until the roosters crowed.

"It's just the one bag," she said, standing up straight when he approached. The move sent her large aviator sunglasses sliding down from her hair and covering her eyes and she pursed her lips in an endearing combination of annoyance and amusement.

"I've been up since three Eastern time," she said, sliding the glasses back into place on the top of her head. "You'll have to forgive me."

There was nothing to forgive, because when Caleb caught sight of those startling hazel eyes staring back up at him, he realized he was completely and utterly fucked.

Rhylee's going to have a field day with this.

As were the guys, not that Caleb ever had any intention of letting them know that he felt like he'd just been struck by fucking lightning.

Her expression changed and he realized he was just standing there, just watching this stranger—their *guest*—in the doorway and not saying a goddamn word.

"Nothing to forgive," he said, and God, he knew his accent came out worse when he was under duress, but this was fucking ridiculous. "Let's get you checked in."

And let's hope she's only here to see the sights.

Caleb had never been a very good liar. But given that he was thankful as hell for the thick wooden desk between him and their new arrival, he had to admit that maybe, just maybe, there was a part of himself hoping she was here for something more than the fresh mountain air. Well, he wasn't going to call out his own lies, was he?

"Ms. Wedgeworth?" he asked, busying himself pulling her reservation up on the computer. "You just booked?"

For whatever reason, that seemed to make her blush and damn if the sight of those soft, creamy cheeks turning pink didn't make Caleb's body burn. He tried to remember if there was ever a time when a woman had called to him so instantly, so viscerally, and he came up blank. In fairness, he wasn't entirely sure he could remember his own name right now, given the way she was looking at him.

God, the things I could do to those lips.

Which was nothing. He was not doing anything to those lips or to any other part of her. His friends, his sister, they knew that Becca had walked out and taken Caleb's boot-stomped heart with her, but they didn't know the things she had said when she'd left, didn't know the extent of the damage her betrayal and pinpointed words had left in her wake—and he had no intention of ever telling them.

Just like he had no intention of doing anything to Ms. Skylar — fucking *Skylar*, the name was as beautiful and soft and sweet as she was — Wedgeworth.

"It was an impulsive trip," she said with a smile that held a hint of mischief. "And a friend's prodding."

Caleb knew all too well what good-intentioned friends' proddings could lead to and he allowed himself a small smile.

"Well, we're happy to have you." He finished her reservation and was about to breathe a sigh of relief that she really was out in Duchess for the view, when the second reservation popped up.

His gut clenched, his dick hardened and his mouth went dry all at once.

"Let's head on down to your cabin, Ms. Wedgeworth," he managed, "Then I can give you a tour of The Ranch."

Chapter Three

Skylar hadn't been imagining the way his voice dropped. And she knew she hadn't been imagining those burning looks he was sending her way—or the very irritated ones that seemed to follow. It was almost like this built, bold mountain man was attracted to her and oddly...upset about it?

Skylar, on the other hand, was far from upset. After having booked her stay right there in Little Cuba, Skylar had felt a weight lift off her shoulders. Oh, she was nervous, sure. A woman didn't head west with goals of realizing—*disproving*—her dark sexual desires without questioning her sanity just a little bit. But Ev and her husbands had been so unruffled by the conversation about her night of pleasure—beyond checking to make sure that Skylar was okay—that it had made her feel...normal about the whole thing.

As if there were anything normal about wanting to find the perfect balance of pain and pleasure to put her right over the edge, or to submit herself fully and totally to another person like she hadn't spent years trying to build herself into the capable, independent woman she was. Having three of the smartest and most successful people she knew — and three people who were far from conventional themselves — tell her that wanting something beyond the conventional and staid was *okay* had gone a long way, and meant that by the time she had arrived at the Sinclair Ranch, Skylar had been ready, willing to see what The Ranch held for her.

The Ranch.

She wondered if Mr. Moody Cowboy with the fine-looking behind was on the menu. Because even the way he had said it — '*Then I can give you a tour of The Ranch*' — had a visceral part of her body responding, her nipples tightening and her inner thighs clenching. It made her uncomfortable and a little bothered, and not the least because she had taken to wearing thin, lacy bralettes without wire, and they did little when it came to concealing peaked nipples. She tugged the sweater around her front and smiled at the cowboy.

"Call me Skylar," she said, hoping she didn't sound overenthusiastic.

What's the politeness protocol for a sex club?

A question she should have Googled on the way over. The first flight to Denver, where she'd had a four-hour layover, had been the perfect opportunity to nap the rest of her alcohol off, but where she would have splurged on the in-flight internet on the second flight to Montana, she had been seated next to a sweet little old lady who had taken out her knitting bag and shown Skylar photos of her grandbabies. Googling etiquette for getting fucked by strangers hadn't seemed…*right* given the circumstances.

"Skylar." Cowboy stuck out his hand and she reached out her own, intending to give him a hearty shake. She hadn't counted on the feeling of his rough, calloused hand in her own, the way his touch had her wanting for something she wasn't sure she was allowed to want. It was clear that there was a powerful control below the surface, that he could follow up on everything she saw in his eyes and so much more, all with the tip of his hat. This man didn't just look the part of the cowboy, with well-loved denim jeans and a flannel shirt that hung over a form-fitted white tee, as if all of it had been molded to his body.

I think I'd like to be molded to his body.

She had thought the cowboy hat was for effect, but something told Skylar that this Montana man was the real deal.

"Caleb," he replied. "Caleb Cash. It's nice to meet you, Skylar."

Nice wasn't exactly the word Skylar would have used. Hell, she wasn't entirely sure she even knew the words for how this stranger made her feel. Maybe it was just the place. The rustic decor, the knowledge that somewhere, behind the photos of bald eagles and lucky horseshoes nailed to fresh wood, there was a hidden haven for the things she had found herself desiring.

Yup, blame it on the place.

"Where are you coming from?" Caleb asked. He came around to her side of the desk and picked up the suitcase she'd had to pay overweight fees for like it weighed nothing more than the folder of check-in information he had handed over. "Your cabin's this way."

Skylar followed him and did *not* check out his backside in those worn jeans, thank you very much. "DC," she replied, stepping back out into the fresh fall air and taking in, far more than she had upon first arriving, the incredible sights around her. There was a reason Ev loved Montana so much, and Skylar didn't think it only had to do with finding the loves of her life.

Or, apparently, their favorite sex club. Lucas Vallejo wasn't a very subtle man.

"DC." Caleb tilted his head and she caught a glimpse of dark green eyes. Those eyes held secrets, power and control and she found herself wanting to know more. "You're a long way from home."

Skylar grinned. She was, wasn't she?

"I'm looking for adventure," she replied. "And from what I've heard, Montana is full of wild things."

Caleb stopped walking and turned to face her, and Skylar definitely wasn't imagining that shard of desire in his eyes then, the way his dark, full lips parted in promise, how his muscled body clenched tight, as if in restraint. He was the man they pulled in to win the game, the wolf who ran the pack. She didn't know him from Adam, but it was there in the way he held himself, in the way he wanted to instinctually care for her, in the way his expression asked questions of her she'd never thought she'd want to answer.

"You heard right," he replied, carrying on as though she hadn't caught him in some sort of moment. "We've got bison, wild horses, a lot of big cats. We get raptors out this way too, mostly owls, but eagles, hawks." The way he spoke of the wildlife, Skylar didn't get the impression that he was only trying to change the subject, but also that he was genuinely interested, excited by the world around them. It was catching.

"What's the best part?" she asked. "Of living out in this natural splendor?"

Caleb chuckled, a sound as rough as the sea, and slowed down his walk, taking them off the main path and allowing her to walk beside him.

"It's a secret," he said, his voice more teasing than it had been. Skylar flushed, hopeful he couldn't see it from under the brim of that dang hat.

"It doesn't have to be a secret from me," she countered.

"Oh, I think it does," he replied. "For now, at least." He placed the suitcase down. "We're here."

Skylar had been so caught up in the way his voice had changed, how the *for now* felt more like a *if you're good*, how it had resonated deep in her bones and made her *want* to be good — like that made any sense — that she hadn't taken in her surroundings until that moment.

The cabin was tucked off to the side of the main path. While it had decent visibility to the main lodge and several buildings off in the distance in the other direction, and the path was lined with lights at regular intervals that she assumed turned on after dark, it was deeply private, a hidden spot on the mountainside that felt like her own.

Caleb pulled out the key and unlocked the door, then motioned for her to go inside.

"The internet isn't great out here," he admitted, "but there is a password in the folder I gave you. Movies under the television and extra blankets in that big chest over there." He indicated across the room and Skylar nodded. The cabin was beautifully furnished, a smaller version of the main lodge, with a fireplace in the center of the living room and a cozy rustic vibe around the whole place that had Skylar wondering if she was ever going to go back to her apartment in the center of metropolitana.

"The red folder has disclosures, questionnaires and rules." He didn't need to explain what for. Limited though her knowledge was, Skylar had read through The Ranch website and knew they were thorough. "You marked on your entrance information that you're a beginner. We ask that you familiarize yourself with the welcome packet at your earliest convenience." It didn't sound like Caleb was asking her at all.

A shiver ran down her spine and Skylar clenched the wood of the doorjamb to keep from showing just how much his powerful presence was affecting her.

"That won't be a problem," she said, managing to almost sound distracted as she disentangled herself from the door wandered through the cabin. It wasn't overly large, a spacious bedroom and the living room with a small kitchenette area off to the side, a bathroom with a skylight and a back porch. She opened the back door and turned back to Caleb.

"Is that a hot tub?"

He tilted his head. "It might be."

"For starlit hot tubbing?"

By myself, of course. Of course.

"If that's your idea of a good time."

Skylar had the sense that this cowboy of few words had other ideas for a good time—ideas she found herself quite interested in.

"And what's your idea of a good time, Mr. Cash?"

Oh goodness, all this Montana air had made her *bold.*

Skylar was woman enough to admit that she liked it, liked releasing the hold on herself she had apparently been keeping close and tight for her entire life.

Caleb the Cowboy raised his hat and she was able to look deeply into those bright green eyes for the first time since arriving. Goodness, it should have been illegal for a man to have such lush lashes, and the humor, the intrigue that she found looking back at her... Damn if it didn't make something in Skylar's belly flip.

"Are you sure you want to know?" he asked. A large pillar supported the back porch and Caleb leaned against it and crossed his ankles, looking for all the world like a good old boy back from the farm. It was the expression in his eyes that told Skylar differently, the way he looked at her with a kind of familiar heat— one all too similar to what she had experienced in Greece.

Except that while Caleb might be able to give her what Kostos had given her, a place to explore what she wanted, what she found herself *needing* with no question or judgement, but he would do it in his own way. A way that intrigued her more by the moment.

She stepped closer to him, bolder than she'd been in years, and caught his scent on the fresh mountain air, well-loved flannel, earth and dirt, leather. *Male.*

"More than I should," she admitted. "But I get the sense you're not going to tell me."

Caleb offered her up a dangerous grin.

"I don't think I am," he said, drawled, *drawled*, then, devil take the hot cowboy, he winked at her. "But I might just show you."

This was moving fast, faster than Skylar had expected it to, and though her body ached for the touch that she knew he would offer her, the feel of those strong calloused hands on her skin, stroking and caressing, her mind was still back in the apartment in DC, back wondering if this was just too much, too far a step outside of her comfort zone, to ever really be her.

Caleb must have sensed some of her trepidation, because his expression changed and his smile transformed into all-polite, all-good-old cowboy, who had no more dirty promises or innuendos hidden in those green eyes. She was running on instinct, but it seemed like the tell of a good Dominant was their ability to read a partner without words.

"You're safe here," he said, his voice quiet and gentle, though no less strong for it, and Skylar had never felt so much like a wild animal in her life. "Whatever it is you're looking for, we'll help you find it—but we'll never, ever push you beyond what you truly want. You do understand that, right?"

Hearing him say so, even without saying the words themselves, calmed her racing heart and allowed her to take a deep breath of the fresh, Montana air. This was a wild adventure—a trip taken at the prodding of friends, but at the end of the day, they were all just people and she was in the company of those who wanted to make sure she was okay, safe, and secure…whatever that meant for her.

"Of course," she managed, wishing for the bold woman of a few moments ago. "Well, I guess I'm still trying to figure out exactly what it is that I'm looking for."

Caleb nodded. "We can help with that too."

Why did she wish he had said *I*?

He pointed to the building in the other direction from the lodge, discreetly tucked away so it could only be seen from the cabin and not the main parking lot.

"There's a gathering at the barn tonight," he said, as nonchalantly as if they were speaking of the coming winter snowstorms. "Just a party—nothing more. I hope to see you there."

Skylar nodded, finding herself grateful for Ev's insistence on a shopping trip.

"Thank you," she said, meaning so much more than for the invitation. Even if she left right now, even if she turned away and never looked back, she would have a better sense of who she was and what she needed than she ever had before.

And watching Caleb, after he welcomed her once more, then took his leave from the small cabin, Skylar admitted, in the privacy of the empty room, under a wide-open sky, that she really didn't want to go anywhere.

Chapter Four

The Ranch is an erotic lifestyle club set in the beautiful foothills of the Flint Creek Mountain Range in Duchess County, Montana. It was founded by seven friends, all of whom have been mentored by and worked as dominant members of the BDSM community for years. We also employ regular independent contractors and individual members are welcome to bring their own dominant and submissive partners to the club as well, according to our guidelines.

In this packet, you will find:

Our agreements and waiver forms
Our list of rules and regulations
Frequently asked questions about the lifestyle
A glossary of common terms
Information on Montana flora and fauna and our non-erotic daily activities and events

Skylar choked on the cup of coffee she was drinking and nearly spit all over the papers spread out on the bed before her. She had managed to get in a short nap after lunch, but knowing that her time zones were all messed up and that she hadn't slept well the night before, she'd decided that caffeine was a good choice for her pre-game party of one. Curious, she flipped to the back of the thick packet and, sure enough, a map of the county with an information key greeted her, along with the regular events and activities of the Sinclair Ranch. Caleb hadn't been kidding when he'd listed the wide variety of flora and fauna for the area. There were more animals in a mile of land here than she'd seen in her entire life spent in DC.

Hmm, I should sign up for that sunrise hike.

She wasn't certain if they had intended to put her at ease with the incongruous national park tidbits and schedule of farm and nature activities, but they had and with that ease, Skylar returned to the beginning of the packet. The waivers were simple and easy to read, highlighting consent and disclosing the risks associated with certain lifestyle options. Next came the questionnaires, which took a little longer, as Skylar found herself blushing and looking away from the page more than should be expected for how far she had already coming in booking her stay here at The Ranch. For most of the kink and lifestyle options, she hedged her bets and allowed herself to mark *open to trying*, though it made her skin hot, and not only in a bad way, to think about what that entailed.

The rules were short but very informative and she read through them twice. There were limits on drinking and subtle ways to indicate one's interests, and she scanned until she found the play that had sent her running home from Greece, tail between her legs. The gist, as she understood it, was that when it came to dominant and submissive relationships, it was the submissive who handed over the power, rather than the Dominant who took it. Certainly, there was more psychology to be explored there, but she felt comfortable with the ways of expressing herself during play — if it ever got that far — and with communicating her needs to her partner.

I hope it's Caleb.

She hadn't stopped thinking about him the whole time she had been reading the pamphlet and when her eyes caught sight of one of the FAQs — *how do I pick the right partner for me* — her mind went to the quietly controlled way he held himself, to the power behind his strong hands, to the promise in his eyes. She was so deep in dangerous thought territory that she nearly screamed when her phone rang on the nightstand. She picked up, expecting Ev, but was surprised to hear another familiar voice instead.

"Mom!"

Skylar jumped out of the bed as if it was on fire and quickly walked into the living room, shutting the door behind her. Callie couldn't see the rules for the *erotic lifestyle club* spread out on the bed, but that was hardly the point.

"Hey, baby," she said, putting all the love and joy she felt for her daughter every single day into the call. It wasn't that she didn't want to hear from Callie, not in the slightest. Caroline had been the light of her life, the brightest part of her universe since the day she had been born. Through each of the tough days — and there had been very many tough days as a young, unwed teen mother taking on the world alone — Callie had made it all worth it. Hearing her daughter's voice on the phone always made Skylar know what she was fighting for, as though she had done her absolute best in the world—all for the person she loved most.

None of that could combat the odd feeling of talking to her daughter right before going out to a party at a club—a party where she didn't quite know what to expect from where she currently stood.

"Is everything okay?"

"Everything's fine!" Callie replied. Behind her, Skylar could hear the sounds of others talking, music pumped up and the chaos of too many women in too small a space. "I just wanted to say hi before we went out tonight."

"Where are you headed?" Skylar tried to keep the judgment and worry from her voice. Callie was eighteen—by the time Skylar had been eighteen, she had been raising a child on her own for years, working full-time as a waitress and trying to ignore the pain in her heart from a family left behind.

Which was why Callie deserved the chance to enjoy her youth, in the way Skylar never had.

"There's a volleyball party tonight," she said. "Nothing crazy, I promise."

From the sound of Callie's voice, the party really was nothing crazy, but Skylar's parental instinct surged to life nonetheless and she had to fight to tamp it down.

"Just promise me you'll be safe," she said. She'd spent the last nearly two decades doing her damnedest to ensure that Callie knew she was loved and supported and would always have a safe place to go back to. That wasn't about to change just because her little girl was at college and living her own life now.

"Of course, Mom!" Callie replied. "Oh, did I tell you I got a ninety-eight on the last chem lab? Professor's way harsh, but the material is so cool." Before Skylar could answer, the call was muffled and she could make out only the tone of voices in conversation.

"Okay, I'm back. What are you doing?"

Skylar looked at the open cosmetic case on the coffee table and the black skirt and rose-adorned top she had hung from a hook on the bathroom door, then out the window up toward the top of the mountain.

"Cozy night in," she said, hating that she had to lie to her daughter, and hating more the idea that this was something she had to figure out before she could be honest. The relationship between mother and daughter was stronger than steel, but there were certain things Skylar needed to learn all on her own.

"New book?" Callie asked.

A glance over to the pile of books peeking out from her suitcase, which Skylar got the distinct impression she probably wasn't going to read.

"Definitely something new," she said with a smile.

"Oh, Kaitlyn's calling me—gotta go." Callie's voice was excited. "Love you, Mom, talk soon!"

And just like that, she was off the line—and probably off to dance the night away at some frat house or other.

There had been a lot of reasons why Skylar's life had turned out the way it had, and certainly not all of them could be blamed on her parents. But when it had been tough for her to let Callie off on her own—the first sleepover, the first movie date with friends, the first time she had driven—Skylar had reminded herself that not having freedom, feeling confined within the walls of her own life, had made her vulnerable, had pushed her far away from the people who were supposed to love and protect her. The people who had ultimately turned their backs on her.

Early on, well before she had any idea of how to raise a child, let alone how to live in the world, Skylar had promised herself that she would never make Callie feel denied or constrained. Sure, she wanted her to be safe — proper sex education had been first and foremost in her mind, as were issues of consent, drinking and driving, sexuality, all of it. She'd covered the bases, then a whole lot more.

But she also trusted her daughter, in the way Richard and Daphne Wedgeworth never had, and for that Skylar could wish Callie a night out with friends and not worry until she heard from her again.

But since she wasn't worrying over Callie, she now had nothing to occupy her mind with or keep the jitters from the night at bay. She wished Ev were here with her, wished she wasn't so nervous to walk up the small mountain path toward the illuminated barn.

Wishing never got you anywhere.

"What are you afraid of, Skylar Wedgeworth?"

The reflection looking back at her in the dark window was gentle and alluring and sweet and sinful and Skylar knew that the real answer had nothing to do with the wild animals of Montana, nothing to do with walking into a room full of strangers, nothing to do with turning around if the scene wasn't right for her.

I'm afraid I'll like it too much.

Unprompted, the image of Caleb Cash came into her mind, broad-shouldered and big, with strong-looking forearms tan under a layer of fine blond hair. His hands were large and he had the look of a man more than capable of using them.

Won't get to see more of the hot cowboy if I stay here all night.

She grabbed her outfit off the hanger and turned on her favorite pump-up music to get ready for the night.

Worse come to worst, I don't like it.

Best come to best, I do.

* * * *

Caleb expected a few funny looks when he strolled into the barn that night dressed to play, not to manage, but he pretended the looks weren't meant for him. His friends, for all they were as big and mean and dominant as he was, gossiped like a bunch of clucking chickens, and he was already one step away from bolting for the privacy of his small cabin up the hill and the quiet of the night.

Except he wasn't used to quiet nights, even now, even all these months after Becca's unceremonious parting, and the sound of crickets and antelope in the brush wasn't loud enough to make up for the companionship of a lifetime.

What he had thought was a lifetime.

He wasn't used to it, but he still preferred the solitude to the knowing expressions that held just a little too much pity. Just because it gave him too much time to think didn't mean he would rather spend his nights around the buddies that knew him too well and saw too much. He could lose himself in documentaries about the greats and a bottle of the nice stuff and he could pretend that things would go back to normal sooner than later.

Normally had gone out the window the moment he had laid eyes on Skylar Wedgeworth.

Which was why he was here, in the low, intimate lighting of a barn night at The Ranch, where couples and Dominants and submissives and everyone in between walked the luxuriously appointed room and spoke in code. From what he had garnered from the others, clubs like theirs were ubiquitous, especially in the big city, and Caleb often wondered if it wouldn't be easier to host such a place in New York City or Los Angeles. As it was, running The Ranch meant discretion, a quiet eye when the sheriff or park ranger or local politician walked through their door.

The ability of their guests to keep secrets was part of the reason The Ranch was so damned successful, even though it had garnered a reputation that was nearly as much legend as truth.

"You're thinking too much." Dante stood behind the bar, his heavily tattooed arms crossed, dark hair curling just above the shoulder. Like Caleb, his home base was in Duchess, and he'd often post up at the bar, happy to lend an ear to the worries of the day.

Despite the silver ring in his lip and the spidering of tattoos from every sleeve and cuff, Dante Caruso attracted sob stories — and had the ability to send needy souls away feeling far better than when they had arrived. That skill tended to come with an uncanny ability to read his friends, which Caleb was never in the mood for and even less so now.

"Who says I'm thinking at all?" he countered. Dante raised a pierced eyebrow.

"You do," he replied. "When you think too much your jaw gets all tight and it looks like you're grinding your teeth. It's your tell."

Caleb shook his head, then took a healthy swallow of the whiskey Dante had placed down before him.

"Remind me never to play poker with you again," he muttered.

"Like I hell I will," Dante replied. "What's up your ass? Are you feeling weird about that pap from this afternoon or is it something else?" *Of course* Van had told Dante about the sleezy reporter. *No secrets among sinners, apparently.*

"It's nothing."

"And I'm the Queen of England," Dante replied. "Tell me or don't, I'll figure it out."

Caleb couldn't help the soft chuckle, and damn even that felt good after so many months of...not moping, thank you very much, Rhylee.

"My sister here tonight?" he asked. Rhylee kept to her side of the club and he kept to his. In two years, it hadn't been a problem and Caleb was normally perfectly at ease with them both living their own best lives, but he wasn't in the mood for her knowing looks or even worse, her worried ones, and he hoped she hadn't come. Likely she'd know about the reporter too, and that was more than he wanted to deal with.

"Van's been in a good mood, so I'm assuming not," Dante replied good-naturedly. "Why, afraid she'd going to Psych 101 you?"

"No more than you're doing," he replied. "And I'm fine. Just wanted to make sure everything went well tonight."

Which was completely and totally unnecessary. They had long perfected the art of their barn parties and he knew Dante and Van could do it with their eyes closed. He knew, because he hadn't actually been to one since before Becca had left and they'd apparently all gone as smooth as whiskey.

"Sure you are," Dante replied. "I'm sure you're here for quality assurance and not the incredibly hot chick who just walked through the door."

Caleb knew Dante was baiting, but that wasn't enough to keep him from turning toward the door.

Toward Skylar.

Caleb knew hot women. He'd spent time with them, women who were tan and lush, women who looked like they had just emerged from a pool in the Caribbean. Becca had been homecoming queen and Miss Montana 2014.

Skylar wasn't hot.

She was something else entirely.

He didn't know if it was the soft, high cut of her hair, the bold dark lipstick on very bitable lips, or the enticing curve of her ass in that tight, *tight* skirt, but she set his entire body on high alert, made him *ache* in ways he hadn't thought possible—and she'd barely walked through the door.

"Poker tell," Dante murmured, his voice not without humor. "Oh look, she's met the sheriff."

Caleb knew that Sheriff Cade Easton from Wolf Creek was happily involved with former FEMA agent turned S&R instructor Hollie Callihan, along with her other partner and Fire Chief Sawyer Matthews. He knew this, in the way one knew the sky was blue and the harvest came in late summer, and he knew that those two men had no intention of doing anything to jeopardize their relationship with Hollie, who was as smart and adventurous as she was pretty.

But seeing Easton make room for her to take a plate from the food table, seeing him offer that handsome, easy grin, gave Caleb all the proof he needed that his *tell* was definitely rough on the canines.

"I know you're not exactly the sharing-our-feelings type," Dante said, and there was no denying his enjoyment in this unfolding of events, "but you are allowed to move on, Caleb. You don't have to be miserable forever. It ages a person."

Dante had demons of his own, Caleb knew that as well as anyone, and though he wouldn't say it out loud, would probably never say it out loud, he was grateful—for the poking and prodding of his friends, even Rhylee's nosiness. It meant they cared, and he knew that not everyone had those kinds of people in their lives—people who stuck by his side when he was a year into the part of gruff, grunting asshole, and far longer of wondering exactly what to do next.

"Go talk to her," Dante urged. "She's been looking around since she walked in and I think that means she's looking for you."

Caleb didn't like the way those words made his chest get hot and tight, so he didn't respond, merely threw back the rest of his whiskey and watched Skylar Wedgeworth.

He hadn't ever really thought he'd be back here, back to this lifestyle and the room that held so many damning memories for him. But one look at her wide smile and the dimples in her soft, sweet skin, and Caleb knew he had been lying to himself for months. Coming back wasn't a matter of getting over the memories. It was a matter of finding the person who made him want to walk through the door—and he was pretty sure he just had.

Chapter Five

"Quinn Langston." The blonde woman perched on a high cocktail chair before Skylar tapped her chin and pursed her lips. "How do I know that name?"

She had introduced herself as Hollie, a Search and Rescue instructor from the town of Wolf Creek about an hour's drive away. Since Skylar had heard the story of Ev, Lucas and Quinn's come-to-Jesus on several occasions, she was quick to ask if the other woman had ever met them in passing.

"Quinn's in the FBI," Skylar offered. "Along with Ev and Lucas."

Hollie's eyes widened.

"Of course they are!" she said. She was strikingly beautiful, in that girl-next-door way that Skylar had been, up until this point, certain no girl-next-door had ever looked like. She wore a dark red and blue flannel shirt, tucked into very short high-waisted jeans that exposed seemingly miles of long, tan skin. Somehow all at once, Skylar had felt both overdressed and very short, though she hadn't been short since grade school.

Hollie, thankfully, had taken one look at her and decided that a mentorship was in order, which was how Skylar had come to be at her cocktail table, and introduced to both the Wolf Creek Sheriff Cade Easton and the Wolf Creek Fire Chief Sawyer Matthews.

"You're going to have to meet Lily," Hollie continued. "Her husbands run the camp where I work since these two tied me down." She winked at Cade and to Skylar's surprise, Cade Easton leaned over and caught Hollie's wrist in his hand.

"Keep teasing and you'll be tied down for good by the end of the night."

Hollie appeared used to this behavior and just clicked her tongue. "Promises, promises," she said with a staggeringly beautiful smile. "As I was saying, Lily and Maddy, they own the Triple Diamond Ranch in Wolf Creek, that's where your friend got…well, got shot, right?"

It had been a horrible day, when Skylar had gotten the call about the incident at Ev's friend's wedding, and she and Callie had threatened to fly out to Montana on the next available plane. But it had also been the day when Lucas and Quinn had promised themselves to her, their lives to her, and Skylar knew Ev would never change that.

"Is Lily here tonight?" she asked. "Ev would be so jealous — she says she owes everything to Lily Hollis."

Hollie shook her head. "The guys are out on a rescue and Lily's wrapping up things for the fall season. She's a park ranger in the Black Reef Mountains, if Ev didn't tell you."

"She did," Skylar replied. This was…easier than she had expected. Finding mutual friends with some of the beautiful strangers that had been filing into the barn had taken the sting out of the worry she felt. Hollie Callihan seemed normal as any of them, except that she was in a *lifestyle* club with her two husbands. If a FEMA-agent turned S&R expert could do it, FBI agents, park rangers, police officers and firefighters too, why couldn't she?

But even as the conversation with Hollie and the two men flowed and ebbed, Skylar could feel his presence from across the room. She hadn't walked into the barn thinking of Caleb Cash, or so she told herself. It actually was a barn, not that Skylar should have been surprised by that, but from the size of the structure and what she knew went on behind closed doors, they were only in the front room of a much larger building. Strings of sparkling lights and gauzy fabric had been strung from the beams that crossed the roof and gave the room the look of a rustic Pinterest-inspired wedding, rather than something raunchy or untoward.

To one side, there was a large, permanent bar structure and tables of hors d'oeuvres and desserts lined the room. It was, on the whole, a comfortable place, not overly masculine or too bright, not like the dance clubs she'd visited with Ev a few times, only to realize she was far too old to go to.

But it wasn't the decor that had her attention now, not the cozy firepits that lined the barn's entrance or the sweet champagne she had been handed when she walked through the door. No, the only thing on her mind right now was the far-too-handsome cowboy leaning against the bar, looking like he wanted to eat her up from all the way across the room and like he wasn't all that happy about it.

"Skylar?"

Skylar blinked and looked back over at Hollie who was smiling indulgently at her.

"What?"

"I asked if you were staying onsite," Hollie said. Skyler tore her gaze away from Caleb's large, brooding form and looked up to Hollie. While she hadn't been paying attention, Sawyer and Cade had disappeared.

"Oh." Skylar laughed, the sound a little self-effacing. "Yeah, sorry. I'm from DC and this is sort of an adventure that I dived into with both feet. I didn't mean to get distracted on you."

Hollie followed Skylar's gaze and raised a blonde eyebrow.

"You have good taste in distraction," she said. "And I think Mr. Big Bad Cowboy is coming our way. I'll make myself scarce." She slid down from the seat with the kind of grace Skylar had never possessed and paused close to her ear.

"I know this is a lot to take in," she said quietly. "We have a cabin through the weekend, if you need someone to talk to."

She slipped a card into Skylar hands and went off to go and meet Sawyer and Cade across the room.

Thank God for women who know what they want.

Skylar's life had been about what she needed, what Callie had needed, for so long that she didn't know how to go about finding *want*. Even years after the rocking tides had calmed and she knew that, while there was no guarantee of smooth sailing, the skies ahead looked clear, she still struggled with finding things and paths for herself. It was a far cry from the woman she would have been if she had never had Callie. Not that she would make a different choice for the world.

She slipped the card into her clutch next to the waivers she'd signed and made a mental note to tell Ev she had met Hollie Callihan, when the sparkling fairy lights above her head were blocked out by the arrival of a very tall, very broad man.

"Ms. Wedgeworth."

How had she forgotten the timber of his voice, the low growl that made her want to slip her soaked panties down under her skirt and climb onto his lap. Had she been wearing panties. Until her jaunt to Greece, that would have probably been the most insane thing she'd ever thought, let along considered actually doing, but time spent with Kostos had changed her — it had brought her here.

"Skylar, please," she replied on a laugh. "Unless you'd prefer Mr. Cash."

He shook his head. "Can I get you something to drink?" he asked. "We want all our guests to feel welcome here at The Ranch."

"I'll follow you to the bar," she replied. "And you can give me a tour of the space."

He smiled with his eyes and Skylar suddenly felt like it was the most important thing in the world that he smiled for her — in full.

"It's a deal." He held out a hand to help her down from the high chair, and damn if even the simple contact of their fingertips brushing didn't put her whole body on high alert.

Should have worn a bra…

Her small breasts had never really posed a problem before, but the lace body suit had strappy, thin shoulders and she hadn't wanted to ruin the line of the outfit. Given how her nipples hardened into tight points at his nearness, Skylar assumed it was only a matter of time before Caleb Cash got an idea of just how much he affected her.

"We built this place about two years ago," he said. "If you'd believe it, the structure is about three times the size of this room."

She did, and she found herself wondering exactly what was in those other rooms.

"Wait, you built it?" she asked. She could manage an IKEA bookshelf, but she'd never exactly chopped down lumber for a cabin in the woods.

"I helped." He shrugged, as if it were the simplest thing in the world to build a massive barn structure on a mountain. Her mind was flooded with images of him in a pair of worn jeans and boots, the utility belt on his hip, cowboy hat on his head and the sweet summer sun making his bare arms and chest shimmer with sweat.

"I think the biggest thing I ever built was Callie's rocket ship bed," she said without thinking. They neared the bar and she caught sight of the curiosity in his eyes. "You can ask," she said. "You don't strike me as the gossiping type. And it's not hardly a secret."

"Let me guess," he replied. He ordered them drinks from the heavily tattooed and darkly hot man behind the bar and turned back to face her. "Callie is a cat...no, dog."

Skylar raised an eyebrow, unable to keep the smile from forming on her face.

"One more guess," she replied.

"And if I get it wrong?"

"You come stargaze in my hot tub with me tonight."

What in the fuc — hell — no, fuck? What in the fuck, Skylar?

Oh boy. That was something that the old Skylar would never have even considered, let alone said out loud. She winced and turned away from Caleb to look out at the room at large, but he reached out and with two strong fingers under her chin, guided her back to face him.

"That doesn't sound like a punishment," he said, and had she thought his voice was low before, because now it sounded just like honey, honey and whiskey, and her skin burned hot for his touch.

"That was inappropriate." She tried to pull back, but he held her tightly in place — not so tightly that she couldn't move if she really wanted to, but tightly enough that it sent a message — a message her body was happily responding to as if it were still the slick summer night in Greece. Much as she was trying to deny it to herself, she craved the power behind even the simplest hold, and she knew this man could offer it to her.

"Yes," he replied, holding her gaze and stroking one strong finger down the curve of her neck. Skylar made a concerted effort not to gulp audibly. "But what's wrong with that?"

The room around them disappeared, the sounds of chatting and soft music silenced, no more boots on hardwood floors or glasses on tabletops, just her and Caleb Cash.

"We just met," she replied, somehow both totally off balance and absolutely where she needed to be at this moment all at once. "I don't know anything about you."

He grinned then, and damn if it wasn't as smolderingly hot and somehow also deeply adorable, comforting and promising of cozy rainy days and a lifetime of protection all at once. Which was absolutely not the reason Skylar had come out to the middle of Montana. She was in search of answers, but not a lifetime of them.

"And you don't know me either."

"If I guess who Callie is," he replied, "does the invitation still stand?"

Skylar nodded. There was no other choice. She wanted him to join her after the soiree, wanted him to spend the night with her, even if it was nothing more than this, intimate conversation with a promise hovering just below the surface.

"She's your daughter," he replied. "And probably the main reason you feel uncomfortable right now."

"I'm not uncomfortable." The protest came out a little squeaky and Skylar knew Caleb had heard it. Before he could reply, however, a tall, broad man in a pair of form-fitting jeans and a black T-shirt that highlighted serious muscles slid up to the bar beside them and ordered a drink from the man keeping the bar. He was objectively hot, just like the bartender, but neither of them made her nearly so aware of her own desire, the ache to be touched, to have her hair pulled and her skin explored quite like the hot cowboy in front of her.

"Good to see you back here," the man said to Caleb. "I was starting to think you'd gone soft."

Caleb made direct eye contact with Skylar as he replied to the man.

"You never have to worry about me going soft." God, that *voice.*

And the implication behind his words, the way he seemed to promise so much while saying so little, that was going home with Skylar whether she decided she wanted to be part of this community or not.

"Van Hunts." The man held his hand out to her. "Welcome to The Ranch."

"Skylar," she replied. "It's a beautiful place."

He smiled, though it didn't quite reach his eyes and she wondered what kind of demons lurked there. His hair was buzzed short and he had the stance of a military man about him, but one never knew for sure.

"Can't beat the Montana mountains," he replied. His voice was too casual and, thanks to Lucas, she knew when flirting was all talk and no follow-through. "If Caleb leaves you high and dry tonight, come find me. I'll give you a tour of the natural beauty." Like now.

So she just laughed, laughed again when a vein throbbed at the base of Caleb's neck. He did want her, that much was clear. Whether he was going to act on it or leave her wanting all night long remained to be seen.

"Next time my sister ropes you into volunteer work, I'm not bailing you out," Caleb said instead. Van just grinned and wandered off and Caleb turned back to meet Skylar gaze.

"You have a sister?" she asked. This man intrigued her, and she found herself wanting to know all there was to know about him. Had he always planned to run a farm, let alone The Ranch lifestyle club? Was that the kind of thing a person set out to do with their lives, or did they just sort of end up there? Skylar knew a thing or two about *ending up there.*

"Rhylee," he replied. "She makes a daily habit of tormenting Van, which is deeply entertaining for the rest of us. What about you?"

A question that should have been innocuous, but even after all these years had the ability to pierce Skylar right in the still-soft spot of her heart. She tried to smile, but it definitely fell flat.

"I have a brother and a sister," she replied. "But we don't talk anymore."

Caleb tilted his head to the side and watched her, and damn if Skylar didn't feel like he could see every one of her memories, the harshest and most beautiful memories that had passed over the years. There, too, she had the sense that he could be the strength she'd had to be for herself for so long.

"I'm assuming that has something to do with Callie," he said after a moment. "Not that it's any of my business."

Skylar pursed her lips. It *wasn't* any of his business. And yet, there was something kind of refreshing about telling a stranger about those ghosts, as if he might hold on to them for her and keep them safe and away from her mind, here in this little hole in Montana.

Give me your control, your worry, your fear. Let me take care of it for you, let me take care of you.

Kostos' accent had been thick and rich, the kind of food she could indulge in but not eat every day. And yet, it had been that foundation that had called to her so deeply, the ability to give someone else her burdens, her control just for a little while.

"It's okay." Her voice was hesitant, but Skylar had never had the luxury of shying away from difficult topics, and to broach this one promised some form of relief. "You're right. Callie is…" She paused, thinking of her beautiful, grown-up girl, living a fresh new life away from home — away from her. "Callie's almost nineteen now."

Mr. Hot Cowboy hadn't seemed like a man easily fazed, but that pulled him up short, and he paused with his glass of whiskey halfway to his lips.

"That would mean..."

"I had her when I was sixteen, yes."

For so many years, Skylar had felt the shame of that. Daphne and Richard Wedgeworth had made certain she would, made certain she walked away knowing that she had brought a cloud over their family's name, and Skylar hadn't known anything else. But as she had gone from silver spoons to the dishwashing line at the City Street Diner, she had learned how to rely on herself, and as Callie had grown into a beautiful powerhouse of a girl, then a teen and now a brilliant young woman, Skylar had been able to shed the shroud of shame. Mostly.

"You must have been a pretty kickass woman to raise her when you were that young," Caleb replied, his voice holding no judgment, only admiration and respect. "Did you have any help?"

Only Ev and the other girls from the diner, a kind landlady. In the beginning, it had been Skylar and Callie against the world, and they had collected their fair share of vagabonds and status-quo buckers trying to make it along the way.

"Not really," Skylar admitted. "But we got by."

"Seems to me like you did more than get by," Caleb replied. "My mama raised us on her own and let me tell you, Rhylee was no easy kid."

At that, Skylar had to laugh. "And I'm sure you were a dream."

He grinned at her, then batted those unfairly long lashes in her direction.

"I was an *angel*, thank you very much."

"And now?"

His expression grew serious, hot and promising, and all the need that had been simmering between them rose to the surface all once. She wasn't imagining this potent connection, not if the promise in his gaze was anything to go by.

"Now, Ms. Skylar Wedgeworth" — He brought his thumb up to her swollen lower lip and brushed it softly — "I'll be whatever you need me to be."

Skylar couldn't help herself. She darted out her tongue and brushed the very tip of his thumb, reveling in the dark hiss Caleb made at the contact.

"Can I ask you something?"

He drew his hand back and nodded, and she knew that he would only go as far as she wanted him to go. The biggest question was going to be figuring out exactly what it was she wanted.

"What did Mr. Hunts mean by 'welcome back'?"

That clearly hadn't been the question that Caleb had been expecting, but he took it in stride.

"You don't want to know that story," he replied. "It's not a nice one."

Skylar pursed her lips and wondered if maybe Caleb Cash needed someone to take care of him too.

"I think I do," she said, and she meant it.

He opened his mouth to speak, but before he could reply further, her phone let out a shrill ring from her clutch. Where she intended to send it to voicemail, Skylar saw Callie's name flash across the screen.

"I have to take this," she told him. "Excuse me." And before she could turn around and ask the handsome cowboy, *again*, if he wanted to join her under the stars, she opened the call and walked away.

* * * *

Caleb walked out of the back door, then turned around and walked right back in. There was no denying that he wanted to go to Skylar's cabin, wanted to see more of her lush, suntan skin exposed under the stars. Hearing about her daughter, getting even the smallest insight into the kind of life she had lived, it hadn't made him less curious. It had made him want to know everything there was to know about her — and it had made him want to take her into one of the back rooms in the barn and teach her exactly what it meant to belong to someone.

She had seemed genuinely curious when Van had mentioned his return to The Ranch's more illicit activities and Caleb, much to his surprise, had found himself wanting to tell her — wanting to tell her even the things he hadn't told his closest friends or his sister. But those things, all that Becca had said to him before he had left, were still raw, still a painful bruise that he didn't want to poke, and something in him knew that if he went to go visit Skylar tonight, there would be a decent amount of poking. At least, if he got his way, there would be.

He sat down at the counter. The cabin was dark. He had been intending to go to her after all, and for a moment, Caleb embraced the dark. He ran his hand over his hair and thought about how he had gotten to this point. Things had gone so right for him for so long. Then they hadn't. He could have a been a star athlete by now, except he wasn't. He could still be married, maybe even expecting children, except he wasn't. Maybe it was because of this life he lived and maybe it was something else entirely, but Becca had always had an uncanny ability to get to his weak spots. For a while she had done that to help him become a better man, to deconstruct his fears and his vulnerabilities, or so he had believed. But in the end, she had exploited it and though Caleb knew better, though he knew she had wrenched some of the wires free in his brain, he couldn't help but wonder if getting to this point, this sense of loneliness and defeat, was somehow all his fault.

"I know you're not sitting in the dark feeling sorry for yourself."

Van turned the lights on and Caleb blinked in the sudden brightness.

"You're not invited," he said. "And no. I was..." Fuck if he could come up with any reason for why he was here, alone, and not with Skylar in a hot tub in the open Montana air.

"She invited you over, didn't she?" Van asked. For a man of few words, Van had a way of picking up on things Caleb really didn't want him picking up on.

He scrubbed his chin and made a mental note to shave the scruff in the morning.

"Yeah," he replied. "She did."

Van opened the fridge and helped himself to a beer then poked around for something to eat.

"Then I have to offer my sincerest condolences," he replied.

Caleb frowned. "For what?"

"For your dick falling off." Van took a long drink from the bottle in his hand and continued. "I'm assuming your dick fell off, right? Because there can't be any other reasonable explanation for why the fuck you're sitting in a dark cabin by yourself when a beautiful woman invited you over to her house."

"It's not that simple."

"Like hell it isn't." Van leaned on the counter and looked Caleb in the eyes. "She's new to this and she's nervous," he said. "I know you picked up on that because you're good at what you do, and I know that part of you wants to walk over there right now and teach her everything you know."

Caleb sighed. He needed less nosy friends.

"But…" Van stood back up and leaned against the far counter. "If you don't want to, I'm sure she wouldn't mind some company from an American hero."

He tried for humor, but there was a hint of desperation in the way he said the world that Caleb filed away for later.

It's not the same thing. A new partner will help you get over her.

"Don't you dare," he said instead. Images of Van and Skylar in her tub under the stars crossed his mind and he knew that he wouldn't let it happen, knew his friend was goading him and that it was working.

"Didn't think so," Van negged. "But, if you want her, you're going to have to put some effort into it, man. Pretty women like that don't like to wait around until our heads come out of our asses."

Caleb had a thought or two about how Van's head was in his ass where a certain pretty woman was concerned, but he stayed quiet about that. Either his old friend would figure it out or he wouldn't.

He stood from the counter.

"Listen," Van said, coming over to put a hand on his shoulder. "I know you don't want to hear it, but if you want to talk about this…" He waved a big hand around and generally indicated Caleb's entire person. "You've got people here to listen. Your sister may be a giant pain in my ass, but she's worried. We are too."

It was a cold day in hell where Van and Rhylee agreed on anything, but Caleb knew it for the support and family love that it was for him. He nodded.

"I'm okay," he said. "Thanks."

With a final nod to Van, he headed out of the back door and in the direction of Skylar's cabin. Perhaps it had been fear keeping him at home, perhaps it had been Becca's words echoing around in his head. Or perhaps it had been the sense that if he went to her tonight, there was no going back.

Ever.

Skylar adjust the messy ponytail on top of her head for the hundred time, then picked up her wine glass and pretended to read. Much as she loved mystery novels—and she *loved* mystery novels, from the cozy-cottage mysteries to the gruesome serial-killer mysteries, she couldn't seem to get her brain to focus for long enough to read more than a single sentence. This current book, *Clue of the Golden Pyramid*, was the latest release in her favorite series featuring a lady detective and her very attractive, well-behaved police officer contact. Part of the attraction was most definitely how Giselle Bedout and Captain Flynn Montgomery kept ending up in enclosed spaces together, but even the unmitigated flirtation wasn't keeping her attention right now.

She wanted the real thing. She wanted Caleb Cash to come up the path and join her under the stars, and she wanted to find out exactly what was hidden in the back rooms of the barn.

Involuntarily, her thighs clenched, and Skylar could almost feel the way his thumb had brushed her lower lip, could hear his harsh intake of breath when she had darted out her tongue to kiss the tip. Shameless as she felt even *thinking* it, Skylar could admit to herself, under this blanket of beautiful stars in the Montana wilderness, that she wanted to kiss more than just the tip of his thumb.

But it had been more than an hour since she had left the party, and though she could see signs of the festivities going on up the hill, she had the sense that Caleb had gone home. Despite the gorgeous good-old-boy exterior, there was a sadness in his eyes that Skylar wanted to soothe. It had nothing to do with mother's instinct and everything to do with the way that she felt about taking care of someone who was also taking care of her.

At the thought of mother's instinct, she sighed. The call from Callie had brought some of the high of the night down. Skylar had been enjoying the party. She had liked getting to know Hollie and learning more about Wolf Creek and the time spent with Caleb had felt like the world around them had disappeared. But Callie's name had flashed across the screen and Skylar's need to be there for her daughter, no matter what, had become the only thing on her mind.

So she'd slipped into the night, aware that the sounds of the party behind her would only raise suspicion, and answered her daughter's call. It had been an accidental dial but when Callie had realized, she'd gotten emotional on the phone and started loudly whispering about how much she loved Skylar and how proud she was to be her daughter. Five seconds into that and Skylar could tell exactly how drunk her sweet little college girl was.

She'd talked with some of Callie's friends and stayed on the phone until they were back safe in their dorm but after all of that, she couldn't bring herself to go back into the party, couldn't bring herself to switch between those two facets of her life so easily, not yet. Maybe not ever.

And yet, part of her had hoped Caleb would come anyway.

She sighed, drank more wine and tried again with Detective Giselle and Captain Flynn when she heard a sound from around the front of the house. Her heart picked up speed and for a moment she remembered the list of all the wild animals that Caleb told her existed around Duchess, big cats, elk and bison, *bears*.

But when the sound came closer and cleared into the bright light of the moon, she knew that this visitor was the wildest one of them all.

Caleb stood in the moonlight, all big and broad and handsome as could be, and Skylar tried not to question the relief that flooded her, relief that had nothing to do with not getting eaten by a bear and everything to do with the fact that he wanted to see her as much as she wanted to see him. Well, there were *some* good ways to get eaten in the dark Montana mountains…

"You came." Her voice sounded breathy and overeager, and though she had been sitting in literal hot water for more than a quarter of an hour, she only now felt her face begin to flush. "I didn't think you were going to."

Caleb walked closer to her and leaned on the edge of the hot tub.

"Neither did I," he said quietly. "But I've got persuasive friends."

"Did Mr. Hunts tell you he was going to visit me instead?" she asked, remembering how the man who had introduced himself as Van Hunts had given her the *look*, clearly with the goal of making Caleb mad.

He chuckled, and she liked the sound immensely.

"Something like that," he admitted. "Told me I shouldn't let our guests get lonely."

Skylar raised a skeptical eyebrow and grinned.

"So you visit all your guests at night, just to make sure they're comfortable." She placed the book aside. "And here I thought I was special."

Caleb's eyes went dark and he took his hat off, hung it on a hook beside her towel, then caught her gaze.

"Oh, honey," he said, his voice full of wild promise, "you are special."

God, what those simple words did to her. She had lived her life on her own terms, made her choices and followed them through and she didn't regret it. But it had been so long, *so* long, since Skylar had ever had anyone take care of her, and there was a promise in his tone, as if he would dedicate himself to making sure she had everything she ever needed. It was a damn heady feeling.

"Are you going to come in?" she asked quietly, and suddenly it really, really mattered that he was on this journey with her. It wasn't just a hot tub or a shared moment of privacy. It was the start of something.

"Are you asking?" he replied. "We're doing this on your terms, Skylar. Whatever you feel comfortable with, whatever you want." And he was definitely *not* talking about the hot tub.

"I'm asking," she said. "And…I know…that I have control here, I mean. It just takes a little getting used to."

"I didn't bring a swimsuit," he replied. "So, jeans on?"

She shook her head. "Jeans off."

That got another chuckle, dark as a summer storm. She would do a lot to make him laugh.

"I just meant… Wet jeans are uncomfortable."

He started on his boots, but she could see the smile playing out on his face.

"Sunshine, around you a lot gets uncomfortable."

Surprisingly, that made her feel better, like she wasn't the only one of the two of them who felt this insane, magnetic pull for something more, like Caleb Cash, the one who was supposed to be the professional between the two of them, wanted her as much as she wanted him.

He stood up and started on the buttons of his flannel, undoing them far too slowly for Skylar's taste. She allowed herself to watch without shame, to take in the powerful curve of his arm, the strength of a man who clearly worked for those muscles and didn't buy them with fancy gyms or protein shakes.

"I like the way you look at me," he said honestly. The words were hot and raw all at the same time and Skylar bit her bottom lip without thinking, an instinctual response, carnal and needy. Her nipples throbbed behind the thin fabric of her swimsuit. "God, you're pretty."

"You're pretty too." Her voice was a little shaky, but he had pulled his plain white T-shirt over his head and now gave it a soft fold before tossing it on top of his pants. He stood there in the moonlight, tight boxer briefs molded to his legs, muscles rippling down his chest, and Skylar wondered if she had died and gone to heaven.

"Scoot over." His words pulled her from her trance and she made room for him in the hot tub, though she wasn't sure there was enough room for him in the wilds of Montana. He took up space, made it hard to breathe, filled her lungs with the scent of pure, wild man.

"Are you nervous?" Caleb's voice was smooth and gentle, a giant of a man who could coax her up or guide her down, no matter what she needed.

Skylar nodded. "A little," she replied honestly.

"Tell me why."

Tell him why. It had been hard enough telling Ev, or rather, repeating it to Ev when she had been sober, and yet, something deep inside her wanted to tell Caleb everything, wanted to tell him about Greece and that night on the beach and all of it.

"You start," she said instead. "I feel like I know you, but we only met today."

He gave a soft chuckle and the sound rippled through her like warm waves on the beach. How was it possible to feel like she knew a person after barely knowing them a day?

"I think that happens when you come to a place like this," he said in response. "The rules of the real world don't really work here, not in the same way."

"You mean The Ranch?" she asked, still playing around with the idea in her head that she had started her week in DC, jumping out of a plane, and found herself here. She wasn't sure which was scarier—or more exciting. "The club?" She motioned up the hill where the rest of the party was taking place.

"I mean the wilderness," he said. "The Ranch is its own thing, and it's quite a thing, but when folks, especially city folks like yourself, come out to the land of big skies, something happens. I think people need to get back to their roots."

"Life is fast-paced," Skylar agreed.

Caleb nodded. "It is. Why is it fast-paced for you?"

She shook her head. "I said you first."

This was simple, easy conversation, and it brought to mind all of the stilted dates and poor pickup lines at the bar, made Skylar remember set-ups and 'oh-have-you-met' moments that resulted in nothing more than shallow conversations about the local weather — hot for fall, yes — or the latest television program — can you believe they killed *her?* This moment, here with Caleb under a blanket of glistening stars, left every one of those conversations behind. He was like a warm hand on her back, guiding and supporting, but allowing her to take her own steps.

"I run Sinclair Ranch," he said. "And The Ranch too, I suppose. I take care of the businesses on the land and the other comes and go. You met two of the guys tonight. Van, and Dante was working the bar."

Skylar thought back to the heavily tattooed man with long black hair and dangerous eyes. He was hot. Van had been hot too. But neither of them made her toes curl and her breath catch in her chest the way the half-naked man in her hot tub did.

She couldn't help herself. She chanced a look at his exposed chest, at the way rivulets of water ran between his muscles, down farther. It was too dark to see exactly what was under those dark briefs, but the fact that he was sitting this close to her in only a thin layer of cotton had Skylar's mind racing.

"Hey, eyes up here, city girl," Caleb teased. "I'm not just a calendar photo."

She blushed but made eye contact with him despite her embarrassment.

"There are seven of you?" she asked.

"You read the welcome packet." He sounded pleased and that sent a jolt of indescribable pride racing through her. "The Sinclair Seven, they called us."

"Not enough for a calendar," she replied. "And who called you that?"

Caleb grinned and leaned back in the tub. He tucked his hands behind his head and looked up to the open sky.

"Everyone did. That's how we met—right here at this ranch, more than ten years ago."

Skylar sat up. "You've been running a"—she lowered her voice to a furtive whisper—"*sex club* since you were sixteen?"

Caleb snorted. "No. First of all, I was eighteen when I first got hired as a hand here. Most of us had just graduated and needed a way to spend the summer. But we didn't start the club until about two years ago. Beau Sinclair left us the Sinclair Ranch—split seven ways. The club came later."

She thought about that, thought about the kind of friendships that lasted through hardship and humor. Ev was one of those friendships, and Skylar valued it more than she could put into words.

"You're lucky you have people like them in your life," she said quietly.

Caleb nodded. "I am." He looked at her and goodness if he didn't have the most discerning gaze. He could practically see right through her.

"What made you sad there?" he asked.

Skylar sighed. "You're good." She shook her head. "I'm okay, it's nothing serious."

Except that she hadn't had an *after graduation* because she hadn't had a graduation, and she certainly hadn't made an inseparable group of friends that would bond together after all those years apart to create a new business and share some of their deepest secrets.

"Did you finish high school?" Caleb asked. There was no judgment in his voice and Skylar had the impression that he was used to people underestimating him because he looked a certain way and spoke a certain way. She could understand the feeling.

"GED," she said with a smile. "And an accelerated bachelor's into my master's online a few years later, but I'm most proud of the GED."

"What do you do, Skylar Wedgeworth?" Caleb asked. "I don't even know."

She grinned. "I'm an art dealer," she said. Even after all these years, even after she had struggled to create her business from the ground up, then realized they weren't just making enough to live, but they were making enough to live really well, Skylar still felt the rush of excitement that her job offered her. She loved it and she knew exactly how lucky she was that she got do something she enjoyed so much every single day. "I specialize in women artists, with an emphasis on crafting and textile specifically, but I've done a little of everything."

Caleb tilted his head and grinned. "I'm not sure where you came from or how it is that you walked into my life, but I feel like you've just changed the course of it."

It was a heavy statement and it should have scared her, should have been the last nail that sent her back to

DC after her adventure out here. It should have—and coming from anyone else, it *would* have. But Skylar couldn't deny, not to herself and not to him, that she felt the same undeniable truth. It didn't matter that they had only met a handful of hours ago. It didn't matter that they'd shared two brief, if powerful conversations. She knew Caleb Cash now, and that changed everything.

"I want you."

"I want you too," he replied. "I've wanted to touch you since the minute you walked through my front door. But we're not doing that. Not tonight."

Skylar pouted. She couldn't remember the last time she had pouted, but *God*, he was sitting right there, hot and wet and covered in moonlight and she wanted to know what he tasted like, how he felt under her fingers.

"You've never done this before." It wasn't a question. "And I think you need time."

That he was making such a decision for her was testament to the fact that they'd already started—and she was letting him.

"I've done it," she insisted. "Once. In Greece. That's kind of why I'm here."

That was exactly why she was here, in this moonlit mountain hot tub with a stranger who wasn't a stranger, hoping he would change his mind and haul her into his lap at any given moment. "I needed to know." She needed to know if the heat and desire that had pooled in her belly when Kostos had given her a command was real or imagined by the light of a Mediterranean moon. She needed to know what the woman who wasn't Skylar the Mom or Skylar the Wedgeworth actually wanted out of life. Was this the missing link, the reason she'd never found the right partner, the person that made her want to throw caution to the wind and beg for things she had never realized she wanted?

"Tell me what you need to know, Skylar." His voice was different. He wasn't the subtle, gentle giant he'd been a moment before, wasn't digging into her past with empathy and understanding. He wasn't asking, either and the reality of that had her sitting up straight in the tub and squirming a little more than she should, given the company.

"I need to know if I want it." Her own voice had changed just then, breathy and soft, like she wasn't quite sure but couldn't quite stop herself.

"What do you want?" Oh God, he was good. They weren't even touching and yet, she could feel the innate need to do exactly as he told her to like a caress across her skin.

"To be told what to do."

That had been the part of it that had hit home. Some women like the line of pain and pleasure, and others simply liked the pain. She could appreciate some of that, or would be able to, if she had ever been given the chance. But it was the submission, the giving over of control and responsibility and choice, that had made her so aroused she could feel her thighs grow damp and her nipples ache. She squirmed, but the wet swimsuit offered little relief and the expression on Caleb's face just made her all the hotter.

"Then stop moving."

She whimpered, fucking *whimpered*. Any doubts that she wanted this were summarily squashed in this moment. Her reaction hadn't been a momentary lapse of judgment on an adventure in Santorini. It had been real, and this was all the proof she needed that she wanted this, craved it like she had never craved anything from a man before.

"See, Skylar, I like telling you exactly what to do. I like the image of you down on your knees begging to suck my cock, waiting until I give you permission. I like that you have to say yes, that your body is aching for me and you want it just as badly as I do."

Kostos had looked like the kind of man who would experiment with hedonistic rituals behind closed doors. He'd had long, dark hair and sinfully pretty eyes and a cat's smile that promised pleasure he had well and truly delivered. Caleb didn't look like that at all. He looked like the poster child for happy, all-American family man. He wore flannel shirts and tipped his hat.

But in this moment, Skylar knew he was exactly the man he promised. The Ranch was as much his domain as the open Montana hills and if she said yes, if she gave her permission over to him, gave him her body, he would more than make her happy she did.

"Now, you're probably thinking that I'm either going to make you do it tonight, pull you into my lap and kiss that pretty smile right off your full pink lips, or that you're going to touch yourself the second I leave this hot tub. I bet you even have a secret little bag hidden in the bottom of your suitcase that you thought you weren't going to use this week."

He leaned over and placed two strong fingers under her jaw.

"Neither of those things is going to happen tonight, Skylar," he said, his voice low but incredibly firm. "I'm going to step out of this tub without touching you the way I really want to, and I promise you that's going to be harder for me than it is for you. Then I'm going to leave. And you're going to go to bed, wanting and aching and unfilled."

"Caleb…" It came out like a moan and he bit his lower lip.

"You are going to taste so sweet, but we're not rushing this. I want you to want it as much as you think you do."

He was guiding her into the submission. Through the haze of lust and the growing ache between her legs, Skylar could see that. He wanted her on the edge, wanted her to be fully committed to what they were going to do, to try, before they got started.

"Do you understand?"

She nodded, not quite trusting herself to speak, for fear of what exactly she was going to say.

"Try again, Skylar," he said. "I know you want to say the word. Go ahead."

It had been on the tip of her tongue, nothing less than a base, natural instinct that screamed out from within her.

"Yes…Sir."

It felt like the most perfect thing she had ever done, like the last piece of a puzzle fitting into place, and she knew this was it. She couldn't walk away, couldn't pretend this had just been a funny chapter in the book of life. She needed it—and she needed it from Caleb.

"So sweet." He rubbed her bottom lip again and the touch was practically explosive. "I'll see you tomorrow, sunshine."

He climbed out of the tub then, and she missed his touch only until she caught sight of the enormous bulge visible through wet briefs. He caught her staring but didn't say a word, undoubtedly part of the luscious torture he was planning to inflict upon her until he felt she was ready.

I'm ready now.

At least, it felt that way. But it was possible, it was probable that he did know better and that was something Skylar was going to have to go along with until he said otherwise.

"Remember, no relief," he told her, tugging on his jeans and sliding into his boots. "And I will know, so don't try to lie to me."

Part of her wanted to lie just to find out what would happen if she did, but another part of her felt the urge to please him far more, a desperate need that rippled throughout her entire body, even now, as he denied her the pleasure she so ached for.

"Sweet dreams," he said. He placed a soft kiss on her forehead, then disappeared into the Montana night.

Chapter Six

Caleb was pretty sure he was the masochist. He didn't have to tease Skylar the night before, didn't have to force her to sit on the edge of her desire and walk away. He could have had her right there in the tub and she would have liked it. Hell, she'd wanted it. But she hadn't wanted it enough and Caleb needed her to be so desperate for him that she couldn't remember her own name.

He'd told her that she wasn't allowed to get off, but the rule hadn't applied to himself and he'd stroked his swollen cock to completion the second he'd stepped into a hot shower after leaving her cabin. Against images of Skylar submitting to him, the desperate, anticipatory, curious look in her eyes — for him — it hadn't done much good. And now he was out on an early morning ride, trying to will his stupid dick down to avoid saddle-induced injury, and failing miserably.

The one thing he could say was he hadn't lost the desire. In the nearly year it had been since Becca had walked out and, if he were being honest with himself, in the months it had been leading up to her walking out, the lifestyle that they catered to here at The Ranch had no longer felt like his own. He'd wondered, when he'd been alone in his bed, if it was the kind of thing a man grew out, wanting something depraved and desperate, wanting a woman so on the edge that she teetered above her own pleasurable destruction at his command.

He'd wondered those things, then he'd wondered how it was that none of his friends seemed willing to walk away from this life, how none of them seemed to feel the growing distance between indulgence and pleasure and who they were. Gabriel and Rafe, they weren't home much, and Bastion had life on the road, Reece was — well, wherever it was Reece spent his time, but when they came back to The Ranch — and they always came back to The Ranch — they walked through the door of the barn like no time had passed, like this was as simple as sitting in a favorite chair or trying on a comfortable, worn pair of Levis.

Then again, none of them had watched the woman they thought they'd love forever turn tail on a life they had built together — and he hoped to God that none of them ever would. Becca hadn't just left him alone in this lifestyle. She'd tainted it for him.

But now, with the sun sleepily blinking pink and orange over distant mountains, Caleb could at least be relieved that he hadn't lost the ache he'd so long accepted as part of who he was. Just as Skylar's desire to submit to him had come from a place of need and base carnal desire, so too did Caleb's need to control, to promise and care for.

So, though he was getting the imprint of his zipper permanently tattooed on his cock at the mere thought that Skylar was somewhere on the property, wet and wanting for him, for everything he had promised her the night before, he could at least rest easy in the knowledge that Becca hadn't taken that part of him with her when she'd left. Not permanently.

Rhylee pulled her horse up beside him. "Heard you had a run-in with the paps."

God save him from meddling little sisters. "Do you guys have a text chat I'm not a part of?"

Rhylee reached into her saddle bag for a thermos of coffee, which she handed over. "Don't tell me you've forgotten how small towns work," she said. "But yes. We gossip about you behind your back."

He shook his head, then drank from the thermos to avoid letting his smile show. There was nothing quite like rich, dark coffee and the morning mountain air to make a man feel like a man. He glanced at his watch. "I was going to ride down to the quarry, but we've got a half-dozen guests signed up for the morning ride. Want to take them with me?"

She nodded and drank from her own thermos, then glanced out to the mountains, streaked with fresh golden light from a sun that had just tipped over the horizon. In his quest to deny that he needed help, that anything might be going wrong his life — when indeed, a whole hell of a lot had gone wrong in his life — Caleb hadn't been paying attention to those around him. At least, not enough. It was possible Rhylee's need to check on him was just her way of pretending she was all right. It wouldn't have been the first time a member of the Cash family kept their emotions to themselves.

"You okay?" he asked. "Aren't you supposed to be at the lab today?"

She turned to him, and damn it, he had missed something going on with her, though the sadness in his sister's eyes was gone so fast that he had to wonder if he had even really seen it.

"Not until this afternoon," she replied. "I'm waiting for some sample results to come back from the lab in Helena and they won't be in for a few hours."

"You didn't answer the question."

"Hm?" She turned back to face him and smiled, a smile that looked real, that probably fooled enough people she thought it would work on him. But while he'd missed that she was even going through something, he'd known Rhylee her entire life, been there through all the pitfalls and all the victories, and he wasn't buying it.

"Fine, but tell me when you're ready."

"You first," she replied. "I know you've been ditching the pain meds, but it still hurts, I can tell. And you haven't been to your PT check-in since…"

Since Becca left.

There were a lot of things he hadn't done since Becca left. He hadn't taken a partner, hadn't embraced the dark, dominant side that had been a constant companion for years, hadn't told any of them what she had said as she had demanded a divorce.

"Point taken," Caleb replied. "I'll lay off. But if you do want to talk."

She gave a curt nod. "I know."

It had always been like that between them, the Cash kids against the world. Even back when they had actually been kids, Caleb had been lucky enough to call his sister a friend.

"I saw the new girl drive up yesterday," she ribbed, turning her horse around to head back to the lodge. "She's pretty."

Caleb only sighed. Sometimes he didn't like his friends that much either. But on this, for reasons he had no intention of sharing with his little sister, he could agree. Skylar Wedgeworth was damn pretty. And she was on his mind.

* * * *

Is there anything sexier than a man on a horse?

Skylar was waiting with the small group of other early morning guests when Caleb and a woman bearing a striking resemblance to him brought their horses ambling into the area near the corral. He wore that same dark cowboy hat and a pair of faded, comfortable-looking jeans that did nothing to hide the powerful muscles of his thighs as he guided his horse toward them.

I'd like him to guide me.

She would *not* feel ashamed for that deeply erotic thought—it was too early in the morning for shame and Caleb Cash, in a fleece-lined flannel jacket, was too damn sexy on the top of his horse for her to feel bad about pointing it out to herself.

"Good morning, folks. My name is Caleb, and this here is my sister, Rhylee. We're going to be taking you on a ride this morning. Is everyone dressed warmly enough?"

Skylar glanced down at her own outfit—snug jeans, a warm flannel and a fleece vest on top. According to the pamphlets—not *those* pamphlets—this time of year Duchess would be cold in the morning, warm mid-day and cold again at night. Given that her body had been hot with wanting the night before, she was going to have to take their word for it.

She glanced up at Caleb, hoping, against her better judgment that last night had been some kind of fluke, that maybe her body had been running on adrenaline or...hell, she didn't know. It wasn't like she could blame jet lag for making her body ache and for making her mouth say words she'd never even thought of before.

But the truth was she had tossed and turned for most of the night, her nipples achingly hard, the heat between her thighs blooming into something that would ultimately drive her to madness if it wasn't managed properly. One glance at the hot cowboy on the back of a wild beast and Skylar knew he could handle her — again and again and again.

The only question was, how long would he make her wait?

Part of her had wanted to go against his directive the night before, if only because she had needed some goddamned relief so she could get to sleep, but they had only just started their game and if she wasn't able to handle one night of being kept on the edge, she didn't think that would bode well for the rest of her time spent here.

After what had felt like hours, Skylar had eventually fallen to sleep, only to be met with dreams nearly as erotic as what she had to assume went on behind the closed doors of the barn — which had made her even hotter, needier, and more desperate to see Caleb again.

Partially because she knew she wasn't getting back to sleep and partially because she had hoped he'd be the one leading the ride, she'd joined the older couple from upstate New York, Marion and David, newlyweds from Chicago on their honeymoon, Kat and Alice, a lone traveler named Zeke and a father with his son, Alan and Bryce, as they'd met near the stables before the sun had fully risen. These were regular guests, guests who didn't know what on behind the closed doors. Guests that came to the Sinclair Ranch, and not The Ranch.

Skylar felt like she had a secret — one that made her a little giddy. It was odd, this sensation, of keeping something hot and wonderful hidden from the world around her, of passing through a normal morning routine with strangers like she didn't want to open door number two. And yet, she liked it.

Caleb and Rhylee dismounted and, along with the man Caleb had referred to as Dante and who'd mysteriously appeared in the corral, they gathered the horses and saddles everyone needed to get moving.

Finally, he brought one out for her. It was a beautiful Tennessee Walker with a shiny black coat and mane that looked softer than her own hair — which she had actually washed this morning, *thank you very much*.

"You ever ridden before, city girl?" Caleb asked, his voice playful and teasing, but with nothing there to indicate to anyone else that he had been teasing her far more nearly naked in the hot tub under the stars the night before, or that he had instructed her on things no one else would ever know about. It was their secret, the reminder of that potent in the way her nipples tightened and her lips parted in anticipation.

But she didn't want him to know how much he affected her, not here, and certainly not before the second cup of coffee of the morning.

"I've been on the back of a horse, yes," she replied, avoiding the easy, if wildly inappropriate double entendre. Had she ridden before? Not nearly in the way she had wanted to do to him last night, let alone this morning, when he stood there looking scruffy and sexy and all pure muscled mountain man.

"This is Molly." He handed her reins. "Let me help you up."

"Thanks," she replied, and though she wanted to feel his hands around her waist, wanted to lean back into his powerful chest and allow him to help her, it wasn't a great idea. The more she touched him, the harder it would be to stop touching him, and those weren't the rules they were playing by. "But I've got it."

Molly was tall but compared to how tall her own horses had seemed when Skylar had first started riding them, no older than three or four, there was no challenge. Skylar easily slid her foot into the stirrup, gripped the horn and swung her other leg around, the movement as natural to her as taking a breath, ingrained in her bones and blood.

Had life not turned out so very differently, she might have continued on the path of fame that her early dressage shows had brought. But life had turned out differently, and she didn't regret it.

Caleb was looking up at her now, curiosity and interest in those deep green eyes and he gave a slow, promising smile that was for her and her alone.

"You're full of surprises, sunshine," he said, quietly enough for only her to hear. "And I can't wait to discover them."

Skylar damned her tight jeans and wished there were some way to get the relief she needed from those words, but Caleb clearly knew exactly what he was doing to her, teasing and calling to her baser needs, and he was damn good at it. He would probably keep her right on the edge all day long, until she came crawling to his door.

The thought was not as off-putting as she expected it to be and Skylar just sighed, turned her attention to their safety instructions, and began following the small party out of the corral and toward the mountain path.

"It really is beautiful." Marion had come up beside her and pulled Skylar's attention away from all the ways she was planning to torment Caleb back, which was probably for the best, given that she wasn't going to get anywhere thinking like this all day.

"It is," she agreed, and glanced out to the amazing view sprawling before them. There was a reason Montana was known as the land of big sky, and it more than lived up to its name. She thought of sunrises in the city, of how the golden glow would bounce off skyscrapers and the morning dew on cars making their way down busy streets, headed to meetings, to press conferences. She loved DC, but it had never been her plan.

Then again, at sixteen, she'd had a hundred plans, changing every day, fanciful and exuberant in the way of young girls. The reality was the family business, but it had never been her reality.

"It doesn't look like this in DC," she said to the older woman. "I imagine it's pretty easy to get used to."

Marion smiled. Her hair was light, streaked more with silver than gold, and it was pulled into a soft braid she had tucked into her own vest. Despite Skylar's best guess of her being late sixties to early seventies, Marion looked like she belonged out here in the mountains, watching the earth and cultivating herself as much as the crops under the watchful gaze of a Montana sky.

Okay, so that was a little fru-fru even for her, but Skylar couldn't help but wonder if there was some place she looked like she fit. It wasn't Washington. Despite her close friendships there, Washington had been a place she had simply never left. And though she had moved from the gilded cage in Massachusetts Avenue Heights, to a part of the city no one from her former life would ever deign to visit, it was still the only city she had ever known.

"That's why we're out here," Marion said, dropping her voice like she had a secret to share. "David and I are looking for an adventure. The kids are grown now, and we've lived on the east coast for long enough."

The kids are grown now.

Callie wasn't grown. She was still shy of her nineteenth birthday, only a month in living in Berkley and still very much finding herself. But she was no longer in the everyday of Skylar's life, no longer on the morning school run or weekend soccer games or plays and sleepovers and kid-friendly birthday parties. For the last nineteen years, Skylar's life had been about making the best life possible for Callie. And now...

And now she had the overwhelming and terrifying task of making the best life for herself.

One that undoubtedly involved a cowboy who promised one very, very hot ride.

She pushed the thought away, because being horny on the back of a horse with a group of friendly strangers wasn't exactly how she had planned to start her day, and engaged with Marion about her children, then got to know Kat and Alice, who had met while working for Teach For America and were RVing across the country on their honeymoon. The hour passed easily, the sun fully in the sky and the great plains illuminated by the time they reached a ridge with a picnic spot and began to dismount.

"Who wants coffee?" Rhylee's voice was cheerful and she unpacked a saddle bag with several large thermoses, and a breakfast spread of pastries, fruit, bacon, sausages and egg cups. Skylar hadn't realized how hungry she was until the scent of breakfast wafted through the air, and she grabbed a plate and settled down next to the others on a blanket overlooking the mountainside.

"It never gets old."

Skylar turned as Rhylee sat down beside her and nodded toward the bright trees decorating the mountain's edge. It was still September, but the rainbow of fall colors, bold reds, shimmering golds, a bright, bright orange, was magnificent, and once again Skylar felt the pull to Montana, to the wide-open skies and the scent of fresh air.

"Are you from here?" Skylar asked. Rhylee had taken up the rear on their trip up the mountain, chatting with Alan and Bryce, keeping the young boy calm as he learned how to maneuver his horse. She was pretty, not just for the long dark ponytail that hung down her back, and the bright smile, but for the kindness she seemed to show everyone she met. Skylar liked her immensely, felt an aura of warmth and generosity and quiet intelligence, more so now that Rhylee was seated next to her, legs stretched out on the blanket.

She nodded. "Born and raised in Duchess, Montana." There was a note of pride in her voice. She stuck out her hand "Rhylee Cash. I left for school and realized I couldn't stay away. Luckily, I didn't have to."

Skylar thought about that, about what Marion had said of never wanting to look around and realize she'd never left a place. If she left DC, would she go back? Like many choices she'd had in her life, it had been well and truly off the table for years.

"Skylar," she replied, shaking Rhylee's hand. "And that is lucky." She meant it. "What do you do?"

"I'm a hydrogeologist," Rhylee replied, with such ease that it actually made Skylar laugh. She knew more than her fair share of brilliant people. Ev and her husbands were some of the top-performing agents in the FBI, for a start, and she worked with talented artists from around the world. But Rhylee was probably closer to Callie's age than her own and here she was, with what had to be several advanced degrees and a solid job she seemed to love.

"I know." Rhylee let out a small laugh. "People don't expect it."

Skylar joined her. "*Men* don't expect it," she replied. "I'm just impressed. My daughter wants to work in science, but she's not quite sure what that means yet."

"Let me know if I can help," Rhylee offered. "I come from a farming family. It was a bit of a shock to everyone, myself included, when I started working in a lab."

"I'm sure." She laughed. "I might just take you up on that, though I think she has one or two semesters before she has to decide."

That got Rhylee's attention and she narrowed her eyes. "You don't have a daughter in college." She sat up straighter and gave Skylar the once-over. "Nope. No way."

Skylar shrugged. "I know," she said, mirroring Rhylee's earlier words. "People don't expect it."

Rhylee grinned and Skylar knew that, at least for the time she was here, she had a friend in this happy, kind young scientist. And if that made her miss Kennedy, miss having a sister in more than just name, well, she wasn't going to think about it.

"There's too much smiling going on here." Caleb came over to the two of them and settled on an overturned log near the edge of the blanket. "Zeke's making eyes at you, Rhylee. Better go put the poor man out of his misery."

Rhylee raised an eyebrow, split her glance between Caleb and Skylar, and apparently came to a decision, because she stood up.

"Don't be a stranger, Skylar," she said then walked over to where Zeke was, indeed, watching her like a lost puppy.

"Is she going to break his heart?" Skylar asked Caleb, trying not to let the scent of him, the power of his stance and the intense look in those dark green eyes overwhelm her. *Trying and failing.*

"Oh, undoubtedly," he replied. "Rhylee eats men like him for breakfast."

Skylar grinned. "I like her," she said. "She's feisty. And smart."

"She is." Caleb was looking at her with such intensity that she felt it all the way to her belly, a warm glow that made her ache for something she certainly couldn't have here.

"I get the sense that you'd know a thing or two about that," he replied. "And I think she likes you too. Not that I can blame her."

Skylar swallowed and resisted the urge to lick her lips. Instead, she focused on the mountain vista laid out around them. She was so intent on ignoring Caleb's loaded words, that she almost didn't hear what he said next.

"Did you break your promise last night?" he asked. "After I left?"

His voice was low, quiet enough so none of the other guests milling near the picnic table could hear them, but also a timbre that radiated through her body, made her ache and sit up taller in a desperate need to alleviate some of the anticipation burning through her.

"No." Her own voice was shaky. God, how could he have such an enormous impact on her so quickly? It was like she gave over to a part of herself when she was in his presence, something she had been hiding from and ignoring for so long. It was terrifying and wonderful all at the same time.

"No," he repeated. "Did you want to?"

"Yes." It was an easy answer. She had brought the small pouch of toys, thought a hundred times through the night of getting up to get them, of bringing herself the pleasure she so desperately craved. But then she thought of his expression, of what he had asked of her, of how he seemed to know exactly what she needed even more than she did, and she had resisted, hard though it had been.

"Poor sunshine," he murmured. "You must be feeling very frustrated right now."

It should have been ridiculous. Instead, it was hot, achingly, painfully hot, and Skylar simply nodded.

"That's too bad." He stood up and indicated for the others to join them, but not before whispering. "You're just going to have to wait."

Skylar covered up her wanton groan with a cough. She focused on helping with cleanup before climbing back onto Molly and following the trail back down the mountain. Whatever this was, whatever she was doing here, giving over to a strange man with the ability to turn her panties wet with a single spoken promise, she was in far too deep to turn back now.

* * * *

Caleb really considered taking a break and a very cold shower when they got back down the mountain, but a busy ranch didn't run itself. Still, no amount of fixing fencing or shoveling hay was able to distract him from the way she had looked, that damnable expression in Skylar's eyes when he'd asked if she wanted it. She hadn't just wanted it. She'd needed it, him, on the same visceral, undeniable level he had needed her.

He'd taken the small group back to the lodge, grabbed a real breakfast and spent the morning trying to convince himself he wasn't in trouble. But it was no use. By the time lunch rolled around, he could admit, if only to himself, that if Skylar gave him that look again, the one that she had when he'd asked if she'd wanted it, then he was as cooked as a Thanksgiving turkey. He didn't just want her, he craved her like fresh water, like she was the sweetest, most natural thing he had ever tasted.

I haven't even tasted her yet.

But he would. He would do a lot more than taste her.

He joined their guests in the mess hall for lunch and tried to will his traitorous cock down, but it was little use. Thoughts of Skylar had his mind occupied, and he had the feeling they weren't going to go away anytime soon. It was late for lunch, and there were only a few people still milling around the hall, but he caught sight of her from across the room, seated by Rhylee and Dante, and he walked over to the table.

"I thought you had to go back to the lab," he said to his sister, in lieu of greeting. "You can't mooch off us forever."

Rhylee just glared at him. "Consider it retribution for all the torment you put me through over the years."

"Not our Caleb." Dante reached over and tried to grab his cheek and Caleb narrowly avoided him. "He's a saint, an angel."

Across the table, Skylar raised an eyebrow, amusement clear in her expression. If anything, *she* was the angel, full pink lips, a glorious smile, brilliant blue eyes that made him feel special just for being seen by her.

He dug into his chili and flipped Dante the bird.

"You have a job too, one that doesn't involve getting in my hair all damned day. And besides, as least I don't look like a delinquent."

"Shop has to close sometimes. I'm an artist and artists need their rest," Dante countered. "And besides, I never got caught by Old Man MacPherson tipping cows."

"You never got *caught*," Rhylee pointed out. "Didn't mean you didn't do it." She nodded to Skylar. "What kind of trouble did you get up to as a kid? These two enjoyed a few sleepovers in the sheriff's office."

Skylar shrugged, an amused smile on her face. "Well, I had a kid at sixteen, so I really don't know who wins."

Dante spit out his coffee, and Caleb grinned. He liked that she didn't hide herself, liked that she was funny and open and willing to share who she was. Most of who she was. He also liked that he got to be the man who showed her something entirely new.

"You win," Rhylee replied. "Officially the town delinquent."

"Weren't you arrested for stealing Mitch Donaldson's Camaro and joyriding it down I-90?" Van sat beside Caleb. He didn't have any food, just a cup of coffee. "As I recall, they couldn't catch you, so they waited until you ran out of gas."

Fire glinted in his sister's eyes and Caleb watched the sparring match with interest. Ever since Van had returned to Duchess—since Caleb had half-dragged him back to Duchess—he and Rhylee had been at each other, pushing and prodding sore spots like it was the only game in town. Judgment day would come for their tentative friendship, and the rest of them would have to be safe underground when it did.

"How old were you," Van continued, "thirteen?"

"Fourteen," she replied. "I had my learner's license."

Skylar coughed and spit a mouthful of lemonade back into her cup.

"You can drive here at fourteen?"

Caleb furrowed his brow. "Not exactly. But you can take the test and drive at fifteen. What you *can't* do is drive a stolen sixty-seven Camaro at a hundred and ten miles an hour."

Rhylee blew on her fingernails and pretended to look bored.

"Borrowed. And maybe you can't, big brother. I bet Skylar could, though."

Skylar grinned. "It does sound like fun."

"See, they say I'm a bad influence." Dante leaned back in his chair and stroked inked fingers through his long black hair. "But it's always the quiet ones. They look sweet and innocent on the surface…"

Dante's words faded in the distance as Caleb caught Skylar's gaze. She did look sweet and innocent on the surface, did look like a nice farmgirl, in her flannel getup, her soft brown hair tousled around her head. But he knew she wanted more, and he knew that he wasn't about to let anyone else give it to her.

"Come to the barn tonight."

That stopped all conversation at the table, and he felt four pairs on him like he had just claimed to be the last living descendent of Jesus Christ himself.

Caleb wasn't worried about the other guests. The mess hall was empty, all but for one other couple that was staying at The Ranch as well, seated at the far end of the room. It was more that he hadn't exactly planned on sharing his whole decision to start up the lifestyle again, not to his friends and not to Rhylee. Already, he and Rhylee had to walk a fine line surrounding the business and the lifestyle. But he had wanted to explore this new thing on his own before they started trying to figure out what he was going through.

He didn't care. He didn't care about his oldest friend's discerning gaze, or even the hopeful look he was sure was in Rhylee's expression. He didn't care that he'd just outed himself as wanting more from this life than he'd been allowing for too long. None of that mattered—not when he was waiting for Skylar to answer, to promise that she'd come to him, that she'd take this journey with him.

Her cheeks were the softest shade of pink he'd ever seen, and he briefly wondered if the rest of her sweet, lush body matched, but when she looked at him, God, her eyes held fire and heat and a wanton need that he had only truly seen a few times in his life. It made him *burn*.

"Okay."

Her response was low, but firm, and not for the first time since meeting her, he marveled at her strength, at how she was brave enough to respond to the question he'd stupidly asked in front of the others. Dante and Van were as much family to him as Rhy, but it had been blind need for Skylar that had him airing their secrets. And she hadn't batted an eyelash.

"I think Reece said he's getting in today," Dante said loudly. "I'm going to see if he's here."

"I'll help find him." Rhylee and Van were quick to leave the table in Dante's wake. Then it really was just the two of them. Skylar watched him, her dark eyes assessing and curious and oh-so interested. He tried reciting the major league stats for his last years in the game, but no amount of baseball scores could make his dick go down, not when what he wanted — who he wanted — was close enough to reach out and touch.

"I think you embarrassed them," she said with a small smile. Caleb slid over to where Dante had been sitting, close to her, close enough to smell the soft honey scent she used in her hair, to see the flush spreading down her neck, though she tried to maintain a cool, calm demeanor. He could see her though, and he got the startling impression she could see him.

"They don't embarrass easily," he replied.

She cocked her head and watched him for a moment.

"This is because you haven't... been a part of the lifestyle in a while, isn't it?" she asked. "Last night, Van said welcome back, didn't he? Why did you walk away?"

This was not a conversation he wanted to have in the mess hall where anyone could overhear. Hell, this wasn't a conversation he wanted to have *ever*. But where telling his friends had felt like climbing over a twenty-foot-tall fence with barbed wire on the top, telling Skylar was more than a garden gate with an open door that gently welcomed him in.

He sighed. Life had given him its shares of high highs and low lows, but he'd always felt like he could turn to someone—Dante for his humor, Van for a silent drinking companion. Reece would take him away from his troubles and Gabriel would logic him out. Bastion, Rafe, always willing to pick up a call, to talk him off the ledge. All seven of them—such very different men, but always there when he needed support. They'd been there when his dad had died and when his mom had moved to Arizona to live with her sister. They'd been there during the worst weeks of his injury and the world's slowest recovery.

But this was something else entirely.

"Will you tell me tonight?" she asked him, clearly sensing his struggle.

In the warmly lit, comfortable space of the barn, there was room for secrets. Caleb had always believed that.

"Yes." He meant it too. He wanted to know Skylar, wanted to know what else hid behind those beautiful brown eyes, and the curious, crooked smile, and he couldn't ask her to share herself if he wasn't going to share as well.

"Then it's a date," she said. "Now, dressing for the party was challenging enough, but what does one wear to a cowboy-themed sex club?"

Caleb couldn't help the laugh that escaped, and he appreciated her willingness to change the topic.

"You look good in pink," he said, gazing over her entire body. She darted out her tongue, probably an involuntary act, and her breathing got shallow. God, from just a look. She was perfect. "I don't care what you wear over that."

He allowed his words to sink in, allowed himself a single glance at her widening eyes as she took in their meaning, then collected the remaining trays and stood from the table. Then he leaned down to whisper in her ear.

"Enjoy the rest of your day, Ms. Wedgeworth," he said, "because your night is mine."

Chapter Seven

"Why are you freaking out?"

Ev deserved the Friend of the Year award, because she patiently stayed on the video call while Skylar tossed piles of clothing onto the bed and lamented over how each and every one of them were the wrong choice. Of course, it wasn't actually the clothes. It was never actually the clothes.

"I'm not freaking out."

She was definitely freaking out.

"Sky, look at me."

Skylar put down an orange crop top and sighed.

"I'm okay," she said. The truth, even an afternoon tour around the Sinclair Ranch and the dinner time showing of classic Wild West movies hadn't been enough to distract her from the gleam in Caleb's eyes at lunch, from the way he'd told her to wear pink—*and whatever she wanted over it*. He was thinking of her lingerie, of her *in* lingerie, and the thought terrified and excited her in all the best ways.

From the movies and a few books she hadn't been able to put down, she'd assumed that Dominants were more like Dante, like Kostos had been, where sin and seduction laced their every move, darkness that came easily and lent itself to flirtation and need. But Caleb was every bit as dominant in his own way, whispering his directives, giving no quarter on his orders, promising with his powerful gaze, that it would all be worth it.

"Of course you're okay. You've got a super-hot cowboy who wants to take you for a ride," Ev pointed out. "I'm almost jealous."

"I heard that." That sounded like Lucas from somewhere off-screen.

"I said *almost*," Ev turned around to shout. "Listen, Skylar, you clearly want this. You told me you did and you're still there, which means you haven't tucked tail to run yet. Wear something that makes you feel hot and confident. Then go blow Caleb's mind." She muttered something that sounded suspiciously like *and other things.*

Skylar sat down on the bed, her hands full of dresses and silk shirts.

"What if I can't?"

Now there's a sad thought.

For so long, for more of her life than not, she had put Callie and her own survival above all else. When Callie had started go to school and Skylar had been able to continue her online education, she had started to chip away at the helplessness she had felt the day she'd walked away from home, little by little, class by class, each next step toward her career, each celebration, Callie's birthdays and graduations, when she made first string on the violin, when she'd made the varsity volleyball team her junior year.

Her entire life had been wrapped up in Callie's, just the two of them against the world, and while Skylar had dated, had friends outside of other parents from various schools through the years, tonight felt more important than all of those dates combined, and she found herself wondering if maybe seeing Caleb tonight, the strikingly gorgeous cowboy, whose snap shirts bulged at the shoulders and who eyes offered dark, giving promises from under the rim of his genuine Stetson, was a step much, much further forward than merely meeting a man.

Schlocky and cheesy and totally overwhelming as it might be, it felt like the first step toward something that would last.

Maybe even forever.

"Okay, please breathe." And there came the voice her best friend, that sane goddess extraordinaire, walking her right back from the edge. "You turned a little green there. Are you going to pass out?"

Skylar shook her head.

"Look, Sky." Ev wasn't a leading federal profiler for nothing. For better or for worse, her best friend pretty much knew what she was thinking at all times. "I get why this might be a little scary. But there's *nothing* you can't do, okay—especially showing a hot man what's up. You're too much in your own head."

That was pretty much a guarantee.

"Wear the pink lace set we got at Bourdieu's," Ev continued. "And the white dress with your brown boots. It's classy and kind of fits the theme. Plus, he can lift up your skirt, no problem."

Skylar tried to stifle a laugh, but three layers of tulle in front of her mouth didn't help. That was okay, if she didn't laugh, she'd actually be thinking about how Caleb's hands would feel sliding over her back, the strong, intentional movement of him pushing his skirt higher up over her waist until he could see exactly how pink lace looked against her skin.

She'd be thinking about how much she wanted him.

"Pink and white, that's sweet," she replied, but she moved the camera so she could shimmy out of the latest 'not this one' dress and start pulling on the dreamy confection of an outfit that Ev had insisted she buy at the expensive French boutique. Points to her best friend, the lingerie made her feel hot and delectable and all the things that Caleb's gaze made her feel when he looked at her from across the dining room table and promised things without saying a word.

"You're sweet," Ev said, "and a little spicy, but I'm sure he'll find that out soon enough. The point is, does it make you feel good?"

Skylar nodded. It *did* make her feel good. And though she hadn't expected it, hadn't even really wanted it, being here, at The Ranch where hot cowboys were so much more than they seemed, that made her feel good too.

Such was the thought on her mind when she headed up the lit path for the second night in a row, Ev's encouraging words front and center in her mind and a small jangle of nerves in the pit of her belly warring with the glow of anticipation.

Last night had been a get-together, easy, no pressure. Tonight, as she neared the seemingly innocuous barn, lit by the blanket of stars she never saw in DC, Skylar knew that everything was going to change. There was no doubt in her mind that even one hour with Caleb would be one of the most pleasurable turning points of her life.

She stood before the barn door and looked up to the wide expanse of sky above her head. The nerves were there. Of course, they were. She had dived into this new part of her life with both feet, but that didn't mean she was accustomed to trying such wild things all at once. But it was more than that. It was the knowledge that once she walked through those doors, there would be no going back.

And that was okay.

She took a deep breath and walked into the barn.

It looked the same as it had yesterday, as if her whole world wasn't teetering right on the edge, and for that Skylar was grateful. She recognized Hollie and her partners from across the room and gave a small wave, then headed over to the bar. If she was going to do this, she was going to need some liquid courage.

"Do you have any red?" she asked Dante, who was back in his usual spot behind the aged wood bar and looking at her with a very discerning expression on his face. She liked him immensely. He was funny and keen, and seemed to genuinely care about the people around him. Still, even those dark eyes and the promising smile that hid a world of trouble had very little effect when compared to Caleb.

"I do," he replied. "But I think you might want something a little stronger. What's your whiskey?" They had a two-drink limit for the evening for any guests planning to participate with partners, but Skylar's nerves were on full blast and she thought he might be right about that something stronger.

She smiled despite herself. "Dealer's choice," she replied. "Have you seen Caleb tonight?" It wasn't like Dante hadn't been there at lunch when Caleb had been bolder than her, more promising and intense than anything she had ever felt before.

"He came in a few minutes ago," Dante assured her. "I'm sure he'll be out soon enough."

The thought made her nipples tighten behind that expensive pink bra and her thighs clench together involuntarily. Unfamiliar as this whole lifestyle was to her, there was something inherent too, something that went deeper than a life she had been exposed to and straight into the marrow of her bones.

Dante placed a half-full glass of whiskey down in front of her and leaned on the bar. "You have nothing to worry about, sweets. He's going to go nuts when he sees you in that," he said, as if he could read every thought in her mind. "There's something about a beautiful woman in white lace." He kissed the tips of his fingers like a chef and tossed her a teasing grin.

Skylar just laughed and took a sip of her whiskey. It went down smooth, smoother than she had expected, and she was grateful for Dante's forethought. *Liquid courage for the win.*

It was a thought that didn't last long because she sensed Caleb the moment he walked into the room and she turned without conscious volition toward him.

He wore dark jeans that fit those tight, muscled thighs with ease, a comfortable-looking flannel shirt stretched taut across a white tee and that damn cowboy hat, the one that made her think of western heroes and riding…

"Sunshine." He leaned into her space, and damn if she didn't feel every single one of the releases she wasn't allowed to give herself over the last day radiating to the surface, the power of his nearness turning her into a wanton woman. "Aren't you just the most beautiful woman I've ever seen."

She resisted the urge to stand up and twirl around for him, to put on a display for his intense gaze, a gaze that might just get her off all on its own if she wasn't careful.

"Mr. Cash." It wasn't what she wanted to call him, not exactly, but this whole thing was new to her, and there was a big difference between calling him *Sir* in the privacy of the hot tub behind her cabin and in the club where anyone could hear them. Not that there was much of a secret as to why they were here, but the point remained.

"Would you like a tour?" He was giving her all the control, and Skylar was beginning to *believe* that was how all of this worked, rather than just reading it in the packets. He gave the directions, he told her exactly what to do and how to do it, but ultimately, she was the one in control.

"I'd love one." Because she needed to know what was behind those closed doors and because she needed to touch him, needed to feel those strong, workman's hands on her skin like she needed air to breathe. She took a fortifying sip of her whiskey, then accepted Caleb's hand down from the stool. Even that simple touch had her body lighting up and her need blooming into something intense and overwhelming.

"Don't get into too much trouble, kids," Dante called from somewhere behind them, but Skylar barely heard him. She was too focused on following Caleb out of the main entertainment space and through a dark wooden door, into the hidden depths of the barn.

Should have worn looser pants.

He had been hard as a fence post for Skylar Wedgeworth since he'd seen her right here in the barn the night before, but he'd still felt the bulging, rushing heat of his cock thickening when he had caught sight of her from across the room. He loved a woman in lace, and white lace was like waving a red cape in front of a bull. Her dress was simple enough, cinched at the waist for a soft indication of the smooth, slight curves below, but it was the hem, an uneven lace pattern that fell just past mid-thigh that made him hungry. He wanted to flip that dress up over her lower back and caress everything underneath it until she was trembling, begging, desperate for more.

"Welcome to the barn," he said, instead of pushing her up against the closest wall and marring that pretty porcelain skin with beard burn. The hallway off the main room was rustic, decorated in dark wood and images of the Montana mountainside. On the surface, it looked innocuous enough, no whips or chains, no bawdy house boudoir shots.

Skylar seemed to have the same thought.

"It looks like a ranch house," she said. "I guess I've been reading too many romance novels."

Caleb shook his head. "We're just getting started." He pushed open a door to the right, illuminating a large room in a soft glow. This one had a raised dais, with acrobatic loops hanging from rigging in the ceiling. Several plush love seats and comforters formed a semi-circle around the stage, and images flashed before his mind of Skylar lying across the bench in the middle, legs spread wide, pretty pink hole slick and wet and on display for the world to look at—but only his to touch.

"Oh." Her voice was soft, sweet and innocent as that damn white lace, and the sound went straight to his swollen balls. Fuck, he wasn't sure he'd ever wanted a woman as much as he wanted Skylar right now.

"For later," he promised. And it was a promise. He was going to get her on that stage and spread out for him sooner rather than later. "There are others. Come on."

He showed her another room, where the wooden beams that decorated every ranch house were equipped with large metal loops, at four corners, the perfect place to tie delicate wrists and ankles, and one that, at first glance, held much of the same crops, saddles and ropes that one might actually find in a barn. At first glance.

"Tell me what's on your mind," he murmured as he closed that door and guided her down the hall toward their true destination. He pressed a soft hand to her lower back, intent on keeping her interested, careful of spooking her with too much too early on. "What do you think of our little play space?"

He watched her response and was rewarded with the sight of a tight swallow, her parted lips swollen and flushed from where he had to assume she had been biting them. Even her eyes looked dazed and Caleb felt the bone-deep need to put that expression on her face every hour of every day.

"It's beautiful," she replied, and God above, even her voice was husky. Not as husky as it would be after she spent the night screaming his name, but damn if the sound didn't make his balls ache and his cock surge.

"I've got a special room for you," he replied, trying not to let it be obvious that her words affected him, made him *ache*. Because she understood, truly understood. It didn't matter how new she was to all of this, there was something intrinsic in it for her — in a way that after years of practicing hadn't truly been there for Becca.

But she wasn't allowed into this space, nor into the room with Skylar, and so Caleb squashed the thought and slid his hand farther down Skylar's back.

"Would you like to see it?"

She nodded, the perfect combination of hesitant and enthusiastic, and Caleb wondered how the hell he was going to make it through the night. He released her waist only so he could take her hand and walk the few extra feet down the hallway until they came upon the room he was looking for.

His friends had their own needs, their toolboxes, inclinations toward pain and pleasures, toward role play, toward group play, but Caleb's needs were far closer to home. And thus, his favorite room, in the enormous club, with its varied play spaces and tools and toys, was the simplest.

There was a large roaring fire in a fireplace on one side of the room, and a spread of down and flannel blankets before it. Two leather couches, a leather desk, a mini bar, and a bed pushed up to the enormous picture window that looked out over the Montana mountains helped to complete the space. It was the perfect room, but all Caleb could think about right then was getting Skylar on the rug and displayed before him.

"Would you like a drink?" he asked her, after closing and locking the door behind them.

Skylar gave a nod, but it was clear she was taking in the room, settling herself into. He wanted her as comfortable in his domain as possible. She'd be far more willing to give over to everything she wanted, everything she needed, if she felt like she was at home.

"You designed this room, didn't you?" she asked, and accepted the tumbler of whiskey from him.

Caleb nodded. "I have specific tastes," he explained. "This fits them."

Her eyes twinkled, reflected with the golden glow of the fire illuminating the room.

"Will you tell me about them?" she asked. There was a slight tremble to her voice and he knew she was trying to be cool and collected. He wanted her trembling, but not from nerves.

"I will," he replied, bringing one hand up to cup her chin. He slid his thumb down the line of her jaw, watched those beautiful eyes dilate at his touch. "But first, I want to hear about yours."

He indicated the pile of blankets before the fireplace.

"Kneel for me, sunshine," he said. "We're going to play a game."

Chapter Eight

The blankets were soft under her knees, but Skylar wasn't focused on her comfort when she settled into position before the fireplace. All her attention was on the striking man standing before her and the insane effect he was able to have with a single sentence and unspoken promise.

Submission was different. Sure, she'd had her experiences with men in the past, with messy encounters on her knees in a fit of spontaneity. But this felt like it had the night in Greece, like a final piece of her puzzle was falling into place, like she had done this a thousand times before and knew exactly how to sit up straight and press her breasts out and her chin down. She had been doing yoga long enough to know how to correct her own form without thinking about it, and this felt the same, only without years of training.

"God, you're perfect." He sat down in the leather chair nearest to her and crossed one leg over the other knee, a visage of dark, broody cowboy in complete control of himself.

And me.

"Now, I know this whole thing is new," Caleb began. "So, we're going to take it very slow. But if at any point, you want me to pull back or stop, I will."

"Green, yellow, red," she replied. "Keep going, slow down, stop." The information in the welcome packet was seared into her brain.

"That's right, sunshine," he replied. "How are you feeling right now?"

"Green," she said without any hesitation. She wasn't just ready. She was already aching, already desperate for a touch he had been denying to her for two days. Had it really only been one night since they'd shared a hot soak under the stars? Less than a day since he'd teased her on the hike? It seemed like so much more time had passed and her body burned for his promised touch.

"Eager," Caleb groaned. "So pretty and eager." He leaned back in the chair and even in the low lighting of the room, the heat of his gaze warmed her more intensely than the heat from the nearby fire.

"Now, I'm going to ask you some questions," he continued. "And if I think you're telling the truth, then you'll get rewarded. If I think you're holding something back from me, there will be a penalty. Do you understand?"

She didn't trust her own voice, so she simply nodded.

"Skylar."

"Yes," she replied. "I understand."

Caleb's eyes gleamed. "Good girl," he said. It shouldn't have made her wet, shouldn't have turned her body's heat up to eleven to hear such a ridiculous endearment, but hell on earth, it did.

"Here's a simple one," he said. "What do you want to call me?"

Simple my ass.

He leaned forward in the chair, strong forearms braced against muscled thighs, the glint of the whiskey glass in his hands dancing across the room.

"It's right on the tip of your tongue, isn't it, Skylar?" he continued. "Be good for me and answer the question."

Her breathing was tight in her chest and she arched her back and rubbed her legs together, hoping for some desperately needed release.

Caleb's large hand on her thigh stilled the motion.

"No," he said. "Don't move, except to respond to my question. Let's try again—what do you want to call me?"

"Sir." It came out on a breath Skylar couldn't hold back, instinctual and base. "Sir, I... I want to call you *Sir.*"

She couldn't really say how or why she felt that rightness, but there was no other option. Just as she felt the pull to lower her eyes when he spoke to her, to keep her breasts plumped forward and her back arched, she needed to call him *Sir.*

"You do, don't you?" He stroked his thumb across her bottom lip in a rough caress. "You want to give yourself over to me like the pretty little pet you are."

The thought should have snagged, probably would have if she hadn't spent a night in Greece finding out hidden truths about herself.

"Yes," she replied.

"Yes?"

"Yes, Sir."

"Hmm, good." With her gaze lowered, Skylar could make out the growing hardness behind Caleb's jeans, and it pulsed with her words. She wanted to make it do a lot more than that. "You can move now," he replied. "Take the pins out your hair."

She reached up and removed three slender bobby pins that had been holding the left side of her hair in place, then ran her fingers through the loose waves. Caleb held out his hand and she placed the pins in it.

"Next question," he said. "Did you touch yourself last night?"

It was what he had asked her on the mountain top, surrounded by strangers who knew nothing of the secret, dangerous game they were playing.

"No," she replied. "No, Sir."

He nodded, approval in his eyes. "Did you want to?"

"Yes." Shaky and unmoored, she had spent the whole night wondering how he would touch her first. She hadn't expected this prolonged play but the heat between her legs and the pinching pleasure of her swollen nipples were indication enough that her body was on board.

"Tell me, sweet one," he said, his voice husky with desire — desire for her, and hell if that wasn't a heady thought — "how do you touch yourself?"

Skylar's breath caught. How was it that she felt more exposed now, fully clothed save for three missing pins, than in all the times she had ever been with a man?

"I..." She inhaled slowly. "I touch my breasts first," she said, thinking of exactly how she had planned to touch herself the night before, if she hadn't been so intent on making Caleb proud of her restraint. "I take my nipples between my fingers and I pinch them."

"Does it hurt?"

She nodded. "But I like it. Then I cup my breasts together and I squeeze them, stroke my nipples and slide my fingers between them."

This was, with the sole exception of her night in Santorini, the most debauched, exhibitionist, depraved thing she had ever done in her entire life, and Skylar had never liked anything more.

"How does it make you feel?" Caleb's voice was harsh and rich. "Does it make your sweet pussy wet and needy?"

She nodded. "It makes me ache for more."

"For what?"

She looked at the ground and didn't answer for a long moment, embarrassment heating her cheeks until she felt Caleb's large hand under her chin again.

"Tell me, sunshine. I'm asking the question, so I want to know the answer." It was like he was taking away her responsibility, taking away her ownership of the depraved thoughts and giving her a platform to live out her desire without worry or humiliation.

"For my toys," she admitted.

His hand slipped away and she chanced a glance up at him. He was leaning into dark leather, a visage of wild cowboy that had an air of history about it, as though they could have been playing at bandit and brothel owner as easily as this game they had started right here in the modern day.

"Good girl." He repeated the phrase that made her toes curl and enhanced her natural instinct to sit up taller, to do him proud. "Do your earrings come out?"

She nodded. "Most of them."

"Give them to me."

She removed the three studs she had in her left ear and the two she had in her right. The cartilage piercing was something she couldn't take out herself, and the secret one, the one she'd never told anyone about—the one Ev only knew about because of changing room antics—that one was something she looked forward to unveiling to him later. She could already anticipate the dark expression his eyes and the low growl that emanated from his throat when he was on edge.

Speaking of on edge.

"We're going to come back to your toys, but it's time for the next question," Caleb continued. "And remember, I'll know if you're not telling me the truth."

She thought about what he had said, about punishing her for her quiet or deceit, and she had to wonder what kind of punishment he would inflict that wouldn't be more reward.

"What happened in Greece?"

She had mentioned it to him, that memory came back to her through the mounting haze of lust, she had told him in the hot tub that she'd done this sort of thing once. And if there was anyone who would understand, who would get exactly what Kostos had been to her, had awakened within her, it was Caleb Cash.

"I met a man," she said quietly. "On the beach. He took me dancing."

Caleb looked at her with a gaze so discerning that Skylar had the impression he already knew the whole story before she told it, that he specifically wanted her to be the one to tell it.

"Is that all he did?"

She shook her head. "He took me dancing, then…" Then he had taken her to a small bar, with an open courtyard, with moonlight casting a silver haze across fragrant bougainvillea. There had been small canopies and plush floor cushions in rich, lapis lazuli blue, adorned in patterns. From the beds, sheer gossamer silk covers had fluttered in the thick breeze coming in from the sea. The night had been one of visceral sensations, from the moment she had accepted Kostos' strong hand to the moment she'd submitted to a secret desire, heady smells, thick air, flowers as strong as perfume on every caress of the night.

At the moment, she was just as aware of her senses as she had been that night. Her knees rested on sinfully soft blankets, the air rich with the tang of wood and leather and whiskey. The Montana night smelled so different, and yet, it resonated through her with possibility, with anticipation and pinpricks of stars like promises of what might come next.

"Did you submit to him, Skylar?" Caleb asked. "Like you're submitting to me?"

She nodded. "I did." A pause. "Sir."

He chuckled, the sound raw with control and intense in a way she had only ever known from Caleb.

"I will never get tired of hearing that word on your lips," he murmured. "But I confess, I don't know if I have the patience to keep playing this game so slowly."

He leaned back. "My lap just got very cold," he said. "Do you think you could come warm it for me?"

She was up and off the flood in a flash, as desperate for his touch, for his nearness as he seemed to be for her, though Caleb had a far better leash on his control than she did. He spread himself wide, made room for her on those powerful thighs, and Skylar slowly climbed into his lap.

Damn, he smells good.

He smelled like rich earth, like a hard-won whiskey at the end of a long day, like the soft caress of leather against the skin. Skylar squirmed.

Caleb's hands were around her waist in an instant, stilling her movement. It was then that she realized she wasn't sitting on his muscled thigh, as she had originally thought, but was pressed right up against his swollen erection. *Double damn.*

Skylar swallowed.

"Unless you want tonight to be over very fast," Caleb began, "I suggest staying still."

She didn't want to stay still, but she did want his hands to roam across the rest of her body, wanted to feel his touch everywhere, and so she settled and followed his orders. For now.

"Good girl," he whispered into her ear, hot and throaty, the sound vibrating against her skin. "Where were we? Right. You were telling me how much you enjoyed submitting to another man. Is it terrible that turns me on? I do like to watch."

She had never even thought about *watching*, let alone being watched, but damn if the idea of Caleb's heavy gaze on her while she was on her knees before someone else didn't turn on every button and switch Skylar had ever had.

"But I prefer to touch," he continued. "And I prefer to have you screaming my name over anyone else's. Do I make myself clear?"

"*God,* yes."

"Good." He nipped at her earlobe and it was going to be a miracle of the highest order if she managed to sit still for much longer. "Now, I want to know exactly what it is that makes you scream. Is it my fingers sliding up your leg?"

He followed the question with the action itself and even the softest touch against her shin, nothing more than a passing whisper, was enough to set her skin on fire.

"*Yes.*"

"Only that?" When he bent down to kiss her neck this time, he scraped his teeth along the sensitive skin of her collarbone and bit. Skylar clenched the arm of the chair and held herself in place, which seemed to please Caleb immensely. She couldn't help the rushing thrill of her own desire at his happiness.

"No, Sir. I want more."

"Good." He slid his fingers up slightly higher. "You're going to tell me exactly what to do and where to touch you," he continued. "And I will. If I agree with your direction."

She knew what he wanted, filthy words she'd never shared with anyone, the promise of poses she'd practiced only when home alone with no risk of discovery. She wasn't sure she could and yet, she was equally sure she had absolutely no choice.

"So," he continued. "Where shall we start?"

"My pussy." The word was foreign on her tongue, but she ached for release from the building sensations he had been teasing out of her for what felt like the whole night, and she was a half a minute away from just riding him.

"So eager," he murmured. "So fucking responsive. You're going to love it when I play with your pussy, sweet girl. But we need to go much slower than that."

Skylar wasn't sure she could go any slower than she was going right now, but she managed to choke out, "Please, touch my breasts."

"Better." Caleb brought one hand up to her breast and gently circled the outside, and it was growing harder and harder to stay still in his lap under this slow and deeply erotic torture. "Tell me, sunshine, can you come from having your nipple touched? Pinched and licked? Why don't we find out?"

She could actually, more so since getting the small bar put in two years back, but she was more than happy with his intent to discover. So she didn't say a word, simply leaned back into his touch as he slid the zipper on the back of her dress down, slipped his hand under the fabric and cupped her breast again.

"I've wanted to touch you since the second you walked through my front door," he murmured, low and promising as he tormented and teased her with barely there touches that did nothing to provide the release she so desperately sought. "And to see you trying so hard not to move because I told you to, because you're aching to follow my orders, sunshine, you make me want to bury my cock in your tight little body over and over again."

"Please..."

She didn't think about the word before she said it, an escaped plea for mercy, one that brought a jolt of Caleb's cock against her ass in its wake.

"Oh, I like the sound of you begging," he replied. "But right now, I want to make you desperate, put you so close to the edge that you forget your own name, forget everything but the sound of my voice and my direction. Do you know what I'm going do to then?"

It was a rhetorical question, but Skylar wouldn't have been able to answer anyway because his hand had slipped under the lace of her bra and was circling in on the swollen point of her nipple.

"Then I'm going to make you wait there," he told her. "Leave you hanging right at the very top of your pleasure, your body vibrating, your skin on fire, every part of you aching for releasing." He flicked her nipple and Skylar shuddered, shuddered again as he began to move his hand toward her other breast.

"Ah, fuck me, baby." This was said with the kind of raw emotion that nearly had her coming right there without anything more than his two fingers on her. "Tell me you have a silver bar through this pretty pink nipple."

"Rose gold," she managed. "The bar is rose gold."

She wasn't sure why that was the information she was able to come up with right now, when his fingers hovered a breath away from the bar in her straining nipple and his eyes were laden with sin and promise.

"Fucking incredible." He was losing his battle with himself and Skylar felt the desperate need to help, but she was barely holding on as it was. "I can't wait to see you all spread out and shiny for me, slick and shimmering in all the best places."

He slid his rough thumb over the bar and Skylar wasn't able to keep still that time, wasn't able to keep from bucking into his hard body and the very, very hard cock straining against her ass. The pleasure that single motion had spurred within her was enough for a month's worth of filthy midnight fantasies.

"Why not both?" he asked, continuing that masterful torture as if he wasn't driving her closer to the edge of her sanity. "Why just the one?"

She shook her head and Caleb stopped moving his finger.

"And we were doing so well," he murmured. "Try again, sunshine."

Skylar groaned, though she wasn't sure if it was from pleasure or frustration or some combination of her overwhelming emotions.

"It's embarrassing," she muttered, her voice barely recognizable to herself, laden as it was with lust and desire. Caleb stopped moving his fingers again, and Skylar conceded the point. This whole thing was a world away from her comfort zone and if she could be here, practically humping the cowboy, she could definitely tell him why she didn't go through with the second nipple piercing...

"I... They're sensitive," she began. "When I got it done—"

He brushed his finger over the bar again. "Did you come from it?" he asked. "Right there in the shop? Did your panties get hot and wet?"

She bit her lip and nodded. "Almost. I went home and..."

"Fuck, Skylar." His other hand, the one that wasn't driving her absolutely out of her mind with the softest, slightest pressure on the bar in her swollen nipple, stole up her dress and cupped her wet, needy pussy in a single motion. She nearly screamed, and bucked into the movement like her life depended on it. It certainly felt like it did at the moment.

"Tell me every detail," he growled into her ear, "and I'll make you come all over my hand, my mouth. Did you fingerfuck yourself?"

She shook her head. "I used one of my toys," she replied. "My vibrator."

He pushed her panties to one side and brushed her swollen clit, which made her vision dance with pleasure spots and promise.

"I had another toy," she continued, emboldened. "One for my...mouth." Because she couldn't be quiet, and because she loved the feel of a large, if fake, cock filling up her mouth while she rode her vibrator all afternoon, the pulsing pressure in her nipples driving her fucking insane, nothing unlike how she felt right now.

"A cock in your mouth and a toy pressed against your pretty pussy." He toyed her entrance and stilled her movement when she tried to slide into the touch. "All we need now is a plug for your fine little ass and you'll be the perfect picture of a needy, beautiful sub, ready for me in every hole."

She wasn't going to tell him that she had one, silver and jeweled, that she had bought in an embarrassed moment of curiosity and never had the courage to use. No, if he wanted to go searching for that information, he'd find it soon enough, she figured.

Then she wasn't figuring or thinking on much of anything beyond the pressure of him sliding two fingers into her slick entrance and teasing her pierced, swollen nipple as he whispered filthy, achingly erotic promises in her ear.

"Ride my fingers," he demanded. "Sweet girl, that's it, take your pleasure."

She did, with abandon, riding two, three fingers, embracing the sweet burn of him filling her hole, teasing her breasts, opening up the sinful side of her and giving her permission to take what she wanted.

"Are you going to come for me, Skylar?" he asked. "Be a good girl, come all over my fingers."

He brushed her clit and that was it, the build-up, the pressure, the promise, all leading to the moment when she fucking shattered in his embrace, coming and coming hard, pressing into him in her overwhelming pleasure, pulsing and shaking and screaming his name as he gave her relief.

Slowly, Skylar came down and Caleb withdrew his fingers.

"I could watch you come every single morning and every single night." He nipped at her throat. "And it wouldn't be nearly enough. How are you?"

Her bones felt like jelly, her breathing harsh and ragged, satiation slowly spreading across her limp body.

"Amazing," she said honestly. "But you didn't..."

He grinned. "I'll get mine. Don't you worry your pretty little head." He reached into the drawer beside the chair and pulled out a cool water bottle and small package of chocolate-covered almonds. It was a small refrigerator, she realized, outfitted to the style of the room.

"Drink." He pressed the water to her lips. "We're not done."

Even though she felt the glow of a beautiful release, Skylar had sort of figured that. Caleb was a demanding man, and she knew he would want more. Hell, *she* wanted more. So much more.

"Open." She allowed herself to relax into his touch, to accept the chocolate almonds as he fed them to her, to enjoy the moment of complete and utter surrender. And slowly her strength returned, her awareness harsh and overwhelming. One release hadn't been enough, not nearly, and she pressed herself against his still hard erection, hoping to convey as much to him.

"Oh, you want to play?" There was a grin in his voice. "Why does that not surprise me? Go, put your hands on the desk. I want to see you."

Chapter Nine

Caleb hadn't shot off early since he was about fourteen years old, but the sight of Skylar in a white lace dress and high-heeled boots bending over his desk was putting him perilously close to the edge. He didn't know how he'd thought he could get away without touching her, while having her in his domain. The second she had walked through the door and gotten down on her knees, he had been done for, absolutely fucking done for. And now he knew that she had a nipple piercing, knew the sound she made when she came, what she felt like tightening around his fingers, and he was pretty much as good as gone.

"Did you wear pink for me?" he asked, standing slowly from the chair and coming over to stand behind her. His cock gave a throb at the sight, and part of Caleb wanted to push her panties to the side so he could ram into her waiting body. She'd submit to him happily, of that he had no doubt.

But it wasn't about him and it wasn't about reaching release quickly. It was about the ride up, the achingly rich, full, intense ride that was going to make her never want to walk away from this lifestyle, going to cement exactly who she was without fear or worry.

"I did, Sir," she replied. "Would you like to see?"

He stepped up behind her and gave her covered ass a light swat.

"More than you know," he murmured. "But don't forget who's in charge here." Not that he was entirely sure in this moment, because Skylar pretty much had him in the palm of her hand. He slid her dress up slowly, revealing soft, smooth skin, adorned in the pink lace he had hoped she was going to wear. It looked even more spectacular than he could have expected, a soft contrast in the light from the fire, a heat nowhere near the one raging through him.

Then, because *fuck* if Caleb could hold himself back any long, he dropped to his knees behind her and buried his face in the lace between her legs.

Skylar screamed, the sound coursing through the air like lightning, and his cock surged, growing harder and more desperate than it had ever been. Her panties were soaked through, wet from her first release and her increasing need, and the scent of her arousal was a heady, powerful drug. He licked the lace, lapped at the wet fabric, and palmed her beautiful ass, wondering if he might have just died and gone to heaven without even realizing it.

"Sir." She was bucking into him now, and he let her. There would be plenty of time for holding her back, for forcing her to the edge of her orgasm just to make her linger in the space of almost-pleasure, but Caleb himself couldn't wait, not to taste her without a barrier, not to make her come all over his lips.

He slid her panties down, just enough to bare her glistening pussy to him, then spread her legs wide. She obeyed his non-verbal commands like they had been doing this for years and there she was, bare, slick, writhing and moving into the touch he wasn't quite giving her.

Caleb leaned in and licked.

She was everything sweet and wonderful he had ever known, the perfect soft summer woman with a flush, pink behind and a bar through her nipple. Her response, her moans and desperate whimpers — they drove him to pleasure her to the best of his ability, tormenting and teasing until she was nearing her precipice, if the dark need in her voice and the sharp movements were any indication.

"Please, Sir..." She was a rambling mess, and he found he was rather fond of her when she didn't make any sense because he was pleasuring her too much. "Please, can I come?"

Caleb had never heard anything more erotic in the thirty fucking years of his life.

He pulled away from her spread pussy, scraping his stubbled jaw across her sensitive skin as he did. He wanted her to feel him, to remember everything he made her feel, to go to sleep with the imprint of him on her thighs.

"Come for me, sunshine," he murmured. "Come all over my mouth."

Then her licked her again, this time sliding one finger into her tight entrance as he did, using his other hand to circle her swollen clit. She was a woman on the edge, and he had every intention of loving her so good she never worried about another thing again.

He circled her clit and he could sense her release drawing nearer, pushing her higher and closer to the edge, so he brought his thumb to his finger and pinched.

She screamed and came hard, her body pulsing around the fingers he still had buried inside her. It was a fucking sight, flushed, shaking skin, her glistening swollen pussy, every beautiful part of her, unsteady and well-pleasured.

He stood and picked her up, carried her to the rug in front of the fire and sat them both down, Skylar in his lap. She was still trembling from the force of her release, and he smoothed her wild hair and held her to his chest, tried not to think about how good it felt.

"You did so well, Skylar," he murmured into her throat. "So well."

She looked up at him, her eyes bright with lust and pleasure. Her lips were swollen and damn if the sight wasn't one he would remember for the rest of his goddamned life.

"We're not going to…" She sounded disappointed and Caleb's angry cock agreed.

"Not tonight," he replied. He had wanted to move things slowly, but from the moment he had met her, Caleb had been driven half-insane by this woman. The least he could do was slowly introduce her to the lifestyle, rather than go at her like a hungry dog. It wasn't the first time he'd get a little exercise when he got home and it certainly wouldn't be the last. "We have time."

They sat there for a few long moments, and Caleb allowed himself to simply enjoy the quiet, the sensation of another body pressed against his own, the soft and steady breathing of the woman in his arms.

When was the last time I held someone like this?

It had been Becca, of course, but when? The divorce had been finalized a year ago, but their relationship had been over well before that. And this, here in the room he had designed to his fantasy, holding a woman who had submitted to him as if it were the most natural thing in the world, this felt like a first. Even after years of marriage, this felt like a first.

"Are you sleepy, sunshine?" he asked, pushing her hair from her face. "Let me bring you back to your cabin."

She nodded and stood, accepting his help, then righting herself, pulling up those *fucking* pink panties and the strap to her bra. He zipped up her dress before she got the chance.

"Was it what you expected?" The night air was cool when he led her out of one of the barn's back doors, rather than through the main lobby.

Skylar smiled. "No," she said honestly. "But I'm glad I'm here, to answer a different question. I don't think I'd ever stop wondering if that night in Greece was a one-off or something I've been missing for all these years."

They navigated the path with ease thanks to the light of the moon and the generous splash of bold, sparkling stars in the night sky, but Caleb kept Skylar's hand in his own regardless.

"Was it?" he asked, far more invested in the answer than he really wanted to be. "A one-off?"

She laughed, and damn if the sound wasn't like those stars over his head. "I'd say it was more like a three or four off, but..." She stopped walking and looked up at him. "No, I don't think so."

Caleb had been part of the lifestyle for a long time, come across his fair share of women and men who experimented and played in all corners of kink and fetish and eroticism, and not once in any of them, not with a single one of his partners, not with the woman to whom he had been married, had he seen the kind of natural submission he saw in Skylar that night.

But it was new to her — and new to him in a way he didn't really want to consider — and he had no intention of terrifying her with the weight of how perfectly their puzzle pieces fit together. He didn't just like control and power. He craved it like the air he breathed and the sunshine on his face every morning. And Skylar. She was a natural.

"This is me," she said. They were already at her small cabin and he was wondering why he hadn't thrown her over his shoulder and carried her back to his house.

Slow. Going slow.

"So it is," he replied. He took a step forward. Then another one. Then one more, until he was boxing her in against the wood siding, one arm above her head, the other at her side. Her eyes dilated in the soft glow from the porch light and Caleb grinned.

"Goodnight, sunshine," he murmured. Then he bent down and kissed her softly on the lips.

Her kisses, Caleb decided, were positively decadent. He could kiss Skylar all day and night and still yearn for more of her touch, for more of the soft mewls of pleasure that came from the back of her throat. She wrapped her hand around the base of his neck and ran her hand through his hair and Caleb wondered if he really did have the kind of control of himself necessary to walk away from a woman like her.

When she brought one leg up to wrap around his waist, however, and Caleb could feel the dampness on the inside of her thigh against the strip of stomach where his shirt had ridden up under her ministrations, he finally pulled back. If he didn't do it now, he wasn't going to, and he needed to take this slow, even if she thought she wanted something else.

"Dream of me," he murmured. "And don't make evening plans tomorrow."

Her laugh was throaty and rich and she smiled at him before slipping into the cabin and turning on the lights.

Content she was safe for the night, Caleb headed back to his home, his empty bed and thoughts of Skylar Wedgeworth on her hands and knees.

Oh yeah, life could be a whole lot worse.

Chapter Ten

Skylar could still feel his kiss on her lips when she went out to an early morning breakfast in the lodge the next day and she wondered if Caleb might be interested in having her instead of waffles and bacon. She'd slept well, but her dreams had been flush with images of handsome cowboys, fence posts and leather, with the look in his eyes as he had pulled away from her, pained and totally aroused and determined not to act on it.

But he had acted on her, and she had acted on some base and wild part of herself that she had never known existed and now, it seemed, Skylar couldn't get enough.

Did he totally love the pink?

Skylar put down her mug of coffee to glance at her phone and blushed. It should have been too early to blush, but her best friend had the uncanny ability to bring up all the most blush-worthy topics. And it wasn't like she hadn't graphically detailed her self-pleasuring routine to a stranger the night before.

Not that Caleb Cash felt like a stranger, because he didn't, but she was going to need a second cup of coffee and probably a year of therapy before she started trying to untangle why that was.

Nosy, much? Not getting enough at home?

Funny. If I was getting any more, I wouldn't be able to walk. Now spill, are you able to walk?

The truth was, Skylar did have a distinct ache between her thighs. Before Greece, it had been more than a year since she'd been with a man, but Caleb had undoubtedly left his touch. And the faint rub of beard burn between her thighs that she had discovered in the shower that morning.

It was a good night.

Bitch. I did not take you to all the best boutiques in the city to get an answer like that.

"Sister or best friend?"

Skylar glanced up from her phone to see Rhylee Cash settling at the table beside her. She smiled at the other woman. "Best friend. Though she might just lose the title if she doesn't quit being so nosy."

Fine. Be that way. See who comes to your rescue with the next fashion emergency.

I'll call you later, clingy bitch.

Just got a case. I'll call you when we're home.

She left a long string of heart and kiss emojis that make Skylar smile and she turned back to Rhylee. "You have a best friend up here?" she asked. "There seems to be an awful lot of testosterone round these parts."

That made Rhylee roll her eyes. "You can say that again," she said. "And I do, down at the lab. But the nights can get awfully cold."

Skylar narrowed her eyes. "So, the vibes I got off you and…"

Rhylee pursed her lips. "Tell me about her," she interrupted. "Or about you. How are you liking our little home on the mountain?"

Skylar knew all too well when someone needed a change of topic and she wasn't about to push her new companion into uncomfortable territory, even if there was no denying the obvious connection between Rhylee and Van—heated though it might have been.

"It's amazing," she replied honestly. "I can totally see why you wanted to come back here after college."

Rhylee nodded. "Wouldn't have had it any other way. And I'm totally open to talking to your daughter about the STEM fields, whenever she's ready."

Skylar sipped her coffee. "She'd love that. The girl wants to be an astronaut and a marine biologist and an environmental scientist and also a Hollywood producer. She's capable of achieving any of them, but I think it might be hard to do them all at once."

Though if anyone could, it was Callie. Skylar had been young, so, so young when she'd first become responsible for another person, but she'd been dedicated to raising her daughter with the mindset that she could be anything she wanted to be. For her and for

Kennedy and Richie, there had never been any future outside Wedgeworth Investments and Real Estate. At sixteen, she had already been well-versed in 'Club Conversation', in the casual way with which rich men moved the world around as though they were the only pieces on the board that mattered.

She had been taught how to read contracts, negotiate deals and play hardball, not by parents who had taken her under their wing, but by parents who brought her to fancy dinner parties and met in upscale restaurants with colleagues by coincidence, who chatted about multi-million-dollar deals at her private school recitals and considered bribery and coercion all part of the game.

At sixteen, she hadn't known much about the world. Certainly, she hadn't known how to wait tables or shop for groceries or make a budget. But she had known that she would never limit Callie to a life that Skylar had picked out for her. It seemed she'd done all right on that score.

"Don't you have a job?"

Van Hunts settled down next to Rhylee, and Skylar would eat her coffee mug if there wasn't something going on between the two of them, whether Rhylee wanted to admit it or not.

Rhylee made a face at him. "I don't have to be at the lab until— *Shit.*" She glanced at her watch, then nearly spilled her cup of coffee in her haste to get up from the table.

"Bye, Skylar," she called over. "Talk soon!" And she was out the door and out of sight in the span of four seconds.

"So." Van leaned on tan, muscled forearms and lowered his voice, as if planning to share secrets at a sleepover party. "Caleb."

"What about him?"

What about him, indeed, except for the way that he could make her reach the pinnacles of pleasure with nothing so much as a dangerous look in his eyes. Oh and except for the way she was desperately aching to go back to the barn, right now, with the sun barely over the far mountains, but had to wait, wait until night fell and she could get dressed up and become a different person. *The kind of person who kneels on soft rugs in front of roaring fires and strips for strangers.*

"He's had a hard time of it," Van said. He leaned back in his chair, as if she had passed the first scrutinization. "I think you might be good for him."

"You do?" she asked. "Because, as I heard it, you offered to come over to my cabin the other night."

The other night felt like ages ago, the first time she had surrendered to whatever this chemical reaction was between her and Caleb. But it had barely been two days, and Skylar's life was inherently, fundamentally altered. Whatever life she went back to after this, she would not be the same Skylar Wedgeworth.

"I changed my mind," he replied easily. "Of course, I've never been one to deny a woman's most wanton desires, but like I said, I think you might be good for him." It was the tone of his voice, genuine concern masked behind playful flirtation that, despite how handsome Van Hunts was, didn't have nearly the impact of Caleb's promises. Whatever it was that Caleb had in his past, it had hurt him, deeply and in a way that left scars. And though Skylar ached with something she didn't understand to know the man better, to, even more insanely, help him heal some of those scars, she was all too familiar with wanting to keep the past hidden. If Caleb wanted to share, he would.

"How magnanimous of you," she teased. She liked Van. He reminded her a little of Quinn. His quietness, the reserve and strength in his posture and behavior, was comforting, even if it did make her sad. She would bet a fair bit of money that he hadn't always been like that, hadn't always been the dark figure alone at the bar.

"I aim to please," he replied. He placed his hand on hers and the gesture was not one of flirtation at all, but something more carnal, more instinctual — the need for human contact, for connection, for reassurance. "Take care of him," he said quietly.

They all had their crosses to bear, their paths hard-won and often lonely. And if part of her wondered if maybe her path wasn't going to be quite so lonely moving forward, well, it wasn't something she had to explore right now. As she had long learned on her own hard-won path, sometimes it was simply best to take each day one at a time and see where the road led her.

"I will," she replied. And Skylar meant it.

Caleb didn't have the right to feel jealous. Hell, he couldn't ever remember the gut-churning sense of envy he felt right now in years of marriage, and that was certainly indicative of information he wanted to keep locked away tight. But as he looked over at the dining room table, where Skylar and Van sat too close together, and *held hands*, he felt a little like chopping down with nothing more than an axe. Not that he should have anything sharp within reach at the moment.

"Town looks different." Reece Prescott looked different too. In the months since he'd been back to Sinclair Ranch, his hair had grown out and he now sported a full beard where there had only been stubble the day he'd taken off for the mountains. Though Reece's hair was pulled back in an elastic, Caleb could see blond streaks against the brown, evidence of time spent in the sun, and some carnal part of him wanted to go running for the woods too.

Whatever he was feeling about Skylar Wedgeworth was, apparently, terrifying enough to make him want to brave the mountains of Montana.

"Some shell company has been buying up the land," Caleb explained, though he never took his eyes off of Skylar and Van, even as they broke apart and she moved back to cup her coffee. That simple sight, all cozy and morning soft, had him yearning for something he had no right to.

"That sounds super cool and above board," Reece replied drily. "I'm assuming they're after the mineral rights?"

"That's my guess." It hadn't been only his guess, either. Duchess was a small enough town and families had set up roots there for generations. To have a sudden influx of cash and the removal of town staples hadn't passed without notice. "It's got people nervous, if you want the truth. Either the company's offering a lot of money, or it's something else."

"Threats?" Reece asked. "Or blackmail?"

Caleb shrugged. "Pick your poison. It's reeks, either way."

As if just talking about it was enough to make it happen, his damn phone range. It wasn't always the same number, but it was always the same message.

Still, given that it could be any number of clients or vendors calling, he picked up rather than sending the call to his mailbox.

"Caleb Cash."

"Mr. Cash, I'm glad I caught you."

He wasn't going to be so glad when Caleb caught him.

"I told you not to call here again." Even if he hadn't already been revved up by the sight of Van and Skylar laughing at the breakfast table, he would have been sufficiently annoyed by the call. The organization, a company that had identified itself only as Magnet Enterprises, had been bothering him for months now, and as the mood in Duchess had shifted from annoyance and skepticism to outright suspicion, he felt less inclined to be polite.

And yet, if this company had been able to get Billy Walterson to sell the general store that had been in his family since the 1800s, there was probably a lot of other things they could do. It was best that he didn't antagonize them to the point of reaction until he knew what he was really up against.

"I thought we might be able to come to some kind of agreement," the man on the other end, who had not yet identified himself, said. "My client is willing to be *very* generous." The way he said the word *generous* brought to mind the snake in the garden, only this time, Caleb felt quite inclined to resist temptation.

Across the dining room, Skylar laughed at something Van said, and Caleb amended the thought. He was inclined to resist *some* temptations.

"We're not interested." He spoke for his friends, but he knew they would agree with the statement. When Beau had left them the Sinclair Ranch, there had been an unspoken agreement that it would stay within their family. With the addition of The Ranch, which they had built from the ground up, they weren't going anywhere for any amount of money.

He certainly didn't need it, not with the income from businesses and the simple life he lived on site and neither did Van. Gabriel was a successful venture capitalist with a lot of extra zeros in his bank account. Rafe — well, Rafe had a country's coffers at his disposal, Dante's shop was booked solid for months, Bastion was a list-topping artist and Reece was far more content with a backpack of granola bars and a sleeping bag under the stars than the lap of luxury, though Caleb had it on good authority that his reporting skills were in high demand. Whatever Magnet Enterprises wanted from them — and he had a few ideas — money certainly wasn't going to be the way in. He didn't want to particularly think about other available options.

"This conversation isn't over, Mr. Cash," the man replied. "We're very interested in your land. Expect another call from us soon."

Oh yeah, that definitely sounded aboveboard. Right.

"Did we speak of the devil?" Reece asked, looking him over with a knowing expression. "You look like you just ate a sour gumball."

Caleb grunted a laugh. "We did. And it sounds like they're not planning on going anywhere. I just wish I had a better idea of who they are and what they're after."

Reece looked thoughtful. Though he was driven to wander, spending months traveling the world or exploring the mountains in his own backyard, he was an expert reporter and photographer and had produced more than one investigative piece that had pulled suspicious activities from businesses and governments out of the shadows. His California-surf-dude vibe covered up a lot...and didn't change the fact that Reece could rope a steer like no one's business, either.

"I'd say I'll look into it," he replied, "but I think you should ask Gabriel. If we're talking big money, he might have his ear to the ground."

It was a good idea and Caleb nodded. If this organization was going to come after him and after the people he cared about most, after the land left to him by a man who had felt like a father, he wanted to be prepared.

"It's good to have you around," Caleb said with a grin. "How long are you in town for this time?"

Reece shrugged. "I was thinking Turkey next," he replied. "I want to do a piece on religious architecture in Europe, but we'll see. Things don't usually go as I plan them, you know?"

Things didn't usually go as Caleb planned them either. Not a career in the major leagues, not a wife and family with the woman he'd loved for most of his life. Not even the affair he thought he'd be able to walk away from whenever Skylar Wedgeworth decided she'd had enough of this fantasy and returned to her everyday life. And damn, if that wasn't the scariest thought of them all.

Chapter Eleven

This time, Skylar didn't call Ev for advice. She had a sense of what she was doing here now, and with it, a feeling of belonging that she couldn't shake. The weird part, the part that should have scared her but didn't, not right now as she pulled on a denim skirt and those fashion cowboy boots she'd spent too much money on in a boutique downtown, the weird part was that she wasn't entirely sure she wanted to shake that feeling of belonging.

She had made her choices in her life, choices she wouldn't take back for the world, not after a lifetime of happiness with her daughter. But for them, she'd had to trade in family, distant though hers had been, had to trade in the friends who had all pretty much turned tail the second she no longer shopped at the same stores or went to the same private school. At the time she had blamed them, but hindsight had her understanding that had the tables been turned, her parents would have prevented such acquaintances too. More than enough time had passed for her to no longer mourn those young adult friendships.

And she had friends. Ev and the women from the diner from back when they had all been trying to get on their feet. She considered a lot of the women she'd worked with to be friends and she had her circle of companions in the parents who had raised their kids as she had raised Callie.

But to speak with Van and Rhylee, to watch the easy banter between Dante and Caleb, it was to see a created family, a family stronger for the corners of the world from where they had all come. Caleb had told her there were seven of them, and Rhylee too, of course. Seven brothers forged in the fields and the dirt. Seven friendships that hadn't just withstood the test of time but flourished in it.

She couldn't help but feel safe in a place built on camaraderie and loyalty and brotherly love. And if it went further than that, well, she'd think about that when all was said and done.

So instead of calling her best friend in a fit of panic over what the night might hold, she put on a dark red lipstick, tousled her hair and walked out of her cabin with confidence. If there was one thing she was innately beginning to understand in her time here in this amazing fantasy world far from her life at home, it was that she would always have the power.

The thought drove her up the hill, up to the familiar structure that still held so many secrets, through the doors and to the bar, where a smiling man with reddish blond hair she had never met before leaned against the wood.

"You must be the gal who's got Caleb's tongue all tied," he said, pouring a drink for her before she could ask for one. "Reece." He placed a tumbler of whiskey on the counter and stuck out his hand. "Nice to meet you."

"Skylar." She shook it, then picked up the glass. She'd be a whiskey drinker for real by the time this trip was over. "Let me guess, you're the outdoorsy one?"

He smiled, two neat rows of bright teeth. "What gave it away?"

"The tan lines," she replied honestly. "And I don't think I could even picture Caleb with long hair."

"If that's what you wanted, I'd consider it." He was behind her, pressed against her back and whispering into her ear, and Skylar lost the world around her, lost the room and Reece and the whiskey drink in her hand. It was just them, just her and Caleb and the way he made her feel with nothing so much as his husky, promising voice.

"I don't think you would," she replied, but her voice was shaky with the effects of his nearness. She yearned for him, yearned to see him and touch him and have him in every way she could think of. And then some.

"Feeling feisty tonight, honey?" he asked. Oh, she was definitely feeling something. "I see you met Reece. He's our resident wanderer." Reece did have the look of a wandering soul about him, but Skylar was much more interested in the downhome cowboy who was pressing sizable evidence of his arousal into her backside.

"And if I am?" she asked. "Feeling feisty?"

"Then I'm just going to have to show you what happens to cheeky women around here," he replied. "How do you feel about a little local adventure?"

She felt like she'd go just about anywhere with him and willingly. Rather than saying so, she pressed back into his body and circled her hips. Caleb brought his hands to her waist and stilled the movement almost immediately.

"You've gotten rather bold," he murmured. "Playtime is over — say goodbye to the nice bartender."

"Nice to meet you." She gave Reece a cheeky grin, feeling wild and flirtatious as the handsomest, most enticing man in the room staked a very public claim on her and guided her into the privacy of the hallway. He had been holding back up to this point, focused on making her feel comfortable, making her want the things she claimed to, but Skylar didn't want to wait for him anymore. She didn't want to imagine the feeling of his powerful body inside of her own. She ached to feel it for real. *Every hard, throbbing inch of him.*

"Are you behaving like a brat to get my attention?" he asked. His movements were gentle and slow, almost so gentle and slow that Skylar didn't realize she was pressed up against the hardwood wall until Caleb was towering over her, one muscled arm above her head and the other at her waist. "Or is just because you can't help yourself, sunshine? Because you know what happens to girls who behave like brats around here."

Her voice was breathy and laden with lust and want when she whispered in reply,

"What happens?"

God, she could look at that grin, promising and dangerous and erotic heat incarnate, every day for the rest of her life and still she would want him with unmatched fervor.

"You really want to know?" he asked.

More than anything in the world.

She nodded.

His hand was on her thigh then, moving slowly up her exposed skin until he hit the hem of her skirt. Skylar inhaled sharply and Caleb paused.

"I thought you wanted to know?" he asked. The game of cat and mouse was for her sake, to keep her comfortable in this new unexplored world of power and control and desire, but damn if it wasn't *working*, wasn't making her pussy wet and her nipples hard behind the soft silk bralette she wore. She instinctively clenched her thighs together in a desperate attempt to get some release, but it didn't work.

"I do," she managed. "I want to know. Please...Sir."

He clearly loved hearing the word on her tongue as much as she loved saying it because he moved his hand up farther at that, brushing rough, work-calloused hands over her skin until she was writhing in the cage of his embrace, half-begging him to move farther up, to *just please touch her.*

"Where?"

She'd never really gotten the appeal of sexy talk. But then again, Skylar had never done anything like this before either and she very, *very* much got the appeal of it now.

"My pussy," she managed. "Please."

"You tell me what you want," Caleb murmured against her throat, "and I'll give it to you. You stop talking, I stop moving."

Voicing her desires out loud. She got it, even as her face flushed with the embarrassment of actually having to say it. She'd had her share of partners in the years since her daughter had been born, but the couplings had been fairly textbook, low lighting, light foreplay, furtive kisses, a couple of hard thrusts, and game over.

This was something else entirely.

"Please touch my pussy," she managed, because dammit, in for a penny.

"Like this?" His touch was so light she wondered if she was imagining it and she strained into him for more contact, but Caleb brought his other hand to her waist and held her in place.

"You're driving," he told her. "Tell me where to go or the ride stops."

She *did not* want the ride to stop.

"More," she demanded. Goodness, she did sound *very* demanding. "Stroke my pussy, please."

He did as she told, and she almost sighed at the hot flood of release that followed the contact.

"Take my panties off." For someone in control, her voice sounded an awful lot like begging. But Caleb slipped his finger under the elastic on one side, then the other and pushed her panties down her legs, gently brushing her mound as he did. Skylar had to bite her lip hard to hold back a scream. She was already so swollen, so aroused, it would be a miracle if she made it through the night.

"My clit," she managed. "Stroke my clit."

He did, light, not nearly enough contact for her, and all sense of embarrassment or shame disappeared in her desperate journey for release.

"Harder," she said. "Make it… Pinch me."

Caleb groaned, the sound low and carnal from the back of his throat, and she wondered if she could push him far enough to take her right here in this darkened hallway where anyone could walk by. Damn, she was learning an awful lot about herself today, wasn't she?

"How hard?" he asked. "Enough to make you scream? Enough to make you cream all over my hand?

Or do you want my fingers inside you when you come?"

"Inside me." She was definitely begging now. "Please, fill my pussy." The feeling of him fingering her from the night before like a branded memory and she didn't just *want* it now. She needed it like air or water.

Caleb, thank *God*, seemed to agree. He slid one thick finger into her slick hole while still circling her swollen clit, and Skylar and Caleb's moans tangled together in the quiet of the hallway.

"You're so fucking tight," he growled. "I can't wait to feel you coming around my cock, taking me deep. Is that what you want tonight? Tell me."

"I want you to...fuck me." A lifetime of raising a kid had made it hard for her to swear, but there was no other way for her to put it, no other way for her to articulate the need coursing through her veins. "Right here."

His laugh was low and rich, like the whiskey from the bar, and it made her feel just as warm and bold and fearless.

"And end the night so soon?" he asked. "I have plans for you, sweet girl." He brought his other hand to her chin and tipped her up so their gazes met. In his eyes she saw a firestorm of lust and oncoming chaos, and no doubt the same one was reflected in her own gaze.

"Tell me."

His grin was dark and dangerous. Predatory.

"If I tell you," he began, moving his fingers achingly slowly in and out of her tight entrance, "will you come on my fingers?"

She nodded. "Please, yes..."

Was there pride in his eyes? She didn't want to think about how that made her chest swell and her need to keep the expression there all the time.

"Good. Then let's start with how I'm going to make you come right here in this hallway where anyone could walk in on us. And you're going to like it, aren't you, sunshine? You're going to do your best to keep quiet, keep from screaming my name while I stroke your sweet, tight pussy, but you secretly want someone to hear, want someone to see."

"No..."

He stopped moving and Skylar opened her mouth to protest, but the words died on her tongue.

"Yes," she admitted, if more to herself than to him. "I want someone to see you touching me."

It wasn't about them joining in. It was about the reassurance that she was submitting to him, that he was the only one who could have her, even while others watched. If that was true or not outside this space, Skylar couldn't bring herself to care right now. All she knew was that she needed more of his touches and his dark, dangerous words.

"That's what I thought," Caleb half-groaned. She liked that he seemed to be losing himself to the lust and to the game as much as she was, liked that he wasn't as calm and cool and collected as he usually was.

"Maybe I'll let them watch," he murmured. "If only so they could see how I mark you, how well you listen to me, sunshine. How well you do exactly as your told."

She nodded and arched into his touch all at the same time.

"Anything."

His eyes blazed.

"Then, I'm going to carry you into the room, strip you bare and spread you out on the blanket in front of the fire."

His movements were growing faster, more erratic, as if he was as desperate for the scene to unfold as she was, and Skylar was along for the ride, for every brush and stroke and seeking promise.

"And I'm going to tell you to touch yourself," he continued. "To spread your legs wide and open your sweet, swollen pussy for me, to fingerfuck your hole until you can't take anymore and just before you come, I'm going to tell you to stop."

His fingers stopped moving then, and Skylar really did nearly scream.

"Will you stop?" he asked. "Or will you come even though I told you not to?"

"That depends," she managed. "What will you do to me if I disobey?"

He didn't say a word, just slid his finger free from her body and started to step away.

"No," she managed, half-frenzied from the scene he was painting in her mind, from the almost-touches that just weren't quite enough. "Please, I'll...I'll be good, I promise."

She meant it.

"Good girl." This time, Caleb pressed two fingers to her hole and the added pressure on her singed nerve endings was nearly too much.

"Please, Sir, please." She was begging in earnest now and she didn't give a good goddamn.

"Please?" he prompted.

"Please can I come?"

He brought his other hand up to her breast and caressed one swollen nipple through the fabric.

"Do it, sunshine," he demanded. "Come all over my fingers. I want to feel your hot release on my skin."

The floor fell out from under her, stars popped behind her eyes and Skylar gave over to the pleasure, to the achingly, powerful, beautiful release he gave her, shards of hot white lust and need prickling across her body until she was shaking and riding his fingers slower and slower, her lip swollen from being bitten, her breathing ragged.

Caleb slowly pulled his fingers free and her body protested, wanting more even as the tingles of her wild release still wracked through her.

"Open." He pressed slick fingers to her lips and she parted without question, allowing him entrance, tasting herself on his skin. It should have been too much, but there was that damn look in his eyes, the look promising her everything if she just did as he said, and she instinctively sucked his fingers deeper, taking as much of him as she could until he slowly pulled out.

"You're so fucking beautiful when you come," he growled. "I want to see it again. But first."

He pushed her up against the wall and Skylar brought one leg up to his waist so she was half-riding and half-climbing the tall, muscled cowboy. *Save a horse...*

Then he leaned down and brought his mouth to hers. The kiss wasn't gentle. He had been gentle before, but now they were both high on passion and drive, evidence of Caleb's arousal pressing hard against the inside of her leg, and Skylar didn't want gentle anyway. Then he was bringing his mouth down to her neck and leaving hot, demanding bites on the column of her throat. She hadn't thought she wanted that bite of pain to go with her pleasure, had always assumed it wasn't for her, but right now, under his ministrations, Skylar didn't just want it, she ached for it with the same carnal desperation that had first made her call him Sir the night under the stars.

"Take me to your room," she said quietly, because she couldn't think of it as anything other than his room. It was all Caleb, rustic and rough, beautiful and full of promise.

"God, yes." Rather than letting her leg slide back down to the ground, he cupped her ass in his hands and pulled her other leg up so she was wrapped completely around him, moving them as if she weighed nothing. But Skylar wasn't paying any attention to that. All she could think about now was the way Caleb's mouth felt on her, the stroke of strong hands on her skin, on the curve of her hips and ass.

"I spent the whole damn day wanting you, honey," Caleb murmured into her ear. "I got hard just from watching you walk across the room. You're so fucking perfect."

She felt perfect when she was in his arms, felt like the kind of woman who could take on the world — believed she already was that kind of woman. Theirs was a game of give and take, of promise and deliverance, and it left her feeling satiated and desired and more in control of anything than her life had ever given her before."

"I wanted you too," she admitted. "I like looking at you when you work."

She had been preparing to head out on another hike when she had seen him slinging hay bales and damn if the sight of a man in flannel and work boots wasn't going to be her aphrodisiac for the rest of her life.

"Mmm, maybe I'll take a break next time and work on you." He reached around her and opened the door to the room they had shared the night before. A fire was already roaring in the grate and the room smelled of campfire and pine and fresh mountain air, and Caleb.

"Please." It came out on a husky, rough sound, and Skylar briefly wondered if she would ever go back to sounding normal, rather than a wanton hussy. She found she didn't much care.

"Please lay you out on the rug and watch you play with yourself?" he asked. "Please rip off your clothes and take you until you can't remember your own name? Please what, Skylar? You're in control."

She wasn't in control of anything right at the moment, but she understood, even through the haze of lust and need, that she was in control of this.

"Please touch me," she replied. "Sir."

"Always so polite." He walked them across the room and settled her on the back of the couch, which made it all the easier for Skylar to spread her legs and welcome him in. Caleb brushed his thumb over her lips, and the taste of her desire was still there on his skin, a heady combination that made her ache for depraved, wicked things she knew she would have before the night was done. "It's like you were made for me to touch." He slid his hand down and pulled her forgotten panties off over her boots.

"I'm keeping these," he told her, before tucking them into his pocket. "And I don't want to see you wearing another pair of them to visit me at night." The gleam in his eyes promised punishment of the most pleasurable order if she disobeyed, and Skylar internally warred with doing exactly as she was told and finding out what he had in mind.

"Turn around, beautiful girl," he murmured. "Place your hands on the couch, just like that."

She was already feeling exposed — and delightfully turned on from it — when he pushed her skirt higher up her legs, until it was completely bunched at her waist and she was on full display for him.

"Spread your legs wider, that's right. I was to see you."

It shouldn't have been arousing, but damn it, she could feel the heat of his gaze, and her pussy clenched on nothingness from the sheer eroticism of his perusal.

"You're so lush and pink and wet," he murmured. "Your pussy must be aching right now, just desperate for my touch."

Skylar whimpered, *whimpered.* "God, yes, please."

She wasn't expecting him to touch her. Caleb loved the tease, loved the buildup and the promise, but in that moment he brought one strong, calloused hand to her swollen folds and stroked. She moaned, and bucked against the couch, her need growing into frenzy.

"That's right, ride my fingers." This time, he slipped two fingers inside her just to start, pumping slowly and steadily in and out of her tight hole. "You're so responsive, Skylar, all slickness and need."

She wanted to reply, wanted to tell him that he was the reason she was panting and moaning over the edge of the couch, but then he was circling the tight ring of her ass with his slick thumb and all she could do was gasp. It was the softest caress, and the deepest part of her found that it wasn't nearly enough.

"Has anyone ever touched you here?" he asked, his voice low and rough and demanding but oh, so gentle all at once. She shook her head.

"Have you ever touched yourself here?"

The fantasy had been a fleeting one on occasion, but she hadn't actually done it, too overwhelmed with the priority of it all to get aroused by it. But now, with Caleb's thumb just *there* just at her tightest entrance, and the jolting, insane pleasure from the simplest touch, she wondered how much else she had been missing out on.

"No..." she managed. "But I wanted to."

His thumb dipped, just a bit, just enough to make her gasp.

"Good." His approval sent another thrum of pleasure racing through her. "Because I'm going to take you here. Not now. Not right away, but sooner than later you're going to be begging me to take you, to fill each and every one of your holes so you're full and stretched. And I will."

The image was streaked with heat and eroticism and Skylar really didn't think she could take any more.

"Sir." She didn't give a damn if she was begging. She just needed some kind of release. "Please, Sir, fu...*fuck.*"

He pressed his thumb past her tight right of muscle and Skylar screamed them, clenched the back of the couch and instinctively pressed back into him. It felt strange, but in a new and delicious way, wracked with pleasure and something wicked and sinful that made it all the better.

"That's right," he murmured. "Give yourself to me. I've got you." She didn't doubt it for a second. Caleb slid his fingers from her pussy and pressed his thumb a little bit deeper. "Can you come from this, baby?" he asked. "From my finger in your ass? I think you can."

She rather agreed with him.

"Tell me to," she asked. Begged. "Tell me to, please."

"Do it." He rolled his finger around. "Come from me playing with your tight, pretty little asshole."

She did, shattering into a thousand pieces, then a thousand more. Her body clenched around him and the burn was beautiful and bright and made her feel wild and uninhibited and completely untethered.

He withdrew slowly and gathered her in his arms, holding her body close as the powerful wave of erotic desire crashed through her. He was going to make her come again and again before the night was through, she was sure of it, but there was something so truly pleasurable in the way he simply held her, brought her to the edge of her pleasure and carried her over with ease.

And for that, it wasn't nearly enough to have him play with her and not get the opportunity to play with him in response. Coming out to The Ranch had pushed Skylar from her comfort zone, but she was ready to take things to the next level, desperate to explore the powerful muscles that held her now, aching for the hard arousal she had seen only in the shadow behind his briefs in the light from the moon.

"I want you." It was bolder than she could ever remember being, and yet, it was also right. It felt good to be bold and Skylar didn't want to hold back any longer. "I want to give you pleasure, Sir. The kind of pleasure you give me."

He peered down at her, where she sat on the back of the couch, and his gaze was heat and molten and promise. She could also see the restraint there, and she ached to be the one to pull at its edges, to have Caleb give over to her the way she had been so willing to give over to him.

"You can trust me." She hadn't meant to say the words, but they felt right too, like the perfect way to explain all the things he made her feel. She wanted him, yes, but it was so much more than that. It was the giving over of her control, the trust burgeoning between them, the promise that she would care for him as he cared for her if he would only accept it.

"I know, sunshine," he murmured, and she really believed that he did. Whatever was happening here between them, whatever was developing in the new space she was allowing herself to become out here in the wilds of Montana, it was so much more than hot, hot, hot sex.

"Then, please?"

He quirked an eyebrow and the corners of his mouth tilted up in the whisper of a smile. Mr. Toughman Cowboy didn't like showing his weakness. He liked being the one in control, liked being the one who held all the cards. And yet, from just the few days she had been at his mercy, Skylar had a soul-deep understanding that she was actually the one with all the power.

"Please what?" he asked. "You know how I like it when you get specific."

The evidence that she liked it as well was in the slick desire coating her inner thighs and the way her nipples were hard, painful points behind her tank.

"Please can I suck your cock?" she asked. "I want to make you feel as good as you make me feel. Sir."

Heat blazed through those beautiful dark eyes, and Skylar knew that she was getting under his skin, breaking down his defenses.

"Do you want to?" he asked. "Take me in your mouth and swallow me? Is that what you want?"

Like nothing she'd ever wanted before. She nodded.

"Then go ahead, sunshine. Touch me."

She practically moaned her sigh of relief and reached for the buckle at his waist, undoing it before she dropped to her knees before him. Caleb Cash made for one hell of an image, towering and lording over her, the sight of his throbbing cock tucked behind worn denim proof enough of his power and dominance.

She tugged his jeans down enough that she could see those navy boxer briefs, similar to the ones he'd been wearing in the hot tub on her first night out in Montana, and she sucked in a breath. He was big, bigger even that she had expected from the feeling of him pressed against her back.

"Do it," he demanded. "Touch me, Skylar. I want to feel your hands on my skin."

She tugged the band of his briefs down slowly until his large cock was freed from its confines and sprang out to meet her. *Holy shit.*

"Do you want it?" he asked, his voice husky with his own desire. "Do you want to taste me? I've been dreaming about the sight of your lips wrapped around my cock since the minute you walked through the door. Show me what it feels like."

She didn't have a choice. She slid one hand up to cup him in her palm, throbbing and hot, smooth skin over his rigid, pulsing manhood. And because he had asked so nicely, because she was desperate for the taste of him on her tongue, she did as she was told.

The ragged swear that tore from the back of his throat was satisfaction enough, but it was the hand on the back of her head stilling her in place that had hot arousal flooding her, making her writhe against the floor in desperate, seeking release.

"Fuck. *Fuck.*" His voice was guttural and harsh. "Your hot little mouth is like heaven, Skylar. I know this is turning you on. Go ahead, touch yourself while you suck me. Fucking angel."

She did as he asked, sliding her finger between her slick, swollen folds as she sucked him deeper, and palmed the rest of his swollen length with her other hand. It was hot and depraved and made her want him all the more.

"Stop."

She stopped moving, stopped sucking, stopping rubbing her own swollen clit in the desperate race for release, though her body screamed in protest.

"I want you, Skylar. All of you. And I don't want to wait any longer." He helped her up, walked her over to the couch and settled down, legs spread, that powerful cock jutting upward. He reached into the stand beside the couch and pulled out a string of condoms, then unwrapped one and expertly slid it down his length. Even the sight of him fisting that large cock as he prepared himself for her was enticing and intoxicating.

"Take it all off," he told her. "I want to see you."

She wanted to see him too, but he was still the one in control, and her ache to follow his directive was stronger than ever. So she did as she was told, pushing the bunched skirt down until it hit the floor, then pulling the tank and bralette off in a single movement. She bent over to unzip the shoes, but Caleb stopped her.

"Shoes stay," he stated. "I fucking love the sight of you in those boots." He shifted so there was room for her on both sides of his broad, muscled thighs. "Now come here."

Her legs were a little wobbly as she walked over to him and waited for his next order, which came as a wordless pat of his thigh. She climbed onto his lap, all too aware that he was still allowing her so much of the power, keeping her on top, controlling the speed and movement.

"Ask for permission," he demanded, evidence of his own desperation taking root. Skylar wasn't in the mood to stall either.

"Please, Sir, can I ride you?"

He brushed one rough thumb over her bottom lip, the movement leaving sparks of electricity in its wake.

"Yes, sweet girl," he murmured.

She didn't need to be told twice. She lowered herself slowly, allowing her body to grow accustomed to the size of him inside her, the throbbing of his wide cock, as she took him inch by inch deeper into her.

"You're almost there," he promised. "Feel so good around my cock. Your pussy is so fucking tight around me." He pulsed again, intentionally, she had no doubt, and Skylar yelped as rivulets of pleasure burned through her. She needed to move against him more than she needed air to breathe.

Caleb must've known, because when she finally bottomed out on his enormous erection, he took her hips in his hands and with gentle, powerful movements, pushed her back up, then down again, controlling her speed and angle and movements, until she was doing it all on her own, a slow descent into madness, one blinding orgasm at a time.

"Take me, sunshine," he murmured. "I want to feel you squeeze tight around my cock when you find your release. Give in."

It was easy, giving in, when Caleb's hard, pulsing cock sent waves of pleasure coursing through her entire body, when his seeking hands found her nipples and toyed with her swollen breasts, when he pulled with a strong grasp on the back of neck and kissed her until all

Skylar could think about was her pleasure and the wild need to submit for this man.

"Come, Skylar. Finish for me."

This release was a gentle riot, the cresting of an enormous wave in slow motion and she fell over the edge in as if through water, the pleasure so extreme and wild that all she could do was give in to it, give over to it, ride it, and him. She heard Caleb groan and he gripped her waist hard and he gave over to the pleasure as well, filling the condom, pumping hot and hard into her, bringing Skylar right to the edge of her completion.

"Wow."

It was the only word she could think of it, and she nearly said it again, but was saved from repeating herself by his gentle kiss on her lips.

"I need to take care of this," he murmured, indicating to the space where their bodies were still joined. "Otherwise, I'd say let's stay just like this all night long."

She rather liked that idea, but he was right to be cautious and she slowly slid from his body, her own protesting the movement away from him. Caleb looked just as wrecked as she felt, his hair mussed from where she grabbed it, his lips swollen and the hedonistic glow of pleasure bright in his eyes.

"There's a second bathroom in there." He motioned to the door she had previously thought to be a closet entrance. "I want you waiting for me on the rug when I come back out."

She nodded and dipped into the bathroom, grateful that she didn't have to explain the whole *pee after sex* thing, and for the small amount of privacy he was giving her. If Caleb had looked well-loved, her reflection in the mirror was that of a woman possessed by pleasured, her lips bright red, her hair a wild tangle, her skin flushed with the aftereffects of her activities. Damn if this man didn't drag something from within her that was at once brand-new and bone-deep.

She washed up and finger-combed her hair, then took a deep breath and headed back out to meet Caleb and the promises he held.

He needed a moment. From the second he had caught sight of Skylar Wedgeworth across the lobby of the Sinclair Ranch, she'd had this hold over him, this way of pulling him toward her that made him feel a little unhinged. Part of him had known that it wasn't a safe bet to touch her more and hope the desperate need would go away, but that hadn't stopped him.

And now he was hiding like a coward, because he was pretty sure she could see everything he was feeling written across his face the moment he walked back out into the room. It was just that she was different, took his mind away from Becca, away from the career he hadn't had, made him feel something that wasn't pain or hurt, or frustration, made him want. He hadn't allowed himself to want anything in a long time. Wanting led to losing and he didn't ever again need the experience of Becca driving away.

But he wanted Skylar. In some way that took him very much off-guard and left him wondering what exactly to do next.

And if he was wondering what to do next, she was probably sitting out on the rug feeling very much alone, so he splashed some water on his face, dried it quickly with a towel and went out to meet her.

"How do you feel?" he asked, pausing by the refrigerator for two bottles of water. "Are you hungry?"

She smiled. "I could pretty much eat all the time," she said. "Depends on what you're offering."

She was cute in a sexy way, if that made any sense to his sex-rattled brained. The kind of sexy that started out with pencils pinning messy buns in place and oversized glasses and big sweaters, and ended with wild, bed-breaking, life-changing sex.

"Chocolate?" he asked. He opened the fridge again. "Cookies, pretzels, ice cream? There's also some cheese and meat in here and bread over on the table."

He made a mental note to increase their waitstaff's salary. The hidden staff who kept the rooms in top order were to be commended.

"Ice cream," she said after a moment's deliberation. "But like, let's put the cookies and pretzels into it."

He laughed and carried the supplies over to where she sat before the fire. Her skin caught the flame's soft glow and the light of the moon gave the whole room an ephemeral feeling. Or maybe that was just Skylar.

"Pretzels and cookies in ice cream?" He settled them on a small wooden tray from the table and placed it between them. "I'll have to take your word for it."

She laughed. "When I was pregnant, I ate the weirdest things," she said. "I went through a period where I had to put soy sauce on *everything*. I mean, donuts and cereal and popsicles. Soy sauce."

Caleb must have made a face, because she laughed again.

"Have you tried it since?" he asked. "How is cereal with soy sauce?"

She gagged. "Positively disgusting. By my third trimester, I was down to eating only popsicles. I was really pregnant at the end of summer and just hot all the time. I think the supermarket started double stocking just for me."

He grinned and watched her pop the top on the ice cream before pouring in half the bag of pretzels.

"This is better, I promise. This was actually one of Callie's great inventions."

"I trust you." The words were said in lightness, spoken of trying a new dessert, not the way she had said them in the throes of passion when she couldn't possibly have known what they meant to a man who had given his heart to someone cruel and unkind. In that moment, he found himself thinking of how she might look if she were pregnant now, glowing and beautiful and full of joy.

Don't get in over your head, Cash.

It was starting to look a little too late for that.

"Here," she said, holding up a spoon laden with pretzels and cookie bites. "Try it." He took the bite and enjoyed it but not nearly as much as he enjoyed the expression of excitement in her eyes.

"Delicious," he replied. "But not as sweet as you." It was amazing she could still blush after all they had shared, but her skin turned a rosy pink and all over again he wanted her.

But he held his control over those desperate urges. She was still new to this, still getting her footing in a world of pleasure he'd known for years. And yet, in a way, it was new to him too. He'd stepped out of his own safe haven ages ago, and it had been this woman who helped to lure him back in.

An hour later, they were standing under the stars, the moon catching in the movement of Skylar's hair as she leaned against the hot tub where this whole thing had started just a few days earlier. Had it really only been a few days? Caleb was definitely starting to lose sense of time and space around her.

"Thank you," she said quietly, leaning back and looking up into his eyes, her gaze far too discerning. "Tonight was amazing. I feel... Thank you."

He couldn't help himself. He was beginning to understand that he'd never really be able to help himself around her, and he leaned down and kissed her under the glow of the moon.

"Clear your schedule tomorrow," he said. "I don't want just your nights anymore, sunshine."

It was risky, taking this intense relationship into the daylight like he had any control over his desire, but judging by the look in Skylar's eyes, it was more than the right move.

"I'd like that very much," she said with a smile. "Sweet dreams."

He watched her walk into the cabin, watched the lights go on and listened to the sound of her getting ready for bed before he finally turned and headed home.

With thoughts of Skylar in his head, his dreams were bound to be very sweet indeed.

Chapter Twelve

"So, where did a city girl learn how to ride a horse like that?"

They were seated at the top of a large hill overlooking a lake so pristine it could have been used as a mirror to the sky. Around them, trees in the brightest of golds, crimsons and siennas rustled against the crisp morning breeze. Skylar burrowed under the flannel blanket and Caleb were sharing. By mid-morning, the temperature would be perfect, a breezy fall day with a hint of chill, but the sun was just creeping over the lake on the far side of the horizon and she liked the excuse to get a little closer to Caleb, anyway.

"My family liked to posture," she admitted. All these years later and she was just learning how to tell the truth about the Wedgeworths. "Polo and equestrian racing, dressage...it's all part of the life they lived, so it was all part of the life I lived." She laughed into the thermos of rich hot cocoa he handed her from the picnic basket. "The funny thing is, I loved the horses. I really missed that part when all was said and done."

She had taken Callie riding a few times, when their schedules allowed them to leave the city and head for the farms of rural Virginia, and even this morning, the experience of being back on a horse felt like putting on a favorite pair of jeans, comfortable and familiar.

"We don't have to talk about it," he replied, pulling the blanket up to her chin. Even when they were Skylar and Caleb, she could catch glimpses of his dominant side, of the version that cared for and controlled with equal measure. She liked those small touches probably more than was safe.

"I don't mind," she replied. "To know me is to know Callie and to know Callie is to know that things weren't always easy for us." They hadn't been easy for years, but she had followed the stories of a lot of the friends she had known in high school, had kept up with the gossip of her former life on rare occasion and had known that the person she had become would never have fit into that world.

"Did Callie's father help at all?" Caleb asked, with the kind of fierce protectiveness in his voice she was coming to expect of him. "Did anyone help you?"

She snorted. "Caroline's father was seventeen years old and headed to Princeton because that was where his daddy went and where his daddy went before him." She shook her head. "The Brookes wanted what my parents wanted, to sweep the whole thing under the rug and pretend it never happened."

She sighed. "I believe absolutely in a woman's right to make her choices, and I think if things had been different, that might have been the right choice for me. But when I found out I was pregnant, it made it so clear what was important to my parents—image, status, the family legacy. I realized that I couldn't be the person they wanted me to be, so I left."

He stroked her hand under the blanket, and Skylar took it for the gesture of support that it was and continued her story.

"There was this twenty-four-hour diner I knew about. When I left, I had grabbed all the cash I could and emptied out my bank account as fast as possible, because I knew my father wouldn't let me access that money anytime soon, but I didn't have a plan. So, I just went and sat in this diner for like three days straight, ordering herbal tea and toast."

She couldn't help but smile at the memory. Those had been the days when she had first begun to understand true kindness in dark moments.

"Caroline owned the place. She had owned the place since like the nineteen-seventies or something, and after three days of my being in that same back corner booth, she sat down and asked me what was wrong."

The sun was cresting over the horizon now and it felt just as it had in those desperate hours, a spot of light and hope in dark times.

"She offered me a job." Skylar laughed. "Said I could work as a waitress until I couldn't stand and that she'd hire me back after the baby was born. She even helped me find a room to rent at her sister's. I lived with Rosemond for three years."

"Callie is named for Caroline from the diner, then?" Caleb asked.

Skylar nodded. "I genuinely don't know what I would have done without that woman. But she was there when I needed her and for that I'll always be grateful."

He stroked her leg under the blanket, and even through the denim covering, Skylar found her body was suddenly quite immune to the cold outside.

"Rhylee said Callie wants to be a scientist," he added. "It sounds to me like you did one hell of a job."

It hadn't been easy. There had been days, so many days, especially in the beginning when it had felt like her alone against the world, and Skylar had to wonder if she could really do it. She hadn't been raised to fight for herself...hadn't been raised to take care of herself either. At sixteen, she'd had maids, cooks, au pairs, a driver. At sixteen, she was suddenly forced to learn how to make rice and wash her own clothes at the laundromat down the street and make a budget for herself when all she had ever been taught was how to spend money. It had been a humbling and, at times, overwhelming education in the truth of life for most people.

"I'm very lucky." She meant it. "Callie is the most important person in my world. Now that she's off at school and settling into her own life, it's time I start to do the same, you know?" It had been the reason behind her trip to Greece and the reason she had agreed to come on this wild adventure into the Montana mountains. It had led her to Caleb's side, whatever that meant for them.

"It seems to me," Caleb said, moving around so he could hold her in the brisk morning air, "that you have a pretty good sense of yourself. Strong, confident, capable of tackling adversity. That's far from nothing, sunshine."

It was *far, far* from nothing, when he put it like that. They had barely known each other for a few days, and already she felt like Caleb could see into some part of herself that had long been hidden. It was overwhelming and comfortable all at the same time, just like submitting to him made her answer questions about herself, about her own desires.

"Why do you call me that?" she asked him. She leaned back into his chest, and God, the man was made of solid muscle, all warm, rich male scent taking over her senses and making her want something no sensible woman would want for so early in the morning. "Sunshine?"

Oh God, the way his lips felt against her throat, the heat of him brushing over her skin, it was such an adrenaline jolt, and even while they sat in this romantic spot on the top of the hill, telling each other secrets and holding each other close, she wanted to please him in an entirely different way, wanted to make him proud, to give him what he wanted from her.

"I suppose it's partially because of your name, sky, sun and all that." She felt the words more than she heard them, his lush lips pressed into the dip at the base of her neck that she had apparently never much noticed before this very moment. "And partially because you light up the room brighter than this beautiful sunrise. Forgive me for being bold, but I could get used to your smile."

She turned to look at him, to peer up into his intense, dark eyes. She wasn't the only one feeling out of her depths here, like she was walking the tightrope and one wrong move could send her plummeting. Caleb, for all his strength and control, wasn't entirely unaffected. This went deeper than base lust and desire and meant something more for both of them — if they were willing to explore whatever it was that might be.

She tried not to let the thought terrify her.

"Why do you need brightening up?" she asked after a long moment. She couldn't help herself and bought one hand up to stroke the strong curve of his jaw, brushing the light stubble across his skin. He closed his eyes at her touch, another way of letting her take the lead, even though she knew he was still the one in control. "What happened to you?"

He pursed his lips and let out a low, deep sigh.

"You don't want to hear that story," he said after a moment. "It doesn't have a happy ending."

She wasn't going to be the one to say that whatever had happened to him had brought them to this moment, shared on the mountainside in the morning sunrise, even if it felt like that in her bones.

"Hearing about my privileged and horrible family and how they kicked me out for getting pregnant at sixteen is a happy ending?" she asked.

The corners of his mouth lifted in wry amusement. "You have Callie," he said. "And an amazing business, friends, a life. You've thrived not despite your hardship, but because of it."

She stroked over his cheek, aching for more contact with this man who got to the heart and soul of the matter in a single sentence. How was it that he so succinctly understood and without so much as a hint of judgment?

"Talking about our problems can help," she said quietly. "Your friends are worried about you."

That got him to open his eyes. "Is that what Van was talking to you about at lunch yesterday?" he asked.

She raised a brow. "Were you watching me?" In return, she scanned his gaze. "Were you *jealous?* Wow, you totally were."

And if that made something in the area of her chest feel a little hot and swollen, well, she wasn't going to consider it too much.

"I feel rather proprietary over you," he said quietly. "I know that makes me a caveman, but there's something about you, sunshine. It makes me a little wild."

She could empathize.

"I like you wild," she admitted. "It's becoming one of my favorite things. But you can also trust me with other stuff too. I know what a hard-won life looks like."

Caleb smiled down at her like she had given him something special. It was the way he had looked in the throes of passion the night before when she had told him he could trust her. She hadn't been sure where it had come from then, but in this moment, with the morning warmth and the fresh fall breeze and a sense of opportunity all around them, Skylar had a pretty good sense.

"I was a pitcher," he said after a long, heavy pause. "Top of the minor leagues and headed up. From the time I was three years old, all I had ever wanted to do was pitch a major league game. I lived, breathed and ate baseball and I really thought I was going to make it. We all did because I was."

He shifted behind her and Skylar could feel that weight, the weight of missed chances, the feeling of the life you had expected coming out from under your feet in a single swoop. She knew the sensation all too well, and while she had walked away with a daughter, Caleb hadn't anything to hold on to while he faced his own struggles.

"Something was wrong," he admitted. "But it was the last game of the season and I was determined to make my stand, prove that I had what it took to take it to the big leagues." She winced because she already knew what was coming, had heard the story so many times before, but that didn't go too far when it came to stopping the inevitable.

"Torn rotator cuff." He rolled his shoulders, putting emphasis on the left one. "You can go back to playing after that. Some people do. But they're never the same pitcher. I had just turned twenty-five, but my career was over."

"Did you?" she asked. "Go back."

He shook his head. "I was never cleared to play again. And even if I had been, I would never have been good enough to follow the path laid out for me."

Under the blanket, Skylar squeezed his hand. The story gave her a glimpse into this man, the one who had become so important to her over such a short amount of time. The one who she still knew so little about.

"So, you moved back home," she replied. "And took back up at Sinclair Ranch."

"Not exactly." He shifted their bodies so she was learning up against him now, and even though the topic was heavy, even though there were questions that needed to be answered, for both their sakes, there was also something deeply enticing, erotic and promising about the way he touched her. It reminded her of the night before and also made her want for so much more than he had given her. She knew Caleb was holding back and she understood why, but Skylar also knew she was up for the challenge.

"So how did it go, then?" she asked.

"I moved back home to nurse up my injury," he replied. "I'd been traveling with the team for a while and there's no place quite like home to feel sorry for yourself, right? Wasn't long after that I reconnected with Becca."

Skylar couldn't say for certain why that sent a shiver down her spine, but it did. Maybe it was the tone in his voice when he said the other woman's name, or maybe it was just that she had become somewhat proprietary too.

"Who was Becca?" she asked, proud of how steady and controlled her voice sounded.

Caleb laughed. "Why? Jealous."

She shot him a look over her shoulder. "Will you answer if I tell you I am?"

He stroked her hair with strong, capable hands. Skylar didn't want to admit how good it felt, how good he felt, all power and strength, from surviving and thriving though life hadn't made it easy.

"Becca was my high school girlfriend," he explained. "We were the all-American type. Varsity captain, prom queen and king, you know? Small-town living."

She hadn't had small town living when she'd gone to school and after Callie was in the picture, it had been GED classes after hours, but Skylar had seen enough All-American high school movies to know the type to a tee—and to know, also, that those picture-perfect relationships had the tendency to go up in flames by movie's end.

"I was nursing my wounds, stuck wondering what the hell I was going to do with my life and feeling like a fool for putting it all on one dream, you know?" he continued. "She made me feel like more than a fallen hometown hero, like I was a person, and I was allowed to grieve this dream. She never told me to man up or pretend everything was all right, and at the time, that was what I needed most."

She hated the sadness and defeat in his voice, hated that he had been forced to give up a dream that had been such a fundamental part of who he was as a person.

"It turns out she wasn't the right kind of person for me. There were things we didn't see eye to eye, fundamental, incompatible things. We've been divorced a year."

She hadn't been expecting that, and she turned around to face him, to look up in those dark, rich eyes and show him he wasn't alone. Though, of course, this was all temporary. Still, she could give him temporary.

"You can tell me," she promised, her voice low and her words as gentle as she could make them. Skylar couldn't be certain, but something about Caleb's movements, about his stilted, harsh posture, told her that even his best friends didn't know the extent to which his ex-wife had hurt him. "Did she do something to you?"

The classic American man, sports hero, cowboy…it would track that machismo in this small town would rule the day, even though his friends and sister seemed progressive and forward-thinking.

"She didn't do anything, no," Caleb said quietly. "But she did know exactly what to say to get me in the gut. That wasn't all of it, of course. We'd been having problems, lots of problems. But she had to get in those parting shots. She got kind of bitter, toward the end. I had moved back home but she had never left it, and the shine wears off the crown when you're not in high school anymore, you know? Part of me thinks she always expected I'd go back to playing. But even if I had wanted to, it wasn't an option. And, after we inherited the Sinclair Ranch, I didn't want to."

"What she said…" Skylar approached the topic carefully. "That's why you haven't been going to the barn or doing any of it. It's why Van said, 'welcome back' that first night, isn't it?"

He shrugged, but it was the kind of shrug that told Skylar she nailed it. She didn't want to have nailed this one.

"What did she say to you?"

Caleb took a deep breath and looked out over the lake. The sun was well over the horizon now and there was a warm glow to the air around them. It wasn't nearly as warm as the sensation of being in Caleb's arms, however.

"She said…she said we're all perverts for running the club. Said that only freaks like rough sex and dominating their partners. She said that no amount of, quote, BDSM, unquote, was going to make up for how my injury had made me less of a man. Something like that."

Once, when Callie had been in middle school, she had been sent to the principal's office for punching a boy in the face. When Skylar had arrived at the school, practically in tears, worried that her sweet, smart, kind daughter was going through something terrible, she had been informed that the boy Callie had punched had reached over and snapped her bra in the cafeteria. She had also been informed that Callie had been suspended and the boy had been let off with a warning.

And she had seen red. She had seen bonfires, in Mr. Strickland's office, and she had yelled at each and every one of the advisors and educators put into place to protect her child. She had yelled at the boy. She had yelled at the boy's parents. She had threatened lawsuits with the full weight of the Wedgeworth family name behind her — which she hadn't had, but had been mad enough to invoke — then she had taken Callie out for ice cream and an afternoon movie and a rousing discussion about a woman's right to her own body.

She wasn't quite as mad as the day her daughter had been forced to deal with both male entitlement and the system designed to protect it in one fell swoop, but she was goddam close to it.

"I swear to...that son of a bitch... If I ever, Caleb, I mean, if I ever — "

Her anger did have some benefit, because it seemed to loosen Caleb's shoulders a little bit and a smile tugged at the corners of his lips.

"Calm down there, Mama Bear," he said, humor in his voice. "I'll be okay."

Except he wasn't going to be okay by pretending it hadn't happened. Sure, their club had its novelty, the fantasy of the location, the intrigue of a band of brothers building something bold and erotic in the Montana mountainside. But it was so, so much more than that. Caleb's domination, his control, his *care*, it was at his core. It made him the person he was, and she would bet her next commission the other men felt the same. To hit so low, to so completely misunderstand the fundamental personality of the man she had promised to love...

"It was cruel," she said, the anger subsiding. "It was cruel, and it was wrong. What you do, what the club stands for, it's about being genuine and true to yourself. It's about embracing who you really are."

That made him smile for real, and she couldn't help but notice the heat gathering in his eyes. She was pretty sure she would always notice the heat in his gaze and the way his body language shifted, ever so slightly, when he wanted her.

"You're right," Caleb replied. "I know that. In my head. But she had shared those rooms with me. She had shared all of it with me. She was the only one I ever partnered with in that room before you. Either she was trying to hurt me as much as she could before she left, or she'd been faking it the whole time. And if she was, then I wasn't doing my job right."

"It's not your job," Skylar put in, pushing the stark truth of his confession about sharing the room for the first time in a year with *her* very much out of her mind. "Especially not with her. It was supposed to be a relationship. Relationships are about trust and communication. If it wasn't working for her, she needed to be the one to say it. I may be new to this, but I understand that part, at least."

He took her chin in his hand and the expression in his eyes when he replied reminded Skylar of a rolling summer storm, coming in hot and full of fire and mystery.

"You understand everything," he said.

Caleb had spent most of his life with a plan. He would train hard and play well, make it to the minors, make it to the majors. When life had thrown the curveball right back at him, he had returned home and settled down, had planned on making a future for himself on the Sinclair Ranch, before they had turned it into the club, then a future with Becca. Beau Sinclair's will and the help of Caleb's persistent and well-intentioned but nosy friends, had made the whole thing easier. *Building a business. Building a secret business within it.* There had always been a plan. Even when it felt like his whole life was on a loose roller coaster cart with no direction, he'd put his head down and focused on taking the next steps. Baseball was, after all, a strategy sport.

But Skylar Wedgeworth, with all her fury on his behalf, the blazing heat in her eyes, her willingness to try anything he offered her because of this inherent and terrifying bond between them, it was starting to make him feel very much like throwing the plans out of the window. He'd been in this business for nearly two years and he'd practiced with his fair share of partners before life and his career had taken a left turn. Never before had he experienced such a coming together of two perfect partners. It was like they were puzzle pieces that had been fitting into other spaces just fine, but now that they had found their actual location within the picture, everything had changed.

"It's new," she breathed. Her face was flushed, and those beautiful, big eyes stared up at him with absolute trust and promise. He hadn't told a soul what Becca had said to him the night she had left, but now that he'd said it to Skylar, to this woman who was proving to be everything Becca wasn't, even though they had only known each other for a few days, it felt like half the weight of the world was off his shoulders. Which was good, considering the ache of the old injury that still lingered there. "It's all new."

He smiled at her, and he'd be damned if it wasn't a little wolfish, a little predatory. Everything about her made him feel wild and animalistic and demanding in all the ways he had missed so much.

"Does it feel new?" he asked, sliding his thumb along the side of her jaw. Her eyes dilated at the simple touch and damn if that didn't bring the erection he had been fighting since he'd first spied her in her cute-ass riding gear that morning to full tilt. "Or does it feel like something you've known how to do forever?"

He'd had partners in the past looking for a way to get their rocks off, and he respected that. Different strokes for different folks — as long as everything was consensual and safe and fun. But he also knew what the face of true submission, true promise, the true and willing sacrifice of control and responsibility looked like, and it made him ache for her in a way that felt like something he, too, had done forever.

"I never realized it was an option," she admitted on a small laugh. "Then, in Greece, I thought it was a fluke, some wild and inexplicable thing brought on by the Mediterranean air. I left early, you know? I think I was scared of what I was learning about myself there."

He brought his hand around to the back of her neck, stroking her skin and running his fingers through her soft, lush hair.

"And now?" he asked her. "Are you scared now?"

She pursed her lips and shook her head and God, if it wasn't a sight he could get used to.

"Good." He would have made her beg more, was becoming deeply accustomed to the sound of desperation on her wicked tongue, but for now, he was more interested in pushing her, taking their play to the next level. She *was* new to this, and that had been why he had taken things slowly for them, but she was also brave and ready to face the next challenge, and he knew she wanted more than he had been giving her. He wanted to give her so much more.

He took the cup from her hands and placed it down near the picnic basket.

"Are you cold?"

She shook her head.

He slid the blanket off her shoulders and dragged her face up to meet his until they were sharing the same breath.

"I've been thinking about kissing you since before the sun came up," he said. "I'm thinking about kissing you pretty much all the time."

She grinned but quickly hid it, her body reacting subconsciously to what her mind was just beginning to accept, and it made him desperate for her, wild and unrefined. So he kissed her, rough and promising. There was nothing gentle in their connection, a clash of tongues and teeth and lips, a giving over and grateful accepting of control and submission.

"Is that all you think about?" she asked him when he pulled back. "Sir?"

He wasn't sure which he liked more, her complete and willing submission or the bratty side that came out when she was feeling feisty.

"Oh no, honey." He tugged her onto his lap. "I think about so much more than kissing you. I think about the way you looked spread out on my rug, the fire caressing your tight, hard nipples. I think about you bent over the couch, with your perky ass in my hand. And I think about making you beg for my touch, my fingers, my tongue, my cock."

Skylar whimpered, fucking *whimpered*, and Caleb found himself doing a play-by-play of the last Billings Mustangs ballgame, just to keep control over both of his heads. A man could get off to the sounds she made alone.

"What do you want now?" she asked.

He raised one eyebrow. "That's my line, sunshine," he replied. "But since you're so eager, I'll tell you. I want you to lie across my lap. Just like that."

Her first expression of skepticism had been replaced with heat the moment she had realized what the position meant, the moment he had caressed her denim-clad ass and tapped it lightly. She bucked under his touch and he leaned down to whisper in her ear.

"Did you like that?" he asked. "Did you like the little rush of pain that comes with so much pleasure?"

She bit her lower lip and nodded, and he didn't correct her, just slapped her ass again, harder this time.

"Here's what's going to happen," he told her, massaging the spot with gentle movements. "You're going to count each of these spankings I give you and you're going to properly thank me for them, for giving you what you want. But you're not going to make another sound. If you do, I start again. Do I make myself clear?"

She nodded and Caleb could have thanked the lord above for it. She wanted this as much as he did, judging by her beautiful responsiveness.

He spanked her.

Skylar arched up, and her voice was aching when she said, "One. Thank you, Sir."

Oh, fuck.

Another.

"Two. Thank you, Sir."

Another. And another. Each time she moved against him, she brushed his swollen cock, and Caleb wasn't going to be able to play this game for very long. He reached into the space between their bodies and undid the button and zipper on her jeans before sliding them down her legs just enough that it revealed her smooth, soft ass, clad in a pair of cute, lacy panties with a crisscross of ribbon running up the back. He palmed her ass.

"I thought I told you not to wear panties anymore," he said. She didn't answer. "You can respond, Skylar."

Her voice was husky and laden with desire when she answer. "I can't go riding without them, Sir," she replied. "Not if I wanted to visit you tonight."

He considered that, considered the tightness of her jeans, now bunched a few inches below the waist, and conceded the point.

"Fair," he murmured. "And they are so pretty. Makes your ass look good enough to eat."

She writhed at his words and he made a mental note to make her scream in some rather creative ways later.

"The problem is, they're also in my way." He stroked down the curve of her ass and came to the soaked lace between her legs. "Oh, you are desperate, aren't you?"

She rocked against him in response.

"That's just too bad, sweet girl." He gently circled the damp fabric, but didn't give her nearly the pressure she was asking for. "Because I'm not done marking your pretty ass."

He raised her hips slightly and pulled the panties down to the top of her jeans so she was completely exposed. Then he spanked her again.

She did scream this time, a tangle of need pouring from her, and he wondered if she might be able to come just from the pleasurable punishment. He might, just from watching the way her ass turned red under his touch. It was a sight he would never forget.

"More?"

"God, yes, please, thank you, Sir." Even among her incoherent babble, she still managed to remember his position of power, to respect it and honor it.

"Only because you asked so nicely." He swatted her three times in quick succession now, sending her writhing and bucking against him, until when he slid his hand lower, into her folds, he found the desperation of her heat and wetness slick over his fingers. He couldn't help himself. He brought them to his mouth and sucked her taste deep and long.

"I could eat your sweet pussy for every meal and not get enough," he half-growled, like the animal she made him. "Do you know what your beautiful submission does to me? It makes me a desperate man."

She was moaning in her earnest now, but she didn't respond without his prompting. So he prompted.

"If you could tell me exactly what you wanted me to do," he began, "and that's not to say I'll do it, what would it be? Go ahead, tell me."

"Sir." She was clearly distracted by the rising desire, the unfilled release he had promised her but hadn't delivered. Yet. "Please."

"Please what, sunshine?" he asked, swatting her ass again. "Use your words."

"Fuck me." She managed that quite succinctly. "Fill my…fill my pussy and…"

"And…"

"Play with my ass."

She said the last so quietly that he was almost certain he'd imagined the request from the deepest part of his desperate imagination. But her skin was flushed and he knew she had, indeed, offered up so much of what he ached for on a silver platter.

"Right here?" He slid his finger between her lush ass cheeks, barely touching, just brushing her tight hole with the softest movements. That she immediately arched back up to meet him was response enough, indeed.

"So fucking perfect," he muttered. "Don't move." He reached over her for the basket that held more than coffee and cookies, for the bag of toys he'd tucked inside with the hope of taking Skylar to new heights. He opened the bag and pulled out what he had been looking for, a small, silver plug with a purple jewel on the end and a bottle of lube.

"Do you trust me?" he asked her, first slicking his finger with lube before circling her hole again. "How are you feeling right now?"

"I trust you." *Fuck*, those words hit him right in the gut. "I'm green. Good. More, please."

He pressed into her tight hole with his finger and her resistance gave slightly until her was able to slide in. Fuck, she was tight there, clenching him and rocking back into his touch. It would take training to get her to take his cock in her tight ass, training he was perfectly happy to help with.

"How does it feel?" he asked her.

"Hot," she whispered. "I feel full, but I want more. It's…so hot." From his perspective, it was about the hottest thing that had ever happened.

"Can you take another finger?"

She nodded. "Please, Sir?"

He pressed into her with the next finger, this time meeting more resistance than before, so he brought his other hand under her and found her swollen clit.

"Relax for me, baby," he muttered. "I don't want to hurt you. Let me in." He stroked her clit and her body gave in to the pleasure, allowed him entrance until he had two thick fingers deep in her asshole.

"Oh, fuck."

"You'll get that soon," he promised. "You're so beautiful like this, sunshine. I love how you look when you open up to me."

"Please?"

He'd bet good money that she didn't even know what she was begging for.

"I'm going to pull out now," he told her. "Trust me."

She nodded, and he slowly pulled his fingers out of her, before placing the slick toy at the entrance to her ass.

"This might be a little cold," he warned. "But I promise it's going to feel so good."

He pushed slightly and the head went in, then more of the bulb, until the entire toy was seated in her ass.

Caleb was pretty goddamn sure he could come just from the sight of Skylar all filled. Her soft, supple flesh wrapped around the plug, made it look snug, like it belonged in the tight hole of her ass and fuck if that thought, the thought of her wearing his toy, of coming home to her ass ready for him, wasn't the kind of the fantasy he would hold on to for years.

"How does it feel?" he asked, half-crazed just from the sight of her. Still, it was his job, the job he loved most in the world, to make sure it felt as good for her. *Better.*

"Full." She moaned the word. "But kind of amazing." He flicked at her clit and she whimpered. "Fine, really amazing. I never realized."

She was so innocent, this soft, beautiful woman who had landed quite literally in his lap, and he was the lucky son of a bitch who got to show her exactly how pleasurable it could be to give up control, to give up shame, to take what she wanted. Even if he was struggling with his own shame, with the remnants of a relationship gone sour, he could still help bring Skylar to her edge, show her exactly how beautiful and powerful she really was.

"The plug is small," he explained. "But fuck if this isn't the hottest thing I've ever seen in my life. You'll be able to take the bigger one soon." He slid a palm over the curve of her ass, just brushing the head of the plug. Skylar bucked against him. "Oh yeah, you're going to like it, too. And you're going to like it when your tight little hole opens to my cock."

He didn't stop her from writhing in his lap. With the delicious friction of her body's movements against his aching, straining cock, he wasn't sure if it was even possible to tell her to stop.

"I don't think you need to be tied up, either," he added. "Some pets do. But you're so good. You'll beg me for the chance to bend over and offer up your sweet, lush body for my enjoyment, won't you?"

He was already beginning to recognize when Skylar was at her edge, and there was no denying that she was getting close. Her movements were frenzied, and her breathing was husky and harsh, laden with desperate whimpers.

"Yes, anything for you, Sir."

"Will you come for me?" He cupped her pussy and stroked gently. "Out here where anyone could see, your ass all plugged up and on display?" The words came out husky and desperate, but for however he sounded, he felt so much more.

"Yes, Sir. Please. Can I?"

"So sweet," he murmured. He stroked over her ass with his other hand again, then tapped it lightly, so lightly she wouldn't have felt a thing, save for the silver plug buried in her tight hole. "Come all over my fingers. I want to taste you." He swatted her ass again, this time stroking her clit at the same time, and Skylar screamed, loud and desperate, and wracked with pleasure, and she came hard, coating his fingers in her sweet release, riding him and taking her pleasure even as he gave it willingly.

Her body went slack against him, and Caleb stroked her hair and back and ran his hands up the sides of her waist because he couldn't seem to stop touching her.

"How are you feeling, sunshine?" he murmured. "Want me to take it out or are you okay to keep playing?"

She lifted her head up, her eyes heavy with lust and her lips swollen and lush. This scene, Skylar in supplication, at his mercy as much as he was at hers, it was something he could get very used to. Was already very used to.

"I want you," she murmured. If could, he would make this woman scream his name every goddamn day of the year. "I want...more."

Her innocence, contrasted with the sight she made now, all flush skin, her ass still in his palm, the plug still tight between her cheeks, was the most sinfully delicious thing Caleb had seen in his entire fucking life.

"You always want more, don't you, sweet girl?" he asked.

She nodded. "From you."

And *that* was the most sinfully delicious thing Caleb had ever *heard* in his life.

Before he could lose himself in her, give over to his baser physical desires like he was sixteen again, he slowly lifted Skylar from where she lay spread across his legs and settled her more firmly in his lap. She let out a small whimper when the plug moved inside her, and Caleb knew that as much as she deserved slow and erotic and promising, that this time was going to be carnal, and demanding as hell.

"I'm going to take you like this," he murmured into her ear. "You're going to feel so full you won't be able to help but come all over my cock. That's what I want. Don't hold back."

He maneuvered himself from his pants without jostling her too much and managed to slide a condom onto his rock-hard cock, even though all his animalistic brain wanted to do was to rut and ride and take.

Then he was guiding Skylar's needy, desperate body over his own, sliding her across his hot, throbbing cock, and feeling like he'd fucking entered heaven itself.

"How does it feel?"

This, through gritted teeth.

"Oh, God." She leaned back against him, rubbing her sweet, lush ass against his groin and making his swear. "So full, Sir..." She trailed off. Then, so quietly he almost didn't hear, she asked, "Does it feel good for you, when the plug is in?"

He groaned a long string of curse words. "Your pussy is wrapped around my cock so tight I feel like I'm going to burst," he managed. "Yes, sunshine. It feels good."

She seemed to take that as permission to move, but he stilled her with a strong hand on the waist.

"But don't forget that I'm still the one in charge here. You may be on top, but, sweet girl, I have all the control."

That wasn't even remotely true, not given how fucking close to the edge he was with the way she wrapped around him like a fucking vice, but he was still her Dom, in this moment, in this scene, in everything, and he refused to let her down by giving over to his own desperate impulses too soon.

"I'm sorry, Sir." She sounded genuine. "It feels good, I..."

"I told you to come as much as you want," he reminded her. "Are you going to coat my cock? Are you going to use me for your own pleasure?"

She only whimpered in response, and he gave over, reached around and found her swollen clit. There was no warning. One flick and she shot off, screaming and writhing and fucking his cock like something wild and uninhibited. Caleb could only hold on by the skin of his teeth.

"Do you clench the plug when you come?" he asked her. "A little extra pressure in your ass that sets you right off the edge, doesn't it?"

She nodded. "It's so good. It's too much."

It wasn't too much. He knew when it was too much, and Skylar was nowhere near it. She needed him to help her find the perfect balance of pleasure and excess, and damn if that wasn't happy to oblige.

"Again," he told her. "Clench around the plug and my cock. Fuck, yeah." She squeezed him so tight it was a wonder she had never done this before. "Come around me again, Skylar. Right now."

He pinched her clit, harder this time, and that did the trick, sending her spiraling, if the whimpers and cries were anything to go by.

"Please, Sir, I can't..."

"You can," he replied. He reached up her shirt and toyed with one swollen nipple. "You're going to come again for me, sunshine, because that's what I'm telling you to do." He squeezed, then leaned down and whispered in her ear. "If you're especially good, if you do exactly what you're told, I might even bring out the nipple clamps tonight, so you can feel that sweet little pinch on your swollen breasts."

The image of her wearing nothing but cowboy boots and nipple clamps was a fantasy he would carry with him for the rest of his goddamned life.

"Do you want the clamps?" he asked, putting more pressure on her hard, peaked nipples. She nodded.

He pinched hard, but not quite hard enough. "You want the clamps, then you're going to have to come for me again."

She shook her head. "It's too much. I can't…"

He brought his other hand to her swollen clit, massaged her breasts and her sweet soft pussy at the same time, while his cock and the plug filled both of her tight holes.

Then he spanked her, right on her swollen, aching pussy, and the sensation was clearly enough to send her flailing over the age, because she clenched hard around him, hard enough to set off his own spiraling release, and he pumped hot cum into the condom while she writhed and bucked into his body, taking as he gave, giving as he took, their combined shouts and curses filling the fresh morning air.

They came down slowly. Caleb's breathing began to return to normal and he massaged Skylar's neck, stroked her hair, caressed her until he could no longer keep her safe while she remained on his lap.

"I need to clean this up," he murmured into her neck.

She nodded, and they moved in unison to slowly pull apart. He dealt with the condom quickly, then turned back to her.

"Take a breath," he murmured. She nodded, her eyes full of trust and locked on his as he slowly pulled the plug free and set it aside. That trust, after their play, after their pleasure, felt more important than anything.

He helped her re-dress, pulled his own pants up, and they shared their second breakfast of the morning, bites of pastry and maple donuts, coffee and hot chocolate still hot from the thermoses. Lazy sleepy cast their tangled bodies in morning glow, and Caleb knew, from her soft, sweet breathing as she dozed in his lap, from the comfort he felt at her touch, from all they had shared in words and actions that morning, that he was in well and truly over his head.

Chapter Thirteen

This time, when Skylar got to the barn, it was to join in the poker game going on in the main room. Caleb, Reece and Dante were seated around the table, along with a few other people she had yet to meet. Rhylee and Van were conspicuously absent, and Skylar had to wonder if maybe all the pheromones were getting to her head.

"Come here, honey." When he took up the mantle of her Dominant, her body reacted without conscious thought, and by the time she climbed into his lap, she was already hot and wet and achingly ready for him.

"Who's winning?" She had never cared about anything less in her life, but if Caleb's version of teasing was to make her sit on his lap until he said otherwise, she would do as he asked.

"Depends on your idea of winning." He whispered this low in her ear, the movement causing his evening scruff to brush against her neck, and Skylar rocked back into him. He stilled her movements with firm hand on her hip. "Because right now it feels an awful lot like I am."

"Flush." This from a beautiful brunette to her right that even in her lusty haze, Skylar could see making eyes at Dante. She didn't blame the woman.

"What?" Was her own blush so obvious that others could see it?

The woman smiled, dazzling and sweet. "Straight flush." She pointed to her cards. A few of the other players at the table folded.

"Annalise," she introduced herself. Skylar smiled and reached over to shake her hand like it was a totally normal thing to do from the comfort of Caleb's lap. "You must be new."

"Skylar," she replied. "And I am, as of..." She thought back. Jesus Christ, what day was it? "Monday...?"

"Time moves differently around here," Annalise said with a smile. "But that's not always a bad thing, of course." She locked eyes with someone across the room, and her face lit up. When Skylar turned, it was to catch sight of a strikingly beautiful Black woman in a suit and heels. Though the attire didn't match the room, she owned it, from her stance to her expression, and Skylar understood what it meant to recognize a Dominant from a mile away, even if they weren't her own.

"Will you excuse me?" Annalise said. It was her cheeks, not Skylar's, that flushed this time, then she was gone.

"What do you think they're going to do in there?" Caleb murmured in her ear. "The same thing we're going to do as soon as I win this next round?"

Skylar swallowed. "I don't know."

"Oh, but you can imagine, can't you?" His words left no room for indecision. "See, Brie travels a lot for work, so they don't get to see each other very often. Which means when they do..."

Skylar had never really thought of other women finding their pleasure as something erotic. She had considered beauty and fashion and all the things she'd thought of in her own mirror, of course, had listened to the stories of friend's adventures, Ev's especially, with her extra partner. But up until this very moment, she had never really considered what went into a scene between two women.

Except as she thought of it now, it wasn't so much that Annalise and Brie were gorgeous, strikingly powerful women who clearly made a statement wherever they went. It was the submission and domination that called her, regardless of sex, the picture Caleb now painted with his words of Annalise on her knees, Brie standing over her with a ruler, of complete and utter trust and communication that could only lead to a night of unbridled pleasure. That was what they were all seeking here, wasn't it?

"I'd offer to let you watch," Caleb murmured, his voice nonchalant as if he had asked her what kind of pizza she wanted. "They like that, an audience. Annalise especially. But..." He nipped at her neck and Skylar tilted her head back to allow him better access, almost without thinking. "You're more interested in being on display, aren't you? You like the idea of someone watching you."

She squirmed in his lap, squirmed again when she felt the hot pressure of his cock against into her thigh. Another thing she'd never really thought about until Caleb. It turned out there were quite a lot.

"I have a present for you, sunshine," he said. He held out his hand and she took his, allowed him to lead her from the main room and down the hall. He didn't stop at the room they had been using, but instead walked them to a door a little way down. When he knocked, a familiar voice called out, and when he indicated for her to go in, she saw Dante setting up tools at a small table. The room was deeply masculine, but she would have known in an instant it wasn't Caleb's. Dark leather couches were set up in the center of the room, with a matching loveseat, and the walls were adorned with dramatic, geometric shapes. It looked like the kind of loft she would see a graphic designer renting for a workspace in DC, and she wondered when he'd slipped away from the poker game to beat them here, in what was clearly his domain.

She hadn't taken a good look at him in the main room, but now she could see his ripped black jeans, the form-fitting Henley that bulged against his muscled arms, the ink escaping from every hem and seam that made her wonder where, exactly, his tattoos stopped. A dark black and studded cowboy hat rested low on the back of his head, but lush dark hair fanned out from below. He was a starkly dangerously, beautiful man.

And completely different from the person she had gotten to know these last few days. Here, in his space at The Ranch, his domination was no longer hidden behind easy smiles and generous flirtations. Like Caleb, the switch appeared to be seamless, a natural part of himself that he embraced. She had thought him handsome and alluring behind the bar, but now she felt very much like she had been happily caged in with two wild animals.

"I've been lenient with you, sunshine," Caleb said, leading her to the loveseat. "Master Dante keeps stricter rules than I do."

None of this should have made her want. She was thoroughly and utterly at the mercy of two of the most beautiful, dangerous men she had ever met, and all she could feel was a riot of arousal that made it hard to think.

"You spoil your pets, Master Caleb," Master Dante said with a wolfish grin. "They're going to expect treats all the time."

Caleb stroked Skylar's jaw, and even that small touch made her arch into him, made her whimper for more. Dante raised an eyebrow, as if to say *I told you so.*

"I like giving treats," Caleb replied. "It's my favorite part."

"Is that what tonight is?" Master Dante asked. "A treat?"

Caleb grinned. God, he was beautiful. As much as Dante was erotic, all vampires of lore and desperation, Caleb seemed to fill something inside her, to equalize a part of her inner soul that had always felt off balance. Or something.

"That depends on if she wants it."

She was right there, sitting practically between the two of them, hard walls of muscle and strength, and they were talking about her like she didn't exist, like she was there for their pleasure and their pleasure alone, and she liked the ever-loving hell out of it.

"Sunshine." Caleb turned to her and she bent her head down until he placed a strong finger under her chin and tilted her head up to look at him.

"She's a natural," Master Dante commented from beside them. He was fiddling with something in a small chest of drawers, but she didn't dare look away from Caleb's gaze to see what it was.

"Mmm, she is." Caleb's voice was proud. "Now, how are you feeling, sweet girl?"

Desperate. Wet. Needy. Depraved.

"Green," she managed. "Sir. So green."

So fucking turned on she was about to slide off the loveseat.

"Good." She would pretty much do anything it took to keep that look in his eyes, pride, approval, desire. For her.

"Remember how you said you only got the one piercing?" he began. He dropped his hand down to the swell of her breast, accurately guessing which nipple held the small ball on the first try, and swiping his hand over the already engorged tip. "Because the pain made you come?"

She bucked up into his touch and let out a small, desperate whimper. He pinched hard.

"Answer me, sunshine."

She nodded. "Yes. I liked it. But I was embarrassed."

Caleb stroked her again. "I don't want you to be embarrassed anymore. Not with me. Not with us. There is no shame in your pleasure, sweet girl. We're going to show you that."

At this, she did glance over at what Master Dante was doing on the small table, recognized his tools instantly. He was a tattoo artist, it only made sense that he would have the skills for a simple piercing as well.

"Now how are you feeling?" Caleb asked.

She took longer to answer this time, the desire, the throbbing ache mingling with that leftover shame. The knowledge that these men wouldn't judge her for her pleasure. They would probably enjoy it just as much as she did.

"Green." She meant it.

"Good. Everything off," Caleb told her. "But keep the boots on."

Stripping was easy. She had been listening when he told her no more underwear. Then she was following Master Dante's instructions to sit back in the comfortable leather chair beside him. He had placed the cowboy hat aside, tied up his dark hair in a knot and damn if the devil didn't look so pretty.

"Any complication from this one?" His tone was all professional until he reached out and flicked her nipple ring, which sent a shot of pure, erotic adrenaline racing through her body. She shook her head.

"No, Sir," she managed. "It healed fine."

He inspected it and apparently found the ball satisfactory, because he reached into the chest and pulled out a small drawer of jewelry, presumably to search for one that matched.

"It's not uncommon," he explained, after he'd found what he was looking for. "Pleasure with pain. I have several piercings, myself." She assumed that the ones in his lip, eyebrow and ears weren't what he was talking about. "You wouldn't be the first person in my chair to come." And he definitely wasn't talking about piercing just then, either.

"Don't torture her, Dante," Caleb said from where he stood at the end of the chair. "That's my job."

Master Dante toyed with her unpierced nipple and bit his lip.

"Oh, but she's so pretty, all laid out on my chair, pink and lush. If you want more pain with your pleasure than Caleb is offering, I've got what you need."

She didn't doubt it for a second. But when Caleb groaned, low and possessive, no promise of another type of pleasure would ever be enough to drag her away.

"I know, I know." Dante pulled on his gloves and held a hand up to cover her eyes before turning on a light. "I can look but not touch." He allowed her to adjust to the brightness, then winked. "Good thing that really fucking works for me, then."

It was starting to become apparent that a whole lot of things really fucking worked for Skylar too. She writhed in the seat, feeling cool leather against her skin and the hot twin gazes of the two dominant men determined to drive her completely off the edge.

"You're in charge, Caleb," Dante said. "You tell me what to do."

Caleb tilted his chin. "Give her what she wants."

"He's good to you," Dante murmured, as he held the tool up. "I like to make my pets wait."

She didn't doubt it.

The metal was cool against her swollen nipple and she wondered if being aroused made the piercing easier.

"Ready?" Dante asked. "It's not too late to say no."

"Ready," she replied. "Please…Sir."

The Sir was a sign of respect, definitely. And Skylar couldn't exactly say how, but it felt differently on her tongue from any time she had ever called Caleb Sir.

He nodded and slid the needle through, quick, professional and capable of immediately turning her body into a writhing, lust-driven mess. She breathed through the ache of pleasure, doing her best to allow him to finish properly, even as shards of white-hot lust wracked her body. *Holy hell...* The first time, it had come as a surprise, the pleasure. She'd been caught off guard and embarrassed and confused, but now, all she felt was a driving, all-consuming *need*. All she could focus on was that perfect, impossible balance between pain and pleasure that had the whole world falling away, until it was just her and Dante's fingers and the slick, cool metal sliding into her sensitive flesh and...

Oh God, oh God, oh God...

She came so hard that and so fast that her vision blurred, and her hips rocked up in impulse and seeking need. Dante's hands were steady and professional, and he guided her through her orgasm with intense, achingly erotic words. *Ride it. That's right take your pain. You've earned it. Embrace the hurt to find your pleasure. You're so pretty when you come in my chair.*

Finally, her breath began to even, and she owned her eyes slowly. Dante's gaze was dark and hooded, as he carefully attached the end of the ball to the piercing.

"Anywhere else you want pierced, pretty girl?" he asked.

Caleb answered for it.

"No, Dante. Thank you."

Dante grinned. The man was sex on a stick, honestly. Just not her flavor of it. "Those do take a while to heal."

She slid up into a seated position and glanced down at her fresh piercing, a soft rose gold to match the first. The sight was deeply erotic, sinful and delicious, and when she glanced up, it was to both of the men eyeing her with intent.

"I think she likes it, Caleb," Dante said. "You're a lucky man."

"Damn straight."

He sat lifted her up and settled her into his lap in a matter of seconds and Skylar let out a squeak and the rough movement, at the electric feel of his touch upon her skin. He had given this to her, a chance to embrace the sliver of delicious pain, to lean into it, rather than fear its meaning.

"How do you feel?" he asked her. "Are you ready to play?"

More than she had ever been in her entire life. If she had been wearing panties, they would have certainly soaked through by now, slick and hot as her wanting was.

"Yes, Sir," she managed. "Please."

"On your knees, then," Caleb told her. Behind the chair, she heard Dante move away, heard him peel the plastic gloves off and toss them in the trash, but she wasn't focused on him, not from the moment Caleb gave her a direction. All she wanted was for him to tell her exactly what to do next.

"Master Dante likes to watch," Caleb explained, oh-so-gently brushing her hair out of her eyes. "He's going to touch himself while watching you make me come and you're going to like that."

She very, very much liked that, if the rush of pleasure that surged through her entire body was any indication. She nodded.

"Unzip my jeans." His words were dark and demanding and Skylar wondered exactly how much trouble she would be in if she came without his permission. "That's good, honey. Stroke my cock. Take it out."

He had spent the last few days lavishing attention on her, so Skylar reveled in the chance to explore his body, to slide her fingers up his long, hard length. His cock was large, the crown swollen and already dripping with evidence of his arousal, and she had to dig her nails into her palms to keep from leaning forward and licking his slit clean.

"Go ahead," Caleb said, as if reading her thoughts. "Give him a good show. Take my cock deep in your mouth, sweet girl."

Distantly, she was aware of Master Dante, his hot gaze matching his hot, demanding fingers that had given her such combined pain and pleasure just a few minutes earlier. But her mind was filled with thoughts of Caleb, of giving him release just as he gave her, and so she focused her attention of tasting him and sucking him hard and deep.

Twin groans echoed through the room, Caleb from above her, Dante from the couch across from them. Skylar's own desperate whimpers joined the fray.

"Put your hands behind your back, Skylar," Caleb murmured. "Hold them there. Use your mouth on me."

She did, feeling the aching, pleasurable sting of the new jewelry in her nipple when she moved, and leaning into it. The first time she had gotten pierced, she'd been overwhelmed by her reaction, terrified of what it had meant, but now she understood, at least a little, that taking pleasure with her pain was not something to shy away from, but something to celebrate. With that thought in her mind, she embraced her task, taking Caleb's throbbing cock deeper in her mouth, all the while keeping her hands behind her back.

"Stop."

She whimpered, the sound something she couldn't control, but she stopped, even though all she wanted to do was bring him to the very edge of pleasure.

Caleb stroked her jaw, and Skylar knew she had to look a sight, flushed and down on her knees, arms behind her back, swollen, freshly pierced nipples on full display. He guided her head off his cock and tuned her to look at Dante. He was spread out on the couch, one arm draped across the back, jeans open and his hand slowly, intentionally stroking an impressive erection. His eyes were dark and intense and filled with intent.

"Do you see the effect you have on us?" Caleb asked, his voice low and whiskey-rich. "It's not just me, Skylar. I'm not the only one who wants to lay you across my lap and claim you as my own every fucking minute of the day. Dante wants it too. He wants to feel your mouth on his cock, your sweet pussy squeezing him, the feeling of your tight little asshole opening for a new toy. But he's not going to get any of that, is he?"

Skylar shook his head, but Caleb's hand on her chin kept her gaze fiercely on Dante.

"Because I'm yours, Sir," she managed. "Only yours." There was approval in the other man's gaze and it was hot as hell, but nothing quite like the sensation of knowing she had said exactly what Caleb had wanted her to say — and that she had meant it.

"Damn straight you are," he growled. His movements were fast and frenzied, but still somehow gentle when he pulled her up to stand. Then he was pressing her against the side of the same couch where Master Dante was sprawled, a close-up, inhibited view of her flushed, aroused body on full display.

"How should I take her?" he asked. Dante flicked his tongue ring and Skylar had the brief wonder of what that ring might feel like against her clit.

"Slow," he responded, keeping direct eye contact with her as he did. "Make her beg for it."

Caleb parted her legs wide which made her sink deeper into the couch. A desperate moan escaped her lips at the slow, teasing contact of his fingers on her skin. It didn't matter that he had taken her hard and rough in the field that morning. It didn't matter that she had spent the last few days learning new and interesting details about her own pleasures and submitted to those pleasure, giving over to the delicious, indulgent sensations of becoming herself. All that mattered right now was that Caleb wasn't touching her nearly enough.

He slicked a hand through her wet folds until before circling her ass, and she bucked into the couch. She was still sensitive there from their play that morning, but in all the best ways, like her body knew exactly how much pleasure could be found with the right partner.

"How do you feel here?" Caleb asked, teasing his thumb at the hole that began to yield to him even before she answered.

"I want it," Skylar managed. "Sir, touch me. Please."

A deep, guttural groan sounded from the couch, where Master Dante was lazily stroking his hand up and down his swollen cock. He rubbed his thumb over his thick crown and it came away slick and glistening. He held it out to her and she sucked his finger deep into her mouth, the taste of his desire salty and hot on her tongue.

"You want to be filled in every hole?" Caleb asked. He still wasn't touching her, but she could feel his hot, predatory gaze sweeping across her back and her ass and her slick hole. "Tell me, sunshine. We're here to please you."

"Fill me." The words were out of her mouth before she thought them, this desperate, wild side of her taking over, giving in to the ride and these two men like she was meant to do it. She couldn't have walked out the door for all the money in her family's offshore accounts. "I want to take whatever you'll give me."

"Right answer, sweet girl." Caleb walked away and she heard him return a moment later. Each second felt like an eternity, and she was grateful that her master was the kind of man who wanted pleasure, rather than denial.

Not my *master.*

"Where's your head right now, Skylar?" Caleb asked, and when he spoke, touched the cold tip of a plug to her ass.

"With you, Sir," she managed. Now it was. He did have a knack for bringing things back to himself. "With the way you're touching me."

He pressed the plug in slightly, and it went easily, slick with lube and welcomed by her desperate body.

"And how am I touching you?" he asked. "What exactly am I doing to you, Skylar?"

"You're preparing my ass…" She tried to move back into the plug, but he stilled her with a hand on the waist. "You're training me to take your cock there."

Before her, Master Dante swore under his breath, the sound rich with heat.

"It's a hell of an idea," Caleb replied. "You all spread out and open for my cock." He pressed the plug farther in. "Begging for it."

"Fuck, more, please…" She had sworn more in the last three days than the last eighteen years.

"Later," he promised. "Right now, we need to focus on filling all your holes, just like you want." With a final movement, he pushed the plug all the way into her ass, and her body accepted it, embraced it, riding the pleasure of the burn like it was something she had been missing all her life.

"Master Dante," Caleb said, his voice intense and raw and like a beacon to the most desperate parts of Skylar's mind and body. "Do you think you could help me with one more thing?"

Master Dante stood, his movement lithe and full of sensual promise. He moved the way she would have thought Casanova moved, like he was making love even when he was fully clothed.

"It'd be my pleasure," he said, with the kind of grin that had Skylar's pussy clenching on emptiness. She needed more, so, so much more than what he was giving her right now, and she didn't care if the whole world knew.

The men apparently had some form of unspoken communication, because Master Dante moved forward on the couch until his swollen cock was just inches from her mouth, and Caleb moved behind her, the tell-tale sound of a condom wrapper being opened filling the air.

"You want us both, sweet girl?" It wasn't a question. Her arousal scented the air, her nipples were hard and swollen, sending new rushes of painful pleasure coursing through her as her body reacted around the piercing. Caleb didn't need to know her body as intimately as he did to know exactly how close to the edge she was.

"Yes, Sir," she replied, her voice confident and husky and like some seductress version of herself that she had never met. "I want to be filled in every hole."

He let out of a long string of curse words, and positioned himself right at her entrance, close enough that she could feel the throbbing crown of his cock nudging her folds open, but not nearly deep enough to give her the kind of release she so desperately sought.

"Open for him," Caleb prompted. She parted her lips and Master Dante moved forward an inch, two, until his thick cock rested just on her bottom lip. Then he pressed in, velvety skin over steel, caressing her lips, sliding across her tongue, spreading the salty, masculine taste of him over her senses.

"So perfect," Caleb muttered, and without another word, he pressed into her.

She had felt full that morning on the mountain, with the jeweled plug thick in her ass and Caleb's swollen cock pumping into her. But with the angle of her body bent over the couch and the added eroticism of having Master Dante sliding between her lips, Skylar felt more full, more taken, desired, more *cherished*, than she ever had before.

And she gave over to it, gave over to Caleb and the man he trusted enough to share her with, gave over to the all-encompassing sensations, and took them like it was the only thing, like the three of them in this room, on this mountain top, were the only thing.

The pleasure came in enormous waves, pounding like nature itself was at the core. It rocked into her, with each pulse and dirty promise from one of the men inside her, turned her over and over again as she got trapped in its swell, and all the while she knew it was holding back, so much more powerful, even, than the cresting tide already shaking her to her core.

When Caleb brought his hand around to her clit and stroked the swollen flesh, she screamed, but didn't allow herself to fall, didn't allow herself to give in until he said so, until all that she had promised him she would do was clear and undeniable.

"Come around my cock, baby." Caleb pressed into her. "Come as many times as you want. Squeeze me. Find your pleasure from our bodies."

And that was all the permission she needed to give herself into the depths of heat and eroticism, all she needed to find her release, to come and come hard, her body pulsing around the hard, welcome intrusions in her pussy and her ass.

Master Dante brought one hand around to cup the nipple he hadn't pierced. He rolled the small bar between thick, calloused fingers, workman's fingers, and the sensation rioted through her body, twisting pleasure and the heated shadow of pain.

"So sweet," he murmured. "If Caleb hadn't put his mark on you, little one, I would. I'd mark you pretty pink skin until you couldn't forget who you belonged to."

With the familiar sensation of Caleb's cock sliding achingly slow in and out of her hot pussy, Skylar would never, ever forget who she belonged to. Caleb ran his hand through her hair and tugged gently so she pulled back, though not far enough to lose Dante's cock from her mouth.

"Again, sunshine."

Her body was still raw and hot from her last release, but that didn't stop the incredible rise of desire blooming in her chest, tingling in her swollen, aching breasts. Her newly pieced nipple was a riot of electric sensations, tightening with desire and the subsequent shots of pain and they tangled together just as she tangled with the two men. So she did as she was told, took her pleasure, embraced what felt so natural and overwhelmingly good, and rejected the shame, embarrassment, any of those things that had been holding her back for so long.

With the freedom of the moment, Skylar came again, digging her nails into the couch, the slick sensation of hot release coating Caleb's still-hard cock. Her breathing was ragged, her nipples burned, and still she would find her pleasure if he told her to. She was beginning to understand that she would do exactly as he told her to, no questions asked.

Behind her, Caleb stroked over the plug, the pressure slight but adding so much to that sensation of fullness and wildness and need, and she bucked back into it, accidentally dragging her teeth over Dante's hard cock when she did. He groaned, and when she glanced up, she caught sight of the erotic storm in his eyes, so she did it again, gently, carefully, giving him the taste of pain he seemed to crave. He stilled the movement of her head with his hand.

"Fucking Christ." His words came out strangled and rich with need. "So fucking good, sweet girl. How is it you know exactly what I need to lose control?" The question was rhetorical. His swollen cock was still buried in her mouth and there was no answer anyway. In that moment, they were all carnal, embracing their natural instincts in ways they could never explain, but followed without hesitation.

She brought her hand around the couch and tucked it into the opening of his dark jeans to find his balls, tight and high, and she scraped her fingernails along the sensitive skin of his sac, which made Master Dante buck forward and swear a litany of words in a language she didn't know but well understood.

"Do it again." He demanded this through gritted teeth. "So fucking sweet." He pushed back into her mouth and she ran her nails across his skin again. Caleb's cock seemed to be growing larger inside her, Skylar understanding his body after just a few days here better than she understood her own.

"You going to swallow me, sweet girl?" Dante asked. "Take what I give you with a smile?"

She shifted slightly so she could look at Caleb without losing Master Dante. His eyes held approval and pride and heat that could only have come from watching her submit to another.

"Yes," he said, the word without question. "You're going to take exactly what he gives you, and you're going to like it."

That seemed to be enough for Master Dante, because he pumped between her lips one more, and Skylar brought her fingers to the base of his cock, and he lost his control, lost his hold on himself, and gave over to the release he had been denying. Thick, salty cum coated her tongue, spurred fresh heat between her legs, made her want to submit for all her days, and she swallowed around him, licking his cock clean until he slowly, gently pulled back.

Her jaw ached, but it was a welcome reminder, a delicious, hot promise of what else was to come and what made her feel like the woman she was, deep inside.

"Did you like that, sunshine?" Caleb asked, all the while twisting the plug in her ass just enough to keep her attention. As if it could be anywhere else. "Did you like being filled up and taken?"

She nodded and licked her lips. "Yes, Sir," she managed, her voice husky and sinful. "Very much."

"That's good," he replied, nonchalant, casual, as if his cock wasn't making explosions of pleasure pop behind her eyes with every thrust. "Because I plan on tying you up and filling every single one of your holes. I plan on leaving you bound and gagged until I feel ready to play. Then I feel like marking you as mine, so the whole damn world knows it."

She wanted to scream *I am yours*, but the depth with which she felt it was terrifying and overwhelming.

"Mark me," she begged instead. "Cover me in your release, please, Master, please."

He stilled. "What did you call me?"

"Master."

Had she gotten it wrong? In all the information packets, there had been some paragraph somewhere, about the proper way to address her Dominant, about the difference between her Dominant and a Dominant, but her mind was too clouded with pleasure and sensation to find the facts anywhere.

"Do it again," he demanded. "Call me Master again and I'll mark all your pretty skin as mine."

Skylar's heart ached with the truth of the word when she said it. "Please, Master," she begged. "Please claim me."

He did, then. He pounded into her one, twice, once again, each thrust pushing her that much closer to the edge of her release. Then they fell together, head over tail into their shared pleasures. She clenched around him and he pulled out of her body, tore the condom free and shot thick, hot ropes of cum across her exposed ass and back, each one feeling like his brand on her body, extending the wracking trembles of her desire, until she was a shaking, swearing mess, leaning on the couch for support.

"Shh, sweet girl, it's okay, shh." Dante was stroking her hair, the devil with the pretty face and the kind eyes and the ability to drive a woman absolutely wild. "Caleb is just going to clean you up. You did so well. So well." His words were that of a friend, of someone she could trust, and they comforted her until she felt a warm wet cloth against her skin and the familiar touch of Caleb's rough hands.

"I'm going to take the plug out, Skylar," he murmured. "Try to relax."

If she were any more relaxed, she would be a medical phenomenon, but she winced slightly as the thick toy came free. Her body was spent and still burning with the aftermath of their play, and yet she would never tire of Caleb's desiring her, never turn down his invitations or his demands. He kissed down her back, gentle kisses meant to soothe, not arouse, and they terrified her so much more than anything they had just done.

"Dante's right," he murmured. "You're so good. Let me take care of you the way you take care of me."

She didn't have it in herself to argue that he had, in fact, been the one caring for her, as their bodies had met and their desires collided. In fact, all she could manage was giving in to his embrace, allowing him to pick her up and carry her to the sofa.

"Rest now, sunshine," she heard him say from far away. "I've got you. I've got you."

Chapter Fourteen

"I've got news on Magnet Enterprises." The morning air was more than brisk when Caleb picked up the call from Gabriel the next morning. He'd had fantasies, of spending the day in bed, wrapped around a hot little brunette who turned him into the man he wanted to be, but the life of a rancher was the life of a man who worked hard, and now certainly wasn't the time to started questioning that.

"Actually, I've got news on Magnet Enterprises because I don't have news," Gabriel continued. Caleb could hear him tapping away at a computer on the other end of the line and wondered where his old friend was right now — New York, London, Beijing? Gabriel's work took him all around the world, but like Reece and Bastion and Rafe, he could never seem to stay away from Montana for long.

"What does that mean?" Caleb asked, walking into the stables to get out of the blustering wind that made it hard to hear the conversation. He didn't like this, didn't like that the town of Duchess had some unseen enemy from distant cities, pulling strings and changing people's lives. Two more business had put up liquidation signs downtown and he'd gotten three more calls in the time since Reece had first arrived back on Sinclair land. Caleb had squarely told the persistent stranger on the other end of the unmarked number to leave him and his well and truly alone, but it hadn't seemed to have made a difference.

"It means they're not showing up in the places you want to show up," Gabriel replied, and Caleb could picture him wedging the phone between his ear as he compared notes and documents. Gabriel was nothing if not thorough. "I'm not just talking about *Forbes* and *Better Business Bureau*, I mean, I've done serious digging and there's no genuine company by that name. Well, there's a vendor that sells industrial magnets called Magnets Enterprises based out of Trenton, but that's definitely not the group you're interested in."

Caleb sighed. "So there's something unsavory going on."

Gabriel barked out a laugh. "You could say that. There's any number of reasons a business doesn't want to be easily identified or traced back to the original source. But when they're buying up property under a cloud of local distrust and there are mineral rights potentially involved, my guess is blackmail, tax evasion, laundering, coercion or all of the above."

That…wasn't great. If they couldn't see the monster under the bed, how in the hell could they fight it?

"Are we in trouble, Gabe?" Caleb asked. "They've become more insistent. The numbers get higher every time they call, but I don't think they're going to be using money to get their way for much longer."

The seven of them, once they had walked off their whiskey hangovers and seriously considered the business, had painstakingly gone over every single detail. The Sinclair Ranch was aboveboard on every single thing, from the way their hen houses were constructed to the specifics of sex club zoning laws for the state of Montana. There had been documents on documents, and they had paid a very successful law firm a very pretty penny to ensure every single faction of their business was well and truly above board.

But that didn't much matter if the organization coming after them was willing to play dirty — and, judging by what was taking place closer to town, they didn't have morality or basic human decency on their side. If this group wanted to claim prostitution or some other illegal act, it would likely do enough damage with rumors and investigations that they wouldn't need to worry about its veracity.

"I'm not happy to hear about any of this," Gabriel replied frankly. "I have a smart friend doing some digging and I think we'll know more in a day or two. But I think we should tell the others. I'm assuming Van, Dante and Reece know."

Reece knew that things were getting worse because he'd been there when Caleb had gotten a call. But Caleb been keeping the truth of just how unsavory things were getting from the others. He hadn't wanted to worry them or overreacting to something that could have been nothing. As it stood, they deserved to know that someone was coming after their home and their business.

"I'll talk to them about this now," Caleb replied. "Bastion's swamped with the tour, but maybe Rafe can help. He knows people." If being prince regent meant knowing people, so much as being known.

"Ten-four," Gabriel replied. "I've got to go—meeting in five. But I'll call you as soon as I hear back from my guy. Best we nip this in the bud as soon as possible."

They said their goodbyes and Caleb shot off a quick text to the other guys, who were waiting for him in the lodge's kitchen when he made his way back down from the stables.

"What's going on?" Dante was sitting on the kitchen island and Van at the table, while Reece leaned back against the counter. Their expressions were troubled, and Caleb ground his teeth. They had a business to run—three business in one, in fact—and the last thing they should have been worrying about was this ridiculous shell company coming into their town and stirring up trouble.

"Gabriel found out that the company that's been calling us is going by the name Magnet Enterprises," he explained. He stopped at the coffee machine and poured himself a mug, hoping this conversation and Gabriel's help would solve the problem without any further worry on Caleb's part. Seemed unlikely. "I thought they might have been responsible for all the changes going on around downtown, and so I had him look into it, to see if he knew anyone who'd heard of them."

"And?" This from Van, who was normally the most patient and reserved of the bunch. Still, he'd been privy to more than one of those calls in the beginning and he knew what the numbers had looked like—numbers that meant major sacrifice.

"And," Caleb replied, "he just called to tell me that they're not showing up in any of the places good types of businesses show up. He thinks we should be on our toes while he looks into it further. We know everything is sound here and up there." He indicated out beyond the back window, up to where The Ranch sat on the mountain top, proud and sturdy. They were just building this new business, barely open two years, important to each of them in his own way. He refused to see it end with some overzealous mogul bullying his way through.

"But it seems they don't much care about the rules. Up until now, they've been offering money for the land. I don't think that's going to be true for much longer."

Dante swore under his breath, and for a second Caleb forgot about this problem, forgot about the future of The Ranch and the Sinclair Seven. All he could think about was the way Dante had sworn when Skylar had sucked his cock deep and Caleb had taken her hard and fast and over and over until she had fallen asleep in his arms, exhausted from her pleasures, and he had held her until she woke. The image stirred something deep in his chest and deep in his jeans too.

"I'm assuming they're after the mineral rights?" Reece asked. His work on environmental investigative reporting was world renowned and he had an intuition for these kinds of things that had proven invaluable.

Caleb shrugged. "That's what Gabriel thinks. That's what would make sense. Either way, they're going to come for us. It's what they've been saying the whole time."

"So we find a way to fight back," Van replied. "I've been raring for a good fight."

"That's because you're a brute and a half."

Nothing spoiled a good men's rallying like the sight of his sister walking through the back door to the kitchen.

"But," she continued, "I happen to agree with you. The company, Magnet Enterprises, you said?" Caleb nodded. "They've called the lab asking for records, soil and water, mostly, but they're getting aggressive. They must think there's something down there or they'd have left town by now."

"Rare we agree," Van said drolly. "But yeah, this company seems like bad news. You tell us if they call you again."

Caleb nodded. Van had known about the first few calls, Reece the one he had been privy too. Caleb hadn't exactly been keeping them a secret, but now that he knew the extent of what they might be up against, it felt good to see the group banding together to protect what was theirs. And speaking of protecting what was his...

"There's something else," he said, before he could rationally consider what that meant, before he could take back the words of strong emotion and vulnerability that would no doubt have his closest friends peering even more closely at his life. "It's not related to that. Don't worry."

Dante spoke first, making it easy for Caleb to avoid admitting things aloud.

"Is this something else related to Skylar?" he asked. "And the fact that you're treating her like she's yours?"

Caleb couldn't remember the last time he had blushed, really blushed, but it couldn't have been more recently than twenty years ago. Still, he felt the telltale sign of heat from his cheeks as Dante continued.

"You're going to have a damn hard time letting that one go," he said. "I've never seen you that in tune with another partner, not even..." He trailed off, the name of Caleb's ex-wife still a sour memory for all them who had welcomed her into their lives. "I've never seen you that way with anyone."

Rhylee coughed. "I'm going to go," she said. "Somewhere. I'm going to go somewhere. I just wanted to drop these off." She placed a covered basket on the counter and turned tail before Caleb could respond. Van lifted the checked towel and the smell of cinnamon and pumpkin filled the kitchen.

"She's going to be the death of me," he murmured, before taking one of the muffins. Caleb wasn't entirely sure the rest of them were supposed to hear that.

"Back to Caleb's not-so-little problem." Dante winked, and it wasn't difficult to see how he'd gotten his reputation as a seducer, or how he never slept alone. "What are you going to do about Skylar? She's only checked in for a few more days." It was a truth that had kept him tossing and turning all night long, despite the deep exhaustion in his bones from the pleasure they had shared.

"I don't know." Caleb scrubbed his face, the stiff bristle of morning scruff rubbing against his hand. "I… I don't know."

"She called you Master," Dante put in. "And you liked it."

That got Reece and Van's attention, and he felt the weight of three of his best friends gazing down at him, even though he was standing. They had forged this business because in the years since the first summer they had shared at the Sinclair Ranch, they had all found their lifestyles were a little different from the norm, a little more intense, and erotic. If anyone knew the importance of him wanting to be called Master, the true and complete submission, rather than the sign of respect that came along with Master Caleb, it was them.

They knew, also, that Becca had ripped his heart out when she had left, that he had been stuck wondering if he had peaked in his earliest years and if he was going to be on his own forever. They might not have known what she said, but they had known how she had made him feel and that was more than enough. Or, at least, it had been. Telling Skylar had him wanting to tell his friends, wanting to get this heavy weight off his chest, so he could get back to living.

"Becca said I was less of a man for wanting to dominate." This came on a single breath. If possible, their gazes grew heavier. "She said she had indulged me for our marriage because she'd always thought I'd grow up, that once I healed and got back on the team, I'd feel like a man again. Of course, I was never going to get back on the team and what we do…" He paused. "How we love…it's not a phase. It's never been a phase. But damn if it wasn't hard to believe it."

The coffee in his hands had grown cold, but he drank deeply from it anyway, if for no other reason than to avoid the very discerning gazes of his friends.

"Skylar has been the one person in a year—hell, in all the time I was married—who's made the shame go away, made me stop questioning why I want the things I want. She's…" *Spectacular, incredible, mine, mine, mine.*

"So tell her that," Reece said matter-of-factly, like it was just that easy to tell the woman who had turned his whole world upside down in less than a week that she was taking over his heart and soul. Maybe it was that simple. "You know how this works, Caleb. You haven't been away that long."

He'd been away a year, longer, away since his wife had stopped playing with him, since their bed had grown so cold and lonely. But, of course, he still had his arsenal, still had a friend in town who could make exactly what he needed to show Skylar all that she was becoming to him. If he didn't lose his courage first.

"It's only been a week," he replied, answering the not-question with a not-answer. It was all rather than saying the fear that was really on his mind of *what if she says no?*

"Sometimes that's all it takes," Dante pointed out. "There are no rules, man. It's different for everyone." They were, of course, talking about the relationship between a Dominant and a submissive. Caleb thought. It was possible there was a much deeper meaning here that he was doing his best to ignore.

"I think I might take a trip into town today," he said quietly. They knew what that meant, what was behind his visit to Ron's metal shop at the outskirts of Duchess. For tonight, at least. When Skylar left, and she would leave, he would deal with the mess of himself that stayed behind. But fear of that mess wasn't enough to keep him from the thing he wanted most in the world.

"Welcome back on the horse, man," Van said. "It's good to have you."

Back on the horse, taking a submissive of his own, felt like pulling on his favorite flannel jacket, like a pair of boots that fit just right. He grinned, the nervous excitement warring with the desire already growing for what the night might hold. "It's damn good to be back," he replied. And, after everything that had gone down with Becca, after the injury that still kept him awake at night, after wondering if he would ever feel like he was, thanks to his ex-wife, truly a man, he meant it. This was where he belonged — he could only hope Skylar agreed.

* * * *

"My advisor thinks I should focus on life sciences, because I want to do something with the environment." The excitement in Callie's voice was contagious and Skylar thought the advisor had an excellent point.

"Is that what you want to do?" she asked. Her daughter was deeply curious, always interested in the next great project or exciting new idea, but Skylar had the sense that this was one of the ones that would stick.

"I think it might be," she replied. "I mean, we have to do something, right? The Amazon isn't going to get better all on its own." It was a familiar refrain, made more dire with each passing year and each natural disaster that threatened towns and communities across the country and across the world. Maybe it was the proud mom part of her brain talking, but Skylar couldn't help feeling that the younger generations were more in-tune and ready to fight than anyone gave them credit for.

"You're my superhero." She meant it. Callie had always been deeply involved, empathetic and not afraid to share the feelings that made her so tuned into the world around her. "Whatever you decide to do, you're going to be great at it."

She could practically hear her daughter smile, then she really did hear a knock on the door to the cabin. That was odd. Caleb had told her to meet him at the barn in — she checked her watch — forty minutes. Part of her ached to see him again and part of her panicked at the idea of being on the phone with Callie while Caleb was in the room.

"Just a second," she called.

"Who's there?" Callie asked.

Skylar swore silently. "Delivery," she said quickly. "Aunt Ev's coming over later, so I ordered Thai."

"I miss you guys."

Skylar sat on the edge of the couch. "I miss you too, stir fry. I can't wait until Thanksgiving break." It was only mid-September. She'd been away from her daughter for just over three weeks, and already it felt like a lifetime.

"Mom, I'm not a kid."

"But you'll always be my kid," she replied. "What are you up to tonight?"

"I've got an essay due tomorrow," Callie replied. "Then there's the game after class, so that, I guess."

"I'm so proud of you." Hot tears threatened, and Skylar was grateful for the second knock on the door.

"Better get that," Callie said, laughing. "Love you, Mom. Talk soon."

"Love you too, stir fry." Stir fry had been her nickname in grade school, but every once in a while, Skylar snuck it in, unable to accept that her beautiful little girl was turning into a woman.

She hung up as she was walking across the room, but when she pulled open the door, she was surprised to see Rhylee Cash on the other side.

"Hi." Rhylee seemed ill at ease, odd considering how comfortable they had grown in each other's presence. "Can I come in?"

Skylar opened the door wider. "Is everything okay?"

"Everything's fine." Rhylee stood near the door and fidgeted. "Look, it's none of my business, but I think you're great for my brother. Like really great. And I just want to say that I know it's complicated and I know you have a life and that you're only here for a few more days, but please don't break his heart. He's had enough of that."

Skylar had to give her credit. It couldn't have been easier to say that, especially since Rhylee probably knew full well that Caleb wouldn't want anyone advocating on his behalf.

"I'm certainly going to try to avoid it," she managed. "But you're right, it is complicated." Made far more complicated by the fact that Caleb hadn't given her any indication that their...well, whatever this was between them, was anything more than the few days of her membership to The Ranch. She knew he cared, knew he wanted to take care of her and keep her safe, but this was a business deal and nothing more.

Even thinking those words inside her own head made Skylar cringe. It was starting to become incredibly obvious to her that this went far beyond a business deal, but what the hell was she supposed to do about it? Rhylee was right, she did have a life.

What's waiting at home?

She had a business waiting at home. And friends. Would her home feel quiet and far more empty without the laughter of a beautiful girl and dinner spent sharing stories? Of course. That had been the reason for Greece. For skydiving. Part of the reason for Montana. While she wouldn't exactly admit to running away from her fear of being alone, she was definitely in no rush to get back.

"Of course," Rhylee agreed. "I don't mean to add any stress to your life. I like you a lot, Skylar. And I love my brother. If you make him happy, and I'm pretty convinced you do, then I like you even more." She sighed. "I'm sure he's being as quiet as a church mouse about what went down with his ex, but it wasn't pretty."

Skylar paused mid-action, staring into her suitcase. "Actually, he told me… A lot of it, at least. And about the injury."

That seemed to give Rhylee pause. "Huh." She worried her bottom lip. "Then he's more into you than I thought. He's a pretty private person. Always has been, but the accident really derailed him. It made him vulnerable to a woman like Becca."

It was Skylar's turn for surprise. "You didn't like her?" she asked. Her first life, the life before Callie and her parents turning her out, had been rife with petty, vicious women determined to rule their social kingdoms. It had turned her off gossip for life, but this went beyond petty talk. She trusted Rhylee, thought the other woman was smart and insightful from just a few shared conversations. If she thought that Caleb's ex had been a poor choice but Skylar wasn't, that had to mean something.

It means I'm in way over my head.

"Becca was manipulative," Rhylee said after a long pause. "She found Caleb when he was raw and unsure of what steps to take next, and she took advantage of that. We were happy that he wasn't floundering after his injury, so it took us a while to realize, and by then it was too late. I think part of her was convinced he would get back into the game or that their being together again would give her all the power it did in high school, but at the end of the day, I just don't think she was a very happy person."

Skylar knew first-hand what desperation for social power did to a person. And she knew unhappy people too, unhappy though they lived in gilded palaces and drove expensive cars and paid their nannies to come to Italy or France or the Maldives. She knew the type all too well.

"It's not your fault," she said. "Not seeing. Manipulative people tend to be pretty good at what they do." Another hard-earned lesson she'd gotten in the school of life.

"I get that," Rhylee replied. "But I can't shake the feeling that I should have said something. He's my brother and I love him. I want the best for him, and she wasn't that."

Skylar nodded. Of what Caleb had told her, of the cruel words she had hurled at him as she had left, she was far from the best. That didn't mean Skylar was the one to take her place, even as the idea settled like a comfortable familiar blanket around her heart.

"Anyway," Rhylee continued, "enough dredging up the past. What are you wearing tonight?"

Skylar laughed. "Are you sure you want to have this conversation? I am meeting with your brother."

Rhylee winced, and that just made Skylar laugh more. "Are you going up there tonight?" she asked. "Anyone you want to see?"

Rhylee's expression was one of complete and utter confusion, and Skylar had to wonder exactly how that was possible. She made have been riding high on hormones, but there was no denying the off-the-charts chemistry between Rhylee and Van. Or maybe it was the kind of situation where everyone around them had to see it first.

"I'm seeing a guy from town," she said slowly, as if Skylar were a child that needed explaining to. "But so far I don't think he's into the scene or anything like that. We haven't talked about it."

Skylar shrugged. It wasn't any of her business. Besides, she had way bigger things on her mind right now.

"So..." She held up a teddy. "Pink or blue?"

Rhylee shut her eyes and grimaced. "Ugh, he's my *brother*."

* * * *

Caleb was pacing. He didn't like being unsettled. He rose with the sun, worked a full day, then went out to his club, to a night with a woman like Skylar. With Skylar. But he was unsettled now, weighed down by the box in his pocket. This was the most unhinged and unsure he had felt since the day of his injury, and that had been for the career he had trained for since he was just a few years old. This was for a woman he had known for a week, a woman who seemed to be turning his life upside with every moment they spent together.

"You called me, Sir?"

She was standing in the doorway to the room they had been sharing, her head bent down in the perfect pose of supplication, her beautiful form clad in a soft pink dress that fell to the floor in folds and made her appear like some Greek Goddess before him.

The box didn't quite feel so heavy anymore.

"Always, sunshine," he murmured, feeling the words in his soul. "I'll always call you." He indicated to the room and she entered it, the sound of her heels clicking against the wood floor and echoing around the room. It still amazed him that she was only just foraying into their world. The way she responded to him, the silent cues she followed, her natural submission, it all seemed so comfortable on her, like she didn't have to think but merely gave over to instinct. He could relate.

"How are you feeling?" he asked. Dante had said the piercing would take time to heal, time before it could be touched or played with, but that wasn't why Caleb asked. She brought out something within him, the part that ached to make sure she was always okay, always feeling good after their time together.

"Just fine, Sir," she replied, tilting her head up and smiling at him. "I'm told it's a faster process for smaller breasts."

Her breasts were the perfect size, perfect for his touch, his mouth, his aching cock, and his whole body screamed at him to take her, to make her his over and over until she couldn't question it.

Until she won't want to walk away.

It was the most selfish thing he'd ever thought in his entire life and Caleb couldn't bring himself to feel bad about it, about any of what Skylar made him want, made him feel.

"I love your breasts," he murmured. "And now, when you play with that hot little ring, you'll think of me."

She blushed a pretty pink to match the dress, to match her sweet, swollen pussy and her flushed breasts, the color, taste, and feel of which he was beginning to know oh-so-well.

"We're going on a walk tonight," he said, rather than allowing his mind to linger, rather than taking her right here in this room, like he so desperately wanted to do. He had other plans and feeling her wrapped around his cock was just going to have to wait. "Will you be able to walk in your heels?"

She grinned and stuck out a foot, clad in a sturdy-looking brown boot. "I think I'll be okay." He couldn't help but return her smile, even as the caveman part of his brain had wanted to carry her up the mountain and into his lair.

"You're prepared for everything," he said, instead. Too bad he hadn't been prepared for her, for the effect she would have on him as he navigated these new waters. He had wondered, briefly, if the effect was merely that she was the first woman he had wanted since Becca had left, but it went so much deeper than that, than want. It was terrifying. "Come."

She took his hand and he led her out the back door and into the Montana night. Above them, a bright September moon was making its way up to hang in the sky. It wasn't quite the harvest moon, still too early in the month for that, but it cast a beautiful glow around them nonetheless, made it easy to navigate the path, even as they moved away from the lights of the barn.

"Where are we going?" she asked. "Sir?"

"You'll see." It was a promise that he'd been planning to ignore since the day she had first arrived, but it turned out that ignoring Skylar Wedgeworth was harder than he'd thought. He held out his hand and she took it, the simple touch overwhelming and comforting all at once, and they walked in companionable silence, easy, fresh-aired and quiet, until they neared his destination.

"Remember how you asked me what the best part of living out here was?" he asked her. In the sparkle of moon and starlight, he could see her nod clearly.

"You said you wouldn't tell me," she replied.

He let out a low chuckle. "You would remember that. Well, then I got to know you. I got to be part of this. And I changed my mind, Skylar. You can know all my secrets."

She ducked her head again, and he knew that meant she was pleased. Pleasing her had become just about the most important thing on his mind.

"Take a look." He indicated forward, to the embankment. She tilted her head in confusion and Caleb couldn't blame her. "Trust me," he said quietly. "It's the very best part of living out here." They edged closer until they were right on top of the small river. It was nothing like Yellowstone River, with its vast, twisting miles of open vista and brush and current. This river was far smaller, a stream, really, that followed the slope of the mountain down until it met the larger rivers at the base.

"Take your boots off," he told her. She toed off her shoes and socks, then snagged a handful of her dress. "Put your feet in." Skylar did as she was told, and he was rewarded with a delighted gasp when her skin touched the water.

"It's a hot spring," she said in amazement. "It's so warm."

"My favorite spot," he told her. "I wanted to share it with you. I hope that's okay."

She turned to him, let her dress drop into stream like some mythical fairy and kissed him hard, their lips a tangle of desire and unspoken promise and fear, fear for what this burgeoning thing between them would lead to—fear of what would happen if they were to let it all go.

"Can we swim in it?" she asked, after finally pulling away from him. He was supposed to be the one in control, the one who cared for her, and yet he seemed to be the one stuck trying to catch his breath. "Or is it too hot?"

"You can swim," he replied. "Come here." He guided her down a-ways, to where the water spilled over rocks in the semblance of a lazy waterfall. The small pool below was no more than five or six feet deep, and twice that around, but it was the largest part of this section of spring.

"This is incredible," she said quietly. "Permission to remove my dress, Sir?" The sound that tore from his lips was part groan and part laugh.

"Permission granted," he replied. "We're secluded here. No one will see us unless we want them to." She had liked that, had liked being on display with Dante and the chance of being caught in the hallway, but he wanted to be selfish tonight, wanted her all to himself as he gave over to the biggest pleasure of them all — asking her to be his.

Before that could happen, however, she pulled the cotton dress over her head, folded it neatly and placed it on a dry rock a little way from the edge. Then she slowly scooted into the water, elegant, painted toes first, smooth, graceful legs, arms, hips, her buoyant, beautiful breasts straining against the surface.

"Is it safe to swim with your piercing?" he asked. He'd be damned if she suffered complications because he wanted to put on a show.

She shrugged. "You're supposed to wait at least twenty-four hours. Better two to three weeks, but I won't be here in three weeks and I'll be damned if I'm missing a night in a hot spring under the stars with you. I'll make sure to clean it really well when I get back to the cabin." She dropped such casual reminders of their fleeting time together, that she was leaving, that their time shared was important. It was hard to find heads or tails in the night.

"You look like a mermaid," he said without thinking. It was a starkly poetic thing to say and Caleb had never exactly been a poet, but she inspired something within him, something that needed to be true and honest. Her skin glistened in the pale moonlight, and her eyes were bright with wonder.

"I can't believe how warm is," she said. "I shouldn't go under the water, right?"

He nodded. "Best not. They say it's not that's safe to ingest with all the minerals."

"Join me?" she replied. "I want to share this."

He wanted to share this too, wanted to share so much more than a single night or a single week. Even if she continued to return to The Ranch, once a year, once every two years, it wouldn't be nearly enough for him, not now that he had gotten to know her, had come to understand exactly how important she was to him.

"I have a present for your first," he said quietly.

Her face lit up. "You've already given me so much," she replied. "This night, everything we shared. You've opened up my world and I'll never be able to truly thank you enough for that."

"You've opened up mine too, sunshine," he said quietly. "That's why I want to give you this. Ask you to accept it." He reached into his pocket and pulled out the box.

Skylar might one day admit to herself that there had been the briefest second of hope that the small box in his hand was an engagement ring. It had lasted for a heartbeat, less than a heartbeat, before her reality had settled back in around her—well, as much reality as a night in naturally occurring hot springs under the stars might really be. He kicked his boots off and settled down on the rock beside her, his feet in the magically warm water, and opened the box.

Inside was a necklace. It was a soft gold that caught the light of the moon, short, like it might land right at the hollow of her neck, and at the center, a simple, strikingly beautiful pendant of a sun.

"Last night, you called me Master," he explained, holding the box open to her. "Master is reserved for those with whom you have a special bond, Skylar. And when you said it, I realized I didn't want to correct you. I didn't want you to call me the same thing you called Master Dante or any of the others. I wanted it all for myself. I wanted you all for myself. Will you accept my binds and be my submissive?"

The word felt so easy on her tongue, clogged only by the heat of happy tears. She swallowed them back and nodded, the sensation in her heart warmer even than the hot springs she swam in, brighter than the moon above them.

"Thank you, Sir," she managed. "It would be my greatest honor." The expression on his face was worth every doubt, every moment of question. He wanted her and she wanted him, and though they had not spoken of the future beyond this moment, this night, Skylar knew she wouldn't be able to let him go that easily.

"The honor is mine, Skylar," he replied. He reached into his shirt and freed another chain, with one with a miniature key attached to the end. When he pulled her necklace free of the box, Skylar realized there was a small lock where the clasp would have been. The idea that he alone could unlock their binds, that she was held to him by this symbol of their connection, was not nearly as terrifying as it should have been. In fact, she ached for it, for the way his talisman would settle against her skin, for everything it meant.

She turned, lifted her hair and the cool metal landed on her throat. Then she felt him play with the lock, securing her binds into place.

"You look beautiful in my binds," he said quietly. "I don't think I'll ever forget this image as long as I live."

"I don't want to forget a moment of this night," she said. "Will you take me here, in the moonlight — Master?"

His grin was sin and pride and heat and he moved toward her, stripping himself of his clothes with wicked speed before lowering into the water. He caught her around the waist and she settled against him, accepting his weight and the power of his straining erection with ease and not a small amount of preen. It didn't matter how often she had him here, below her, above her, around her, Skylar would never tire of the feel of him, would never turn down the chance to explore their pleasure together. She bucked into him and he took the movement, kissing her throat, sliding his fingers along her back, groaning into her mouth as they kissed.

"We can't use the condom in the water," he said. "It's not going to protect you." Even now, even in their desperation to touch and be touched, he was worried about keeping her safe.

"I have the IUD," she said after a moment. "And after I came back from Greece, I got checked. Just to be safe." It wasn't something she had considered up to this moment, but here with him, it felt more right than anything she had ever fantasized about before.

"Skylar." The word came out on a strangled groan, as if he couldn't quite contain himself. She understood the feeling all too well. "I haven't been with anyone since Becca. And I didn't trust her faithfulness in the end, so I had the tests too, but are you sure? I wouldn't hurt you. I'd do anything it took to keep you safe."

She knew that, knew that he really believed it, even if the knowledge that she'd be walking away from The Ranch with almost certain heartbreak was never far from her mind.

"I'm completely sure," she said quietly, perhaps more for herself than for him. For so long, she had been a side note in other people's stories. She had been her parents' trophy to parade around at their clubs and parties. She had been Callie's mother, had dedicated her life to creating a happy, safe, supportive home for her little girl. And she had done so much within those worlds, started a successful business, found lifelong friends. But this, here with Caleb under the light of the moon, in touch with nature and with her deepest desires—it felt like diving headfirst into a moment entirely for herself, taking something she wanted because she wanted it, and not because it would somehow benefit someone else.

"Then come here, sunshine."

In the end, they made love on the bed of the small stream, soft sand below their tangled bodies and the heat from the river keeping their skin warm against the cool breeze of the September night. By the standards of what they had done, it was simple, almost sweet, and yet, it felt like the most adventurous night of Skylar's life, like she was taking the first steps on a new journey she hadn't realized she had wanted until that moment. When Caleb brought her to new heights again and again, then eventually succumbed to his own pleasure, spilling across her heated skin, it felt like nothing she had ever done before. And, as she lay in the moonlight, skin slick with the aftermath of their lovemaking and the hot steam of the river, she knew she would never quite be able to go back to the woman she had been before. Lingering in the back of her mind, as she faded into a blissful sleep and felt Caleb pick her up, felt him carry her down the hill, was the question of what exactly that meant.

Chapter Fifteen

"Stay."

She had meant stay with her that night, stay in her little cabin up the mountain, hold her the way he had been longing to do since the very first moment he had laid eyes on her. In a lustful, sleepy haze, she had clutched his flannel and begged him to stay, and he had, all the while fantasizing about that word having an altogether different meaning.

Stay with me. Forever.

He had given her the binds and she had accepted them, they had come together like it was their very first time, and yet, the question of what came next was ringing in his ears so damn loudly that Caleb couldn't fall asleep if it his life depended upon it, even as Skylar slept, gracefully sprawled beside him in the warm and comfortable bed. If he were a different man or if she were a different woman, he could take these few days as the gift they were. Wrap himself around her, make love to her again, then happily say goodbye when she returned to her life in DC. But he wasn't. She had wrapped herself around him, body and soul, and now he was stuck staring at the wooden beams above his head wondering what in the fuck he was going to do next.

He was almost grateful for the distraction of his phone buzzing against the wooden bedside table, until he turned it over and saw who it was.

Becca.

God *damn* her, intruding into this space with Skylar, taking moments that would make for the best kind of memories and tainting them with her manipulation and her cruelness. God *damn* her.

He ignored the call, but the second he sent it to voicemail, she called again, and his hackles raised. It had been a year since the papers had been finalized and it wasn't as though their communication skills had been all that top notch before she had left, so if she was calling at...two-fifty-three in the morning, there had to be a damn good reason for it.

He rolled out of the bed as gently as he could, careful not to move Skylar, and grabbed his phone to duck into the other room.

"What the hell do you want?" He had wanted to come across as cool and impassive, but the aching hurt of her final words and all she had taken from him, years of happiness and opportunity, imbued his tone.

"To make amends," she said quietly. Even after all this time, even after the irreparable tears in his heart, her voice still made him ache. *God damn her.* "Or rather, some amends. I know I hurt you, Caleb. I know I was cruel in the end and I'm sorry for it. But that's not what I'm calling." Of course she would gloss over the painful memories of their last days.

"Then why the hell are you calling?" he asked. "It's the middle of the night."

"I know." She did sound remorseful, he was willing to admit, but then again, she'd always been talented at playing parts and there was absolutely no reason for him to give her the benefit of the doubt right now. "And I would have waited, but I don't know how much time we have and I wanted to warn you properly."

His gut turned to ice and he stood up straight, pressing the phone to his ear as if that might help her to convey the message faster.

"Warn me about what?" he asked. "What the fuck is going on, Becca?"

She sighed and he wanted to reach through the phone to shake her. They hadn't spoken in more than a year, allowing lawyers to act as their go-betweens, and she called him in the middle of the night with some cryptic-ass warning — that wasn't going to fly.

"I told some men about what goes on at The Ranch," she admitted. "They're buying Daddy's farm and they said they would offer another ten percent if we knew anything about the property."

Caleb couldn't swallow. His chest constricted, and he wondered if this was what the sensation of being buried alive felt like.

"What did you say, exactly?" he asked. "And who the hell are these men, Becca?"

It wasn't great that her father was selling. He had a horrible past with the ex-wife, but her father was a salt-of-the-earth-type man who would have run the family's small dairy farm for the rest of his life if given the choice. Everything Caleb already feared about this unknown company — *Magnet Enterprises* — coming into

Duchess and destroying their way of life was coming to pass.

"I don't know." There was a hitch in her throat and Caleb couldn't even feel bad about it. "I'm not in town anymore, I haven't been since...but when Daddy called me to tell me the good news, he gave me their number and I spoke to someone on the phone. That was around dinnertime."

"Then why are you telling me?" He was exasperated and worried and wondering how the hell it always ended up with him and Becca at a crossroads that would likely determine the rest of his life.

"I wanted to hurt you." He believed it. "I wanted to get you where it really made you feel abandoned and lost. I did that, and I'm sorry. But the more I thought about it, the more I thought about Daddy selling the farm and all of it, the more I realized I shouldn't have said anything. I tried to call them back, but the line was disconnected."

Thank God for the minor miracle of Becca discovering she had a soul at the eleventh hour.

"I don't know when they're coming, Caleb. But I know they will. Daddy told me they paid him three times what that land is worth without batting an eye and with all the stores downtown closing, I don't think they're nice men."

He didn't agree with his ex-wife about much, but this was one of those things.

"Fuck... Listen, Becca, I'm not forgiving you for any of this. But I am grateful you called."

A slight sniffle came on the other end of the line. "There's a lot I don't deserve forgiveness for," she replied. "But I'm sorry, nonetheless. I do miss you, Caleb. And I love you. I wish that were enough."

He sighed. "I wish it were enough too, Becca. Good luck."

He disconnected the phone, stared at the black screen and wondered which of his friends he should call first, wondered how in the hell they had gotten to the situation, when he heard a small sound. When he turned to the noise, it was to see Skylar standing in the doorway, where nothing but his T-shirt and a totally unreadable expression on her pretty face.

Things just kept getting better.

"Skylar, I can explain."

She shook her head and smiled, but it felt more like a grimace.

"There's nothing to explain," she replied. "It's none of my business that your ex-wife calls you in the middle of the night while you're in my bed."

Skylar took a deep breath. With Callie in her life, relationships had been hard, and she hadn't exactly learned at the knee of affectionate, loving parents. Coldness and passive aggression had been par for the course in her home, and though she had done her damnedest to raise her daughter with trust and open communication, she sometimes reverted back to that frustrated, attention-starved sixteen-year-old girl. But this was too important, this thing between her and Caleb, this reckoning that might just make it easier for her to walk away when the week was up, though the thought made her want to howl.

"She had something important to tell me," he replied.

"Like I said," she tried again. "It's none of my business. I don't have any claim on you, Caleb. I'm leaving, remember. In three days, she can call you all she wants and it won't matter to me."

The words tasted like ash in her mouth, and she knew she wasn't doing nearly enough to rein in her temper, but something about hearing him talk to the woman he had loved first, the woman he had loved *only*, who had taken parts of his soul when she had left, like it was no big deal, it had made her see red.

I'm not jealous.

Except it was her own heart that hurt, it was her own chest squeezing with the feeling that she would never get the chance to know Caleb as well as Becca had, never get the chance to…care for him. Because she was going—and even with all they had shared the night before, even with his binds, the necklace he had gifted her in the moonlight cool against her skin—he hadn't asked her to stay.

"It matters to me," he replied, his voice a growl, and she realized he was no longer holding back the emotions he'd once pushed down when it came to talking to her. "It matters to me you know that she's out of my life."

Becca might have been out of his life, but Skylar was going to be out of his life soon enough too, and it seemed there wasn't a damn thing she could do to avoid that.

"Then why the hell did she call you at three in the morning?" This was ridiculous. If she had any hope of walking away from Caleb without breaking her own heart in the process, she was going to have to get a lot better at not caring.

"The Ranch is in trouble," he said. "She was calling me to warn me."

Ice ran through Skylar's veins. She hadn't even been here a week and already this place felt like a sanctuary, the kind of escape people found themselves in. That *she* had found herself in. The idea of it facing problems made her stomach hurt for reasons that had nothing to do with Caleb—or may be only just a little to do with Caleb.

"What's going on?" she asked, and it was suddenly imperative that she knew.

"We've had some guys sniffing around, asking to buy the place," he admitted, and she had to wonder why he hadn't told her that, if their bond had been stronger on her side than on his. But he had given her his binds, hadn't he? "They've been offering money, up until now. Stupid amounts of money for the land. Every time I tell them no, it's more money. But I don't think it's going to be money anymore."

Skylar released a breath, and for the first time since getting out of bed, she realized how cold the floor was below her feet. She had been too young, when she left home, to really see gears behind her family's business machine, but she had sat in at enough club events, heard the whispers of enough of her father's friends, seen the backs of enough closed doors, to understood that business could take many forms, according to those in positions of power. Coercion, bribery, manipulation, blackmail, threats—those were just the beginning.

"What are you going to do?" she asked.

Caleb opened his mouth to respond, but before he could say anything, it was Skylar's phone that trilled from the bedroom. She glanced at her watch—still the middle of the night, and any parent knew that middle-of-the-night calls were the worst kind of calls. Her heart in her chest, she moved quickly across the room and checked the ID on her phone.

Callie.

"Honey, what's going on?" Maybe it was just another drunken call, like the first night she had been out with friends and she had called Skylar to tell her how much she loved her. *It's probably that, right?*

"Ms. Wedgeworth, this is Detective Rodriguez. I'm calling from the Alta Bates Summit Medical Center in California."

Skylar's heart dropped like a stone in her stomach and she half-fell on the edge of the bed, clutching the phone to her ear.

"What happened? Is she okay?"

"She's going to be fine," he said, the words like a shot of adrenaline coursing through her electrified body. "She was struck down by a vehicle while crossing to her dorm. She does have a concussion, a few broken fingers and a sprained wrist, as well as some smaller injuries, but she's going to remain under observation overnight."

Skylar could barely hear the detective over the sound of blood rushing in her ears. She was already up and moving, tossing shirts and shoes into the open suitcase on the floor, rifling through the piles of shit on the sink.

"Is she awake right now?" she asked. "Can I talk to her?"

The detective was quiet for a moment, then she heard the sound of a door closing.

"She's heavily medicated at the moment," he replied. "For the pain. But I can tell the nurses to let her know we've spoken."

She got the rest of the information she needed, aching to demand that the detective wake her daughter up just so she could hear her voice, but knowing that the best thing for Callie was rest and respite from the pain. Finally, bag mostly packed and contact information scribbled in eyeliner on a napkin, she thanked the detective and hung up.

"What's going on?" Caleb was standing in the door, and his presence should have made her calmed, usually would, but right now all she could think about was how he wasn't hers and how Callie was.

"I need to go," she said. "There's...there's been an accident and I need to go to California."

"Let me drive you to the airport," he said. "And you can tell me what happened."

She should have fought him, but he was right. This time of night, the roads were already dangerous and dark. Add in her own harried thoughts and she might well end up in the ER to match her daughter.

They didn't say anything, as she continued her sprinted cleaning, packing her belongings and not looking Caleb in the eye as she did. She wasn't sure she could handle both these emotional tidal waves all at once, and her daughter always, always came first.

The ride to the airport was quiet and heavy. When they were down the mountain and she had a signal again, she checked any and all flights leaving Montana, and was able to secure a spot on a seven am flight to San Jose. It would be another ninety-minute drive to Callie, but it was better than waiting for the four pm flight to San Francisco and it got her out of Montana, which right then seemed about the most important thing in the world.

The airport was dead quiet as Caleb pulled her rented car up to the terminal. He had told her he would drop the vehicle off and have Dante grab him from town, and she had been grateful, yet again, for the ride, as he'd navigated tight, dark mountain turns with ease. Compared to DC, when even flying at four in the morning was busy, it felt like they were the only two people in the entire state, surrounded by the mountains and the stars above them, and the weight of their lives outside of the Sinclair Ranch hanging heavy in the air.

Caleb placed her bag down on the concrete and leaned against the car, his eyes discerning in the hash halogen lights above them.

"Will you call me?" he asked quietly, his voice gentle. "When you see her? Just so I know you're both okay?"

Skylar nodded. The night was cold, September in the mountains, but the chill running up her back wasn't from the Montana air.

"Are you going to come back, Skylar?" he asked her, his voice so laden with emotions she very nearly gave in to her own. *Ask me to come back, Caleb. Ask me to stay.*

Instead, she said the only thing she could say and mean with any sort of honesty.

"I don't know," she said. "I don't know."

Chapter Sixteen

"How is she?"

Skylar jerked her head up at the small knock on the door jamb, and her pulse relaxed only when she saw Ev standing in the hall.

"How'd you get here so fast?" she asked. After the early morning flight, in which she was unable to calm her panicked heart long enough to get any sleep, and the hour-plus drive from the San Jose airport, she'd barely been in the hospital for two hours, during which time Callie had hardly stirred.

According to the doctors, the concussion was of little concern, but monitoring the pain from her broken fingers and sprained wrist was a priority. She had a purplish-green bruise forming below her right eye as well, and small nicks and scrapes across her cheeks and arms that made things appear worse than they were, according to the doctors. She was, in the end, expected to make a full recovery, if she kept up with PT and took the healing process slowly.

None of that had changed the roiling guilt Skylar had been battling all night, mixed with fear and panic and the desire to put Callie in a big plastic bubble until she was ninety.

"Being in the FBI has its perks," Ev said. She crossed the room and handed Skylar a paper bag from the local coffee shop. "How is she?"

"She's going to be fine," Skylar replied, though even the words from the experts felt hard to say. "At least, that's what they tell me."

Ev passed over a cup of coffee from a tray Skylar hadn't even realized she was holding.

"Then she's going to be fine," she said. "Callie's strong as hell, Sky, you know that. Besides, it looks worse than it is."

Skylar tried for a smile at the repeated sentiment, but it came out as a grimace. The hot coffee felt good in her hands, something comfortable and cozy to hold on to, but she didn't try to drink it. Anything she put in right now was likely to come right back up, what with the heady mixture of fatigue and panic and spent adrenaline.

"That's what they keep saying," she said. "But she has two broken fingers and a sprained wrist. How's she going to finish out the semester?"

"She'll type with one hand," Ev replied. "Or we'll get her that dictation software. Or she'll take time off. But you have to let her decide that."

Skylar knew she was right, knew, even before asking Callie, that taking the rest of the semester off to heal wasn't even a question. She'd be pissed as hell about volleyball, but she could utilize the athletic department's resources and trainers until she was strong enough to play again. As far as outcomes went, she could have been facing much, much worse news here in California. But knowing that didn't seem to make any difference.

"Mom..." Callie's voice was croaky, and Skylar jumped out of her seat. She reached for the small cup of water at Callie's bedside and adjusted the straw.

"Do you want something to drink, baby?" she asked. "Or should I call the nurse?"

Callie groaned. "I feel like I've been hit by a truck," she said. "Water, please." After a few sips, which Skylar instructed her to drink down slowly, her voice evened out and energy returned to her eyes.

"It was more like a Ford Focus," Skylar said. "But that's for the better. Do you need pain meds?"

Callie shook her head. "They make me groggy. Maybe just some Advil or something?"

Ev took point on that, and a few minutes later, one of the nurses that had given Skylar Callie's charts came back into the room.

"How are you feeling, Caroline?" she asked. She was young, probably a few years younger than Skylar. Beth, that was her name. When she'd first arrived at the hospital, nothing else had seemed important.

"You should have seen the car," Callie said. She tried to sit up and winced in pain when she used the wrong hand. "I'm fine," she said. "Really."

Beth handed over a small cup of over-the-counter pain medication that she said wouldn't make Callie so groggy and promised to return with a breakfast tray a few minutes later.

"You guys didn't need to come," Callie said, when the room had quieted and it was just the three of them, watching monitors and listening to the beeps of the machines. "I'm going to be okay. It was just a small accident."

Skyla smiled, a genuine smile for the first time since her night in the moonlight and her shared moments of peace with Caleb, a lifetime and a world away. Still, even through her smile, tears — of relief, of guilt, of love and adoration — threatened.

"You may not need me," Skylar said, all the while rubbing Callie's uninjured forearm, as if to prove to herself that Callie was here and alive and fine, "but I need you. I needed to see for myself that you were all right, and I needed to be there for you when you woke up. If you ever have kids, baby, you'll understand."

Callie must have been tired, because she merely smiled, rather than arguing with Skylar about it.

"What about you, Auntie Ev?" she asked. "You don't have kids. What's your excuse?"

Ev snorted out a laugh. "I've got you, wise guy. And I was in Seattle, it wasn't far."

Callie furrowed her brow. "Since when?"

Skylar watched the scene in slow motion, but it was like she was frozen in her spot, unable to stop her well-intended best friend from accidentally spilling the secrets she wasn't ready to share yet.

"Since yesterday morning."

Callie might have been injured and lying in a hospital bed, but when she narrowed her eyes on Skylar, she was discerning and intentional.

"You told me you having dinner with her last night," she said. It wasn't a question. In the chair beside Skylar, Ev swore under her breath. "So, who were you having dinner with, then?"

Skylar opened her mouth to reply, "Oh, did I say Ev? I meant..." But the lie got stuck on her tongue. She could tell Callie it was a guy she had met, online or through work. That was probably what Callie was expecting to hear. But now that she was away from the magic of Montana, now that she was no longer trapped in the spell Caleb had woven around her, it was easy to see that she had been lying mostly to herself. Of course there was no future for them, not in any way that really mattered. She was a mom, first and foremost, and she was losing her grip on the important things if she thought going back to The Ranch was a good idea.

"I've been traveling, actually," she said quietly. "I came home from Greece early, like I told you, but..." Why was this so hard, this coming together of two separate parts of her life that really didn't feel like they would ever come together? Caleb and The Ranch and the lifestyle she had actively given herself over to this past week felt antithetical to her role as a mother, to taking care of Callie. And she knew which she would choose every time.

"Mom." Skylar had to wonder when Callie had become the parent in their relationship.

"I went out to Montana," she said. *Like ripping off a Band-Aid.* "There was...a program on a ranch there. And I spent some time with someone." She sighed. "I didn't know where it was going, so I didn't want to tell you just yet. And it doesn't matter, because I'm going back to DC and back to work."

Callie raised her eyebrow. "A program on a ranch?" she asked. "Sounds like a sex club to me."

Ev had been drinking coffee and she sprayed a mouthful of it across the floor — and across Skylar's lap. Skylar just coughed, too stunned to do or say much of anything for a long moment.

"Well, there's all the proof I need," Callie said with a tired grin. "You went to a sex club. Don't want to know the details but go, Mom." She lifted her non-injured hand in a weak fist pump.

That got Skylar's attention. "How do you know anything about sex clubs?" she asked. They had both always been very open about sex and sexuality. She'd gotten pregnant at sixteen, as much the result of her parents' inattention to their children as it was the shroud of mystery surrounding safe sex, and Skylar had been careful from the get-go to give Callie the information and resources she needed to protect herself.

Still, for all that they had spoken of the mechanics, contraceptives and consent and sexual orientation, for all they had pointed out their favorite TV and movie hunks, they have never strayed into the territory of sharing sex club stories. Skylar really hadn't even thought they would.

Callie laughed, though it seemed to hurt a little. "Don't worry, I've never been to one," she said. "I'm taking a Woman's Gender and Sexuality Class and we did a lesson on erotic novels and the myths and misconceptions surrounding sex clubs in modern media." She grinned. "It was cool as hell, to be honest." She narrowed her gaze on Skylar. "So, what happened with the guy?"

Skylar shook her head, feeling like the floor was moving in two directions below her feet. The last twenty-four hours had been a whirlwind, a series of incredible high highs and some of her darkest lows. She had given herself over to Caleb, accepted his binds, the ones she still wore, even now. Then they had fought over her right to him, and all the while she had been hoping he would ask for more, that he would ask her to stay. And before any of it had gotten resolved, she'd found herself in a hospital in California, heart in her throat as she watched her kid in a hospital bed, only to find that said kid was intimately familiar with the idea of sex clubs and, apparently, had no problem with her mother being part of one.

"We got into a bit of an argument," she said. "And it was for the better, I think. We live different lives. It's a fun week away from real life, but come on, I'm a mom, I run a business. It doesn't fit into my world."

That statement was met with silence, and she glanced between Ev and Callie, expecting to see agreement there.

"Do you like him?" Callie asked.

Skylar nodded before she could stop herself.

"And you like the..." She waved her uninjured arm around in the air, as if to indicate all that they were talking about and not saying aloud.

Skylar nodded again.

"So, the reason you're running away is because *moms don't do that kind of thing*?"

"It's a distraction," she replied. "It means I can't be there for you when you need me."

Callie made a face. "Bullshit." Skylar didn't comment on the curse word. "You're scared of actually liking someone."

When in the hell had her daughter gotten so smart, and was the process reversible?

"You don't understand..." Skylar was actually starting to get the distinct impression that maybe *she* didn't understand. Had she fallen asleep on the plane ride and was experiencing one of the most accurate dream sequences of her life?

"If you mean I don't understand that you're still paying some penance for being a teen mom, I do. But you've given me the most amazing life. We love each other, I love school. You're allowed to have your own life too, Mom, whatever you decide it might be."

Skylar choked, her throat suddenly clogged with the thick, heavy emotions that had been driving her decisions for the last twenty-four hours, for the last week, for the last nineteen years. Making sacrifices for her daughter had felt like the simplest thing in the world. Doing whatever it took to give Callie the life she deserved had been an easy choice. It was taking the step back and allowing Callie out in the world, to make her own fumbles and her own choices, that had been hard.

It had been finding her own identity as she stood outside of being a mother, outside of being rejected from her family all those years ago. Going to Greece, going to Montana, those had been some of the first choices she had made for herself. And every decision she had followed through with Caleb had felt right, had felt like another puzzle piece in her heart falling into place. She had left, planning not to return, blaming it on the fact that he hadn't asked her to, but as much fault lay with her, with the fear buried deep that she was somehow abandoning her other roles to follow this one, when, in fact, they were able to work in perfect harmony.

She held Callie's hand, squeezed it tight and thanked whatever gods might have been listening for a daughter that was so much smarter than her, for the love of a spectacular young woman, and for the hope that Caleb had a little more faith in her than she had in herself.

"Go back to Montana, Mom," Callie said with a smile. "You deserve it."

* * * *

In the end, Callie checked out of the hospital and Skylar brought her back to her dorm, where several of her friends and dormmates had planned a get-well party for her. Callie and Skylar spoke to the dean of students, the athletics advisor and her coach, and Callie's roommates promised both to care for her and to call Skylar for any reason. And, after a long day of running around the school and keeping busy, Skylar was faced with going back. *Going home.*

Montana wasn't home, but part of her couldn't deny that it sure as hell felt like it.

"Call me when you land, Mom," Callie said, gingerly wrapping her arms around Skylar. She had an extra few inches and towered over her like some athletic goddess. Skylar figured most mothers thought of their daughters as goddesses, but hers really was. "I love you."

Simple, powerful, the most important words she had ever said to the most important person in her entire life—which wouldn't change if she took a new and different path.

"I love you too."

Chapter Seventeen

Caleb had never been more grateful for farm work, not even on the day his doctors had told him he would never play professional baseball again. Farm work meant sweat and sore muscles, busy hands and a blissfully clear mind. It meant he could be remotely useful, even as he felt like he was going out of his goddamn head.

Two days. It had been two days since he had driven Skylar to the airport after the terrible call about her daughter, and he hadn't heard a word. Two days since she had told him she didn't know if she would be coming back, and his gut clenched every time he saw a car coming up the driveway or the phone in the lodge shrilled.

'It's none of my business. I don't have any claim on you, Caleb.'

If only she knew exactly how much of a claim she really had. She wore his bonds, and unless she had broken the chain, she still wore them, because the necklace's key was on a chain around his own neck, a reminder of how he had messed up something so incredible. He had asked her to be his and she had agreed and they had done nothing less than make love in the moonlight, and still she hadn't called in two days. Of course, she was probably doing everything she could for her daughter, and he understood that completely. But he also understood that she probably wasn't coming back. He hadn't given her reason to — her time at The Ranch had nearly been up and he hadn't asked for more, hadn't asked her to stay. *Fool that I am.*

It hadn't been Becca that had been the problem, or her ill-timed call that had led to nothing but more worry and stress for the last two days. It had been the look in Skylar's eyes when she had realized who he was talking to. It had been her belief that he didn't want her in any sort of long-term way. It had been his fault for letting her believe that.

Coward.

It was true, of course. Caleb had been honest enough with himself to know that he did want her, and he did want her in a long-term way. He should have just fucking said it. But the fear of the path ahead, of opening himself up again just to have his heart trampled, it had fucking terrified him. Not that Skylar would ever do what Becca had. They were fundamentally different people. But Skylar also had a hold on him he didn't quite understand, and that kind of power had made him want to turn and run in the other direction.

He wasn't a jumpy man by nature. A lifetime of baseball training and time spent around large farm animals had helped to hone his instincts and make him calm, measured and careful in his responses. But when his phone rang in his back pocket a moment later, Caleb nearly jumped out of his skin to answer it. Until he saw that it wasn't Skylar calling.

You could call her.

"Gabriel." It wasn't entirely unusual for them to call when nothing was going on. They did share a business after all, and Caleb knew that life got lonely for his friend, as he toured the world and made his deals. But there was little likelihood that this call wasn't related to Becca's news and threats of the oncoming legal storm.

"I found the information," Gabriel said in lieu of greeting. "My PI friend came through and I have what we've been looking for. But, Caleb, you're not going to like it."

And that was exactly what he wanted to hear, one more scoop of shit salad on the back of hearing from his ex-wife, worrying about his business and watching the woman he cared about to the point where it terrified him walking out of the door, and he was here for more bad news.

"Lay it on me," he said.

Gabriel was silent for a moment and Caleb appreciated that he didn't ask if he was sure. He wasn't sure and he might just say no. "Magnet Enterprises," Gabriel began, "is a shell company, like we originally thought. It exists in an official capacity in name only. There's no contact information and the business's address is just a PO box. But here's where it gets a little weird."

Caleb sighed and gave up on loading gear into the truck. He sat down on the edge of the fence and pressed the phone to his ear.

"Sounds like weird is bad."

He could picture Gabriel's expression, even as the tension grew across the phone line.

"Weird isn't good," Gabriel admitted. "Magnet Enterprises is a shell company for Standard Incorporated, but they don't exist either. We traced them through three offshore banks with a little digging, and found a name, James Halifax. Followed that name through several major cities in the United States, until we got to DC." He paused, and Caleb thought about asking him to stop right there, to not share whatever terrible information he seemed to have waiting on the other end of the line.

"The official company trying to buy the land," he said quietly, "is Wedgeworth Capital and Investments, Caleb."

If he kept speaking, Caleb wasn't sure. The pounding of blood in his ears created a cacophony of waves and thunder and he couldn't hear a damn thing over the sound of white-hot pain coursing through his body.

'I realized that I couldn't be the person they wanted me to be, so I left.'

How much of what they had shared had been a lie? Had she fabricated a daughter across the country so when the wolves came sniffing at the door she would no longer be by his side? Was that why she had fled after Becca's call? Why she had started the fight, claiming it was about them, about their undefined future, when it had really been about her escape, her way of getting out of whatever it was that had happened between them before he realized the extent of her betrayal?

"Caleb, are you there?" Gabriel's voice was worried and rough on the other end of the call, as if he had been speaking for several minutes and hadn't gotten a response. It was likely. Caleb had never felt more detached from the natural world. He was a farmer with the dirt of the earth under his feet and the sensation of falling off the edge of the world.

"If it counts for anything, we didn't see Skylar's name on any of the information we searched," Gabriel tried. But that didn't seem to matter. All that mattered was that he now knew the way she felt coming apart in his arms, giving herself over to him completely, and she had played him for a goddamned fool. He had given her his binds, and though he'd be an asshole about it, underplayed exactly how important she was to him in a desperate attempt to save himself more heartbreak, that didn't change the fact that she had come out to Montana with the intent of getting under his skin. Hell, maybe she had even hacked their computers or taken photos as evidence of what they did at The Ranch. Maybe she had been planning to seduce him into giving up the land and everything that went with it. It didn't matter. All of a sudden, nothing in the world mattered at all.

"I have to go." He hung up without waiting for Gabriel's reply and called Skylar's number, the number he had been afraid to try for two whole days, his actions now fueled by rage and hurt rather than regret. It went straight to her voicemail. He tried again. On the third call, he gave up and threw the phone into the bed of the truck. It would have smashed to pieces with the force of his anger, if not for the alfalfa bales he had piled there just a few minutes before, back when he had thought things couldn't get any worse.

As it had turned out when he had been dropped by the team, when the doctors had told him he would never play professional baseball again, when Becca had walked out of their life and left a gaping, wounded hole, things could always, always get worse. And with Skylar, with the hot razor cut of betrayal she had left in her wake, he didn't think they could ever get better again.

* * * *

She parked the car in a cloud of dust, left her bags in the trunk and ran into the lodge, but Caleb wasn't there. He wasn't in the back of house either and he wasn't in the stables or the corral. She found Dante and Reece repairing a line of fence near the barn and sounded half wild when she asked them where he was.

She hadn't admitted the truth to herself until she was on the second plane, from Denver to Bozeman, that her feelings for Caleb went further than a week-long fling. She hadn't admitted to herself until she was fifty miles on the road to the Sinclair Ranch that she couldn't possibly go back to the way she had lived her life before, not now that she knew him, not now that she had opened her heart and given over her body to a man who understood her in ways she barely understood herself.

And she hadn't admitted, until this very moment, frantic and panicked with the weight of it bubbling up inside her and the man it was for nowhere to be found, that she loved him. She didn't wear his binds for a temporary promise. She hadn't known it at the time, but when she had accepted them, she had accepted them for life, and she was willing to wade into the deep waters and confess the hard and dangerous truths, if it meant the possibility of a life with him.

"How's Callie?" Dante asked, leaning on the shovel. Any other time, she would have appreciated his asking, would have appreciated his caring, but right now she had more important issues on the mind.

"She's going to make a full recovery," Skylar managed. "Where's Caleb?"

Even in her frenzied state, she couldn't miss the look the two men shared, but they pointed her to a small hill by the back door to the lodge. Then she wasn't thinking about Dante or Reece or any of it. She was only thinking about him.

She slowed a few paces before she got to him. His back was turned, his shoulders bunched, tension emanating from every muscle in his big beautiful body. Had it been the call from his ex-wife that had put him in such a state? Had it been the news that the Sinclair Ranch was in trouble of some kind? Or was it her? Could she be so lucky as to have found a man who had missed her in these two days as much as she missed him? Skylar could only hope.

"I almost fucking bought it."

She had never heard such harsh words from him before and she froze in her tracks. His back was still turned to her, and it seemed he tightened up even more with her presence.

"Bought what?" The words, the tone of his normally enticing voice, had chills running down her spine.

"Bought your pretty little act." He did turn then, and she saw absolute fury behind those beautiful eyes. *Fury, pain, hurt. So much hurt.*

"What act? Caleb, what on earth are you talking about?"

"Don't pretend you don't know," he said. He was large and imposing but even now, even with the full of weight of his anger and pain, she didn't fear him. He would never hurt her, with the exception of breaking her heart, but she would have walked right into that trap of love and affection and forever herself, and willingly.

"I don't know," she replied. "I came back because I can't go back to my life without you. It took a smart kid and some tough love from my best friend to see, but I couldn't stay away."

Was it her imagination or were his eyes glistening with tears? *For what?* Maybe the emotions of the last few days had clouded her mind, because she was having a damn difficult time making heads or tails of what was going on right now.

"I wished it were real, Skylar," he half-growled, leaning into the wild beast she knew he kept inside. "I wish it were all real. But I learned a long time ago that wishing doesn't do a damn thing."

"I don't know what you're talking about, but it doesn't matter. I came back to tell you that I can't live without you, that…that I'm falling in love with you, Caleb. I love you."

He didn't bat an eyelash, didn't move at all, and Skylar felt the hot press of tears at the backs of her eyelids.

"I wish I believed you," he said, repeating his words again. He started to walk away, and she followed him, desperation rising in her throat as she realized exactly how wrong things between them had gone.

"Please believe, me," she said. "It's true. I love you. I think I've loved you since the moment I saw you. Nothing has changed."

"Everything has changed."

He didn't elaborate and she didn't have the chance to ask what *everything* was because they were interrupted by the arrival of a large black SUV pulling up to the back of the lodge. It arrived in a plume of dirt and dust, too quickly for the mountain roads, and with the air of city slickers who would be happy to leave the moment they were able. Skylar wasn't focused on them, wasn't focused on the movement inside the vehicle or the sounds of voices as passengers exited. She was watching Caleb intently, trying hard to figure out what Chapter she had missed in the book, when she saw something she would never have expected.

"Kennedy?"

She must have fallen asleep on the plane, because there was no way that she was seeing her sister here, after nineteen years, on a mountain top in Montana as she confessed her love to man who apparently no longer wanted her for reasons she couldn't even begin to understand.

"Skylar?"

Kennedy looked beautiful. Even after nearly two decades, her older sister had an air of elegance and grace that belied little of the conniving woman Skylar knew existed below. Her dark hair was coiled tight and low, and she wore a pantsuit that would have made their mother proud.

"What the hell are you doing here?" Skylar asked, her confusion mounting by the moment. "Father couldn't just get one of his thugs to hunt me down in DC?"

She heard a bored cough from over her other shoulder and turned to see another familiar face she had never expected to see again.

"Richie…" It hurt to say these old names, ones that no longer meant anything to her, not after all this time. The hurt almost overpowered the confusion, but it didn't overpower the mounting fear at the nape of her neck that said the arrival of these two relics from her past couldn't possibly mean anything good.

"It's Richard, now," he said. He'd been just a boy when she had left, thirteen years old and more interested in riding his horses than learning at Father's knee. He had cried in her arms the night she had said goodbye to him, had begged her not to go. It seemed she wasn't the only one who had changed so very much these past years.

"And we're not here for you. We're here for Mr. Cash, actually."

Skylar turned, sure her jaw was about to hit the ground, and looked at Caleb. His expression was that of a man ready for a fight, but that confusion marked the corners of his mouth too. Well, he was going to have to get it elsewhere today, because she was long, long overdue for one and it had come right up to her front door. She stepped in front of Caleb. He still had a head on her, but this wasn't the kind of battle where muscle won the day.

"And what business, exactly, do you have with Mr. Cash?" she asked. "Is the business of blackmailing and threating his company? Is it the business of stealing his land out from under him by any means necessary? Do tell, Richie, what in the ever-loving hell are you doing here?"

Richie…*Richard*…sucked on his teeth and Skylar resisted the urge to grin. She had followed the news and pieces of her family's business, knew of the dirty deals and shady trading that brought them so much money. It seemed unlikely that if Caleb and the Sinclair Ranch were being threatened by some unknown organization and her siblings happened to show up after nineteen years out of thin air, that the two were unrelated.

"Step aside, Skylar. This doesn't concern you." He paused, cocked his head to the side and grinned the way her father had used to when he thought he had an opponent beaten. "Or does it?" He looked back at Caleb. "It makes perfect sense that we would find you in a place like this. After all, you do have a history of acting the slut."

Caleb moved so quickly she didn't see it happen until Richard was on the ground, his hand wrapped around his nose and blood streaming between his fingers. Skylar crouched down at his side.

"See, in order for your words to hurt me, I'd have to care about what you think. And since what you think is that blackmail, coercion and intimidation is the way to get what you want, I don't." She leaned in even closer. "Tell Father that you're going to walk away from Duchess. You're never going to bother the Sinclair Ranch again, and you're going to offer every single business you ran out of town the price twice over if they want to take it back."

He spit blood on the ground and it stained the dust between them.

"Why the hell would I do that?" he asked. "When we're so close to getting what we want?"

"Because I'll go to every major newspaper, every national television program and famous journalist I can find on Twitter and I'll tell them exactly what Father keeps in the safe in the hidden room behind his office," she said. "I'll give them details and evidence and sources."

Richard narrowed his eyes. "You're bluffing."

She wasn't, actually. Skylar knew all manner of what Richard Wedgeworth the elder kept in his safe, and she had taken evidence of it as insurance when she had left. Some was old, probably past the statute of limitations, but she knew that even if he couldn't be legally punished, it could deliver serious blows to his company's upstanding image—and the trust of his investors. She didn't condone blackmail, but she was more than willing to fight fire with fire.

"It doesn't matter if she is." Kennedy stepped forward and Skylar swiveled to look at her sister. Kennedy looked so much like herself and so different too, a woman of polish and shine and luxurious. A woman Skylar had never gotten to meet, not with the way their lives had turned out. "I have all the backups on my server and in the cloud. We're going to walk away from this town, just like she said, and we're never going to look back. And when we get home, I'm walking away from the company. She's our sister, you asshole."

She caught Skylar's gaze and held it, and Skylar could see a world of hurt, of longing and regret for so much lost time. She reached out her hand without thinking and Kennedy took it. Skylar knew this hand, had held it when they were young and had big dreams and big imaginations. So much time had passed between them. Their lives had led them a world apart, but Kennedy was here, now, and that was all that mattered.

Seemingly emboldened by Skylar's touch, she turned back to Richie and continued. "I'm sick of this company anyway, the lying and the cheating. Blackmailing! Threatening! That's not how a good, honest business acts and I've been turning a blind eye for far too long. I don't want to look back in twenty years and realize I'm too much like Mother and Father to change."

The words felt like the fresh spring rain after a long, dark drought. They felt like cool air in a heatwave, like ocean water on her toes when the sun had been beating on her back in a desert of loneliness and loss. They overwhelmed her, made it hard to breathe and even harder to know what to do or say next, and so Skylar just stood there like an idiot, watching the woman she hadn't admitted to missing for so long handing over an olive branch.

"We've done some terrible things to you, Sky," she said. "But I can try to be better."

Skylar nodded. "I'd like that," she said. The tears that had nearly fallen moments early now sprang free for an entirely different reason pressing hot against her eyelids now. "I'd like that very much." Then, without thought or inhibition, she wrapped her arms around her sister and squeezed. It was only a moment, but the touch felt like an eternity, like an answer to prayers from long, long ago. It wasn't too late for them. She could have her sister back.

After a moment, they broke apart and Kennedy turned to Caleb, who had been standing still as the mountain itself since he had broken Richie's nose.

"This is me," she said, handing over her business card. "I'll make sure you don't have any trouble here again. But if you do, don't hesitate to call me." Then she looked at Skylar.

"I'm sorry that it had to be something like this that brought you back into our lives, Sky," she said quietly. "But I am happy for the outcome. When you're back in Washington, I hope you'll call." She handed over another card and when Skylar glanced at it, she smiled.

"Same number," she said quietly.

Kennedy nodded. "Same number." She walked around to the driver's seat of the SUV and paused at the door.

"Get up," she said to their brother. "Or I'll leave you here and go back to city alone."

That seemed to do the trick, and Richie scrambled up, cursing and muttering about lawyers and assault under his breath the whole time. He wouldn't get far — their father had always been into the idea of 'becoming a man' and Richie showing up at home with a busted nose would end worse for him than anyone else.

She watched the car turn around in a puff of dust, watched Kennedy take herself and Richie slowly down the mountain, the large vehicle getting smaller as Kennedy put more distance between them — and yet, so much less distance. Skylar wasn't going to kid herself that connecting with Kennedy again would be easy, but she was grateful for the chance, nonetheless. The thought sat comfortably on her mind until they were well and truly out of her sight. Then the weight of all that had happened, all that had been said and all that remained unspoken, rested in the air.

"Skylar... I..."

It was her turn to keep her back to him, her turn to feel muscles bunched with tension, to refuse to look him in the eye. The arrival of her past in a gleaming Cadillac had been enough to catch her off-guard, but now that Kennedy and Richie were out of sight, the riot of emotions coursing through her veins came to the surface in a single fell swoop.

"No, Caleb," she said quietly. "Don't."

"But…"

She turned to him then, at the sound of desperation in his voice, so different from all the passionate pleas they had shared this past week, so different from the confident, supportive man to whom she had given so much, the man who had helped her to crawl out of the shadows of her own life to become who she really was. She could barely recognize him in the man who stood before her now, and that was more devastating than having lost her family for nearly twenty years.

"You didn't even ask." Her voice came out shriller than she had expected, the catch of tears at the back of her throat making her wild and loosened from the reins that had first brought her back to him. "Fucking hell, Caleb, you just got some false lead from some friend of a friend and instead of asking me, instead of even bothering to tell me, you just fucking assume that I've been lying to you, that I've been playing you and manipulating you?" The tears were from anger and she wasn't ashamed of them.

"I know Becca did that to you and I'm damn sorry for it, but I'm not her. I'll never been her, and if you can't see that, then you don't know me at all." The bitch of it was, that he did know her, just as she did know him. It didn't matter if it had been a week or a month or a year or a lifetime — she knew Caleb Cash and she had thought he knew her. He tried to speak again, but she cut him off.

"You are a goddamned hypocrite," she said, her voice getting very, very low now. "You ask me for my trust, ask me to turn myself over to you in submission, and I do. Damnit, I trusted you with everything and the one fucking time you're supposed to just trust me in return. At least enough to want to know more."

They had an audience now, Rhylee and Van at the back entrance to the Lodge, Reece and Dante coming up from the stables.

"Well, here's your damn trust back. I don't want it." She wrapped her hand around the necklace and gave it a small tug, then remembered that he had locked the clasp and she didn't have the key. "I'm not yours anymore, *Master*." She spat the word out on the ground. "And I never will be again."

Thankfully, Rhylee was at her side in an instant, which meant Skylar didn't have to keep her energy up any longer than she already had.

"Skylar, wait." He called for her, and even in her state, she could hear the absolute devastation in his voice. "Please don't go. I... I love you."

She turned, looked him in the eye and repeated the same words he had said to her not an hour before.

"I wish I believed you."

Chapter Eighteen

When Rhylee came back up to the lodge later that night to grab Skylar's car and suitcases, Caleb made sure he'd gotten there first. He hadn't thought he could ache for the anger and hurt he had felt earlier in the day, but he did now, so overcome with emptiness that he found himself wandering the grounds and not paying any attention to where he was going. This should have been a night of celebration—Wedgeworth Capital wasn't going to terrorize the town of Duchess any longer and Skylar had come back. For him.

Then he'd gone ahead and done the one thing that made it impossible for them to move forward. He hadn't trusted her. Hell, he hadn't so much asked her, had done nothing more or less than assume the very worst, that she had been playing him, manipulating him, taking him down with her pretty words and her stunning smile. She had been right, when she'd said she wasn't like Becca, that Becca had tainted him for trust, for the love of another woman. She had been right, too, when she had said that it didn't matter. It didn't matter. Things with Becca had ended terribly, but he was a grown man, responsible for his own feelings and his own actions, and very, very much regretting the choices he had made today.

"How is she?" He cornered his sister by the car, only to be on the receiving end of a brutal glare.

"Why do you care?" she asked. "That was some rough shit, Caleb. I don't know everything that happened, but I know she didn't deserve that."

"I do care," he said. Even Rhylee's censure wasn't enough to break through the fog that clouded his thoughts. In the years since he had been in the lifestyle, he had made mistakes, but none had ever been so monumental. She hadn't just submitted to him, the night in the water under the moon. He had made promises to her too, promises to care for her, to always support her, to make sure no one ever hurt her again— and he had gone ahead and thrown those promises out without a second thought. He deserved the anger from Skylar, the glare from Rhylee, and he deserved so much more.

"Well, you have a funny way of showing it," she said. "Skylar's going home on the next flight out of here, Caleb, and she's not coming back. I suggest you accept that now."

She loaded Skylar's suitcases into her truck and slammed her door with more force than was necessary, before pulling out onto the dirt path. In an instant, her car was on the main road and taking his last vestiges of Skylar with it.

Instinctively, he reached for the chain around his neck as he had been doing since the night she had gone to California, but, of course, it wasn't there. He had slipped it into her suitcase, with a note, expressing every apology he would never be able to say out loud. Rhylee was right. He didn't deserve Skylar. But that didn't mean he wasn't going to do absolutely everything in his power to fight for her anyway.

* * * *

"Sage, when are you sending me those prints? I have the perfect place to set up a show for you."

She jotted down his notes and ended the call with the promise of more information forthcoming. She had been back at work a week, and it still felt as though she had taken a short trip to another planet, explored epic new lands, defeated evil villains and returned to earth only to see that nothing had changed. Nothing *had* changed — at least, not on the outside. Her home office was still sunny and bright, afternoon light coming in through a triptych of windows and illuminating boxes stacked on the floor and frames leaning against the walls.

Her clients had been happy to have her back in town, and DC still bustled with the wildness of a city where the very future was being written, but it didn't feel the same. She didn't feel the same. Even with her regular calls in to Callie to check in on her progress and healing, even with her lunch dates with clients and her short text chats with Ev, text chats for fear that she would reveal too much to her best friend in person, Skylar knew this was a tentative peace she had brokered with herself.

Her life here in DC was good. It had been great until Callie had left, until Greece, until Montana, until she had finally understood that it was time to make her life her own, until she had been exposed to a world of opportunities that she had felt deep in her bones were the right ones for her. She had been happy, until she had realized how much more there was. She had been happy until Caleb.

She reached for the bottle of antacids she had been keeping in her desk drawer and popped a few, focusing on the fake, chalky fruit flavor rather than considering the real source of the ache in her chest—an ache no amount of medication could cure. To come back to DC after Montana was to go back to vanilla ice cream after trying every flavor in the shop. It was still sweet and delicious, but it was no longer enough all on its own.

It didn't help that Caleb wasn't letting her go. She didn't know if that was for better or for worse, didn't know if she ached for the small packages at the door every day, for the flowers and gifts that came unbidden. Sometimes she listened to the messages he left her every morning and every evening and some afternoons, but most of the time she deleted them, unable to hear his voice without wondering how everything had gone so shit-side up. He wasn't supposed to be anything to her, and yet, in barely a week he had become both the most important person in her life and the one most capable of hurting her.

Her pity party was soundly interrupted by the creaking of her front door and Skylar's heart dropped into her stomach. On top of everything, it seemed like she was going to have to deal with a break-in too, because that was clearly how this month was going to go. She grabbed her phone off the desk and moved into the corner of the room to get a better view of the entryway, her blood pounding in her ears, all hurt and anguish from Montana momentarily forgotten, until…

"Sky, I brought coffee."

"You damn near scared me half to death," Skylar managed, coming out of the room to the sight of Ev standing in the entry, looking beautiful and put together and holding two cups of coffee. Skylar wondered if she would ever feel that put together again, would hold that much of a grip on her own life, her own feelings, ever again.

"It's been a week since you got back and you haven't given me anything to work with here," Ev said. She placed the coffee down on the counter and tucked the spare key that Skylar had completely forgotten giving her into her purse. "Something is wrong, really wrong, Skylar. As your best friend, it's my duty to figure out what the hell is going on."

Skylar sighed and came around the kitchen counter to grab her coffee. Iced, splash of almond milk, one pump of vanilla. Ev knew her coffee order, had her spare key and had been in the hospital not two hours after Skylar herself, when something was wrong with Callie. If there was anyone in the world who would understand, who Skylar could open up her heart and soul to and share her darkest moments with, it was Ev.

Knowing that rationally didn't make it any easier on the heart.

Before Skylar could open her mouth, however, before she could even begin to explain why she hadn't told Ev what was going on—and what explanation would that have been?—Ev stepped around her and into the living room.

"You haven't unpacked?" she asked. "Skylar..."
She hadn't been able to do it. Unpacking would have meant admitting that the whole thing was over, one giant, disastrous waste of time that had irrevocably

broken her heart and left it in pieces on a Montana mountaintop. Unpacking would have meant putting the entire Chapter behind her, and with it, Caleb, with it, the woman she had become in those too-short, blissful days. Her fear of the memories within those bags, the outfits she had worn for him alone, the scent of the fresh mountain air, had even driven her to stop at the local pharmacy to pick up toothpaste and deodorant, so she didn't have to go digging.

"He didn't trust me," she managed. "When it was most important, he didn't believe in me."

That had been the crux of it. He hadn't asked her. Hell, he hadn't even told her what he thought he knew. He had merely waited for her to prove herself until he believed it. For a man who had asked for so much trust, for so much sacrifice, that he wouldn't give her the same in return was devastating.

Ev was wrapping Skylar in an embrace then, holding her tight and allowing her the chance to release all the pent-up, overwhelming, terrified emotions she had been feeling for the last week, for the last two weeks, for the last nineteen years. She had thought, in finding Caleb, in her decision to return to Montana, to return to him, that she had been making a choice for herself, a movement forward in her own life, independent in a way, just as Callie was now independent in a way. It was a chance for her to do something for herself. And she had wanted it desperately.

Far more desperately than he did, it had turned out. It wasn't just Caleb, though that was so very much of it. It wasn't just that her heart had felt cleaved in two by his ability to distrust her so quickly, to give over to the fear and question left behind by his ex-wife with such ease. She missed the woman she had become in Montana too, missed the life she had created in her mind, of morning rides, of fresh mountain air, of a choice. Washington DC was an amazing city and it had been Callie's home, Skylar's home, their entire lives. It was the backdrop to a million memories that she would always cherish. But she had stayed in the city because she had more important things on her mind when she had first found herself pregnant with Callie, then because she had been a young mother, then because of school and work and friends. The draw of Montana had been the first time she had ever wanted to move, and she missed the opportunity now denied her with a painful, hard sensation in her chest.

But mostly, she missed Caleb.

Ev held her as she cried, whispered soothing nothings in her ear the way Skylar had done for Callie when she was little, promised her that it would be okay, that she was strong, and *she* would be okay. Then she offered to have Caleb quietly killed and buried because she *knew people in the FBI*.

"Don't you take a vow to uphold the law or something?" Skylar asked through a wash of tears. "And thanks for the offer, but no. I don't want him dead. I just…"

She wanted him back. She just wasn't sure if she would ever be able to offer him the same level of trust and intimacy they'd had before.

"You don't need to tell me everything," Ev replied, when even Skylar realized she wasn't going to finish the sentence. "Why don't I order us some lunch and help you unpack these clothes?"

Ultimately, Ev unpacked, while Skylar sat on the couch, drinking her coffee and occasionally switching through the television channels. It was the middle of the day and she should have been back at work, should have been tackling new projects and putting out feelers for new clients, but a soft rain had started and Ev had put Joni Mitchell on in the background and the comfort of her best friend helped Skylar to feel more like herself than she had all week. Until Ev made a sound over her shoulder.

"What's this?" she asked.

Skylar looked over the edge of the couch to see the small piles Ev had made, clothes, toiletries, books and work stuff, but she was referring to a small envelope in her hand. Skylar narrowed her eyes.

"I don't know," she said. "I didn't pack that."

Ev handed it over and Skylar's heart double timed when she recognized the handwriting of her name on the front of the otherwise bare envelope.

Caleb.

"You don't have to open it."

If she hadn't been consumed by the weight of the small envelope in her hand, she would have thanked the heavens for friends like Ev, for the support and love she'd had behind her at every stage of this wild and exciting journey. As it was, Skylar could only think about that small envelope, and what the hell it was doing in her suitcase.

"He must have slipped it into my suitcase before I left," she muttered, turning it over and holding it up to the light. It didn't provide any more clues. "I don't know how." Rhylee had gone back up to the Sinclair Ranch to grab Skylar's things, after Skylar had taken refuge at Rhylee's own house close to town, so Skylar's bags hadn't been accessible for more than an hour at the most.

Suddenly, it felt incredibly important that she open the envelope.

She started a small tear. Then her speed increased, her movements driven by desperation and a keen, carnal sense of longing. He'd sent his apologies, in the bunches of flowers and the other gifts, in the voicemails and texts. But she somehow knew that this one would be different. After all, it had been his very first.

Sunshine

His handwriting was straight and bold as if each line were intentional and thought-out.

I know I don't have any right to call you that. As it turns out, I've never had any right to call you that. Everything that happened between us this week was built on trust, communication and openness. My actions undermined that trust and for that, I can never apologize enough.

I can see now that I have been both a coward and a hypocrite – not only was I quick to distrust you, but part of me hoped it was true because I was afraid of how much I had come to feel for you in such a short time. I should have asked you to stay the first time you left, and I should have begged you not to leave the second.

The binds I gave you the night by the waterfall were meant to symbolize our growing relationship in and out of the lifestyle. I no longer deserve to call you mine, and I certainly no longer deserve your submission. That's why I've enclosed the key, so you can free yourself. It is my deepest wish that one day you might decide to put them on again, of your own volition. In the meantime, I hope my actions won't turn you away from our lifestyle and I hope, in time, you can forgive me and look upon all that we shared with fondness. I know I will never, ever stop thinking of our time and I will continue to fight for you, sunshine.

I have always been yours,
Caleb

She tilted the bag and a small gold chain that matched her own slid out, the key to the necklace on the end.

He had sent her freedom. He had sent her a way of out of their...*relationship?* He had given her back the reins as a symbol of his own submission, of his own bowing in supplication, of his own trust and sacrifice and love for her. She gripped the necklace so tightly the chains dug into her skin, but she didn't care. If he was willing to lay himself out so thoroughly for her, if he was willing to show that he understood how he had hurt her, that he knew the value of all she had given him, and that he would lay himself on the altar to beg for forgiveness, then the fight was lost.

Hope beginning to flicker in her stomach, Skylar searched for all the reasons he had hurt her, for the pain she had felt at his callous words, and found it was flowing away from her, a grasp of something gone by the time she opened her palms.

When Skylar looked up, Ev had a knowing expression in her eyes.

"You deserve happiness, Sky," she said quietly. "All this time, you've been punishing him, but you've also been punishing yourself, for all the transgressions, the mistakes, for trusting Caleb enough to hurt you." Damn, being friends with a profiler was a tough business. "But deep down, you know you can trust yourself. And in that, you can trust him."

She *could* trust him. She wanted to trust him. And the fact that he no longer demanded her submission, but left the choice up to her, was proof enough that he understood its value, and that, ultimately, she was in the one in control of it. And herself.

"Don't finish unpacking," she said with a half-wild grin. "I think I need to catch a plane."

Ev's face split into a grin. "Damn straight you do."

Those ridiculous suitcases had gone from DC to Montana to California to Montana and back to DC. And now, same clothes, same cowboy boots, same detective novels, they were taking one last trip back to the wild — and Skylar was pretty damn sure it was where her suitcases were going to stay. But first, she had to make a quick stop at the post office.

Chapter Nineteen

He had given himself a week. He had given himself a week to call and send flowers and text her and grovel. Then he was going to stop. Not because she didn't deserve it—hell, she deserved so much more. He'd catch the moon in a fishing net and string it onto a necklace for her if he could. But he couldn't take any more. He couldn't take missing her this much and he couldn't take thinking about her with the kind of fierce, desperate hope that made a man turn into some wild, unhinged, unrecognizable version of himself.

"Mail came."

His friends had been walking on eggshells around him and Caleb couldn't say he blamed them. They had been there for him, next door and literally a phone call away, when he had first gotten injured and had been facing the complete derailment of the career he'd anticipated for his entire life. But this derailment was so much worse. This wasn't just the sense of lost opportunity, of being set adrift after having had a map for so long. This was a raw, aching wound that he honestly wasn't certain would ever heal, and it had turned him into a real grizzly fucking bear the last few days.

Even Rhylee had taken the hint and kept her distance, and for his sister to read a room and decide not to comment on another person was indicator enough that he was behaving badly. Rhylee didn't scare easily.

Nor, for that matter, did his friends. But Van, venerated war hero and victor of his own inner battles, most days at least, was hanging back from Caleb, as he shuffled a small pile of envelopes in his hand.

"I'm assuming we haven't heard anything more from Wedgeworth?" he asked. Even saying the name made his throat feel too tight, like he was perpetually drowning without ever drawing his final breath.

"No word," Van replied. "Though downtown is starting to look normal again."

Ever since the day Skylar had had it out with her family members — then him — in a turn of events he couldn't have anticipated in a hundred years, the threatening, coercive phone calls had stopped completely. Several businesses had moved back into town and Duchess was thriving again. He supposed he had to be thankful for small favors.

"That's good," he managed. The vaguely positive tone of his voice made Van's expression change and Caleb wondered if it might be easier just to go live on a mountain top somewhere and never speak to anyone ever again. It was pretty much all he felt up to after reliving the look in Skylar's eyes a dozen times an hour, as she realized what he was implying, as he made the biggest damned mistake of his life.

"This came for you." Clearly Van was chomping at the bit to get away from the bear's den, so Caleb took the envelope and gave him a tight nod. He wouldn't have called what the other man did *scurrying*, exactly. But he imagined it wasn't Van's finest retreat.

The envelope was light, decorated in stamps and ink that indicated it had been shipped express overnight and he wondered who it might have been from, even as the smallest flicker of hope ignited in his chest. He squashed it down. He wasn't allowed to hope. He wasn't allowed to take refuge in the fantasy of Skylar forgiving him. He did it anyway.

Until he opened the envelope.

There was no note, no return address, no signature of any kind, but, of course, he didn't need one, not when he slid his familiar gold chain out of the envelope in his hand. His key. To his binds. And her lock.

His stomach fell into his feet, leaden and heavy, and if he had been thinking properly, Caleb would have commended Van for getting the hell out of Dodge. This made it official. This meant there was no going back, there was no Skylar and Caleb, no Sunshine and Master, not ever again, not for him. It was over.

"I was hoping you could do the honors."

His mind was playing tricks on him. Maybe he had entered some dark parallel fantasy world where he heard only the things he wanted to hear. And he wanted to hear her voice.

"When we start again, I mean. I thought you might like to start again."

He turned his attention away from the far mountain, away from the slice of golden sun cutting across plains and hills, and there she was, standing in the sunlight, hair catching the wind, eyes glowing. Even in a fleece jacket and boots, she looked like an avenging goddess, like the queen who knew her place in her land. And she looked very much like the woman Caleb loved.

"Hi." She stuck out her hand. "I'm Skylar." She smiled up at him and Caleb couldn't help himself. He fell to his knees in front of her, dazzled by her beauty, overcome with relief and love and joy.

"Caleb," he managed. "I'm Caleb."

"It's nice to meet you, Caleb," she said. "I think we're going to get along very well."

He stood, picked her up in a single motion and swung her around until she was laughing and swearing at him.

"You came back," he said finally, slowing, bringing her back to standing on that Montana mountaintop, sun in her hair. "You didn't break the clasp on the binds." He had noticed that when he had spilled the chains into his hand.

"I didn't open my suitcases until yesterday," she replied. "That's when I saw your note. I've been wearing your binds for more than a week." The very idea make Caleb want to howl at the moon, but he merely contented himself with wrapping her closer to his body, with holding her tightly so she would never let go. He knew he would never let go again.

"I want to do it again," she said quietly, but he was holding her close enough he could practically hear her heart beating in her chest. "With everything else that happened that night and the week after, I want to do it again. Forever."

His eyes were hot and his throat was tight when he repeated,

"Forever."

And there, in the golden light illuminating their little mountain top, he took Skylar Wedgeworth's hands in his and looked her in the eyes.

"Will you be mine, sunshine?" he asked her. "Will you trust me to care for you and love you and cherish you for the rest of our time?"

She smiled and held his gaze. "Will you trust me to care for you and love you and cherish you for the rest of our time?" she repeated.

"Without a shadow of a doubt."

Her smile widened. "Then yes," Skylar replied.

He placed the necklace back on her smooth skin and locked it, then slipped the key around his own neck.

Skylar's grin widened. "Caleb, a thousand times yes. I love you."

The rest of her words were muffled when she kissed him, hard and clumsy and full of joy and he kissed her back, kissed her until they could barely stand, until they half fell, half sat on the ground, kicking up a mess of dust and dirt, too consumed with thoughts of each other to pay any mind to their clothes or hair.

Skylar was his. Mind, body and soul. And he was hers.

Forever.

Epilogue

"Do you think she'll like it?"

Caleb hadn't been unsure about much where Skylar was concerned since she had found him on the mountain top nearly a year earlier, but as he surveyed the cabin, he found that his palms were a little sweatier than usual.

"Yes, doofus, she's going to love it."

Callie was the spitting image of her mother, a spitfire of brilliance and smart mouth who was never afraid to speak her mind. She loved wildly and openly and had accepted the odd circumstances surrounding their meeting and the six brothers and one sister Caleb came with without so much as batting an eye. He had thought Rhylee on her own was a terror, but when Rhylee and Callie colluded on something—and they colluded on everything from advances in microbiology to hot pop stars—Caleb knew to make himself scarce.

Still, it had been surprisingly easy to go from life on the Sinclair Ranch to life on the Sinclair Ranch with

Skylar and Callie when she was home from school, and today they were finalizing Skylar's life out in Montana with the last touches on her new gallery, a beautiful wooden structure located near the lodge, perfect for the travelers who came through and a setting that matched her choices in art and craft. She had found some amazing local artists and they were already selling successfully thanks to her support, even if she had been working out of one of converted rooms at the lodge. In that time, she had been able to double her attention to female artisans, helping the community in ways Caleb had never even considered.

Without any more nudging from his sister, he had also taken up helping the community in his own way, with coaching at the school. Maybe it was because of Skylar herself or maybe it was because of the kind of man she made him into, with her joyful smile and her unquestionable love, but he didn't hate being around baseball again, and the opportunity to help others on their career only made him feel enthusiastic and engaged. He was a far cry from the man he had been before her, no longer questioning his place in the world or what kind of person he was without the career he had always trained for.

"She's here." Rhylee poked her head in the door. "Want me to stop her?"

Caleb came out to meet Skylar who was walking up the path from the main house in a beautiful floral dress that somehow made her look both sophisticated and rustic all at once. He had taken the city girl out of the city, but Skylar remained her own version of Montana, just like she remained her own version of everything — it was one of the very, very many reasons why he fell more deeply in love with her every day.

"Can I go inside finally?" she asked, but her eyes were teasing and she wore that dazzling smile that knocked him on his ass every time. The gallery had been his moving-in gift to her, an obvious choice that matched her career and her passion with their newly shared home, kept her close to him and gave her an office to contact buyers and artists from around the country.

While she'd had her input on everything important to the space, Caleb had wanted to build it as a surprise and had enlisted the help of his less-enthusiastic friends to complete the process. It had been a fun and exciting experience for them all, but Skylar had been begging to go inside for weeks, and now that it was finally finished, he couldn't wait to share their project with her — the final promise that he wanted her here forever.

"You can go inside," he said, and opened the dark wood door to let in their small group, Rhylee and the guys. Even with half a dozen large cowboys in the room, it was still large and spacious, with several skylights letting in the brightness of the mountains without taking up any valuable wall space.

"We used your dimensions," he explained, coming up to stand beside her, "so you've got space for three to five full shows, and smaller exhibits." He indicated several treated branches suspended on thin, clear wires from the ceiling. "Plus you have hanging room."

With her work in crafts and textiles, she had a lot of art to display that didn't necessarily hang on the walls. That had been the reason for the branches and the hidden nooks and shelves that decorated the space, but which could be removed for larger pieces.

"You also have a quilt wall, a jewelry display and a lounge." The lounge overlooked the mountains, purple in the late setting sun, and was decorated with classical cabin apparel but finished with an upscale shine, courtesy of Callie and Rhylee's input. It also had a sliding barn door that could be closed for private meetings with clients.

Skylar was quiet as she walked around the space and Caleb had to wonder if he had overstepped. He shouldn't have tried to come across the conquering hero to create the space for her, but she had seemed so pleased that he wanted to make her something, wanted to settle them into their new home here together. Maybe he shouldn't have pushed.

"It's amazing."

Her voice was husky and he knew her well enough by now to understand that she was overcome with joy and love, and the feelings surged through his as well, overwhelming and wild. Just one more terrifying event to tackle before the day was done.

"You like it?" he asked, not quite realizing how afraid he was that she wouldn't until he was finished. Her smile was even brighter now than it had been when she walked through the door.

"You thought of everything," she said. She turned to Van, Dante and Reece who were standing by one of the gallery's center walls, looking only a little too large for the space. "I know you all helped so much and it's just a little overwhelming how much you've made this place feel like home."

Beside her, Callie slipped her hand into Skylar's without saying a word, and Caleb's love for his new and surprising family member bloomed all over again. Had she put up any sort of fuss about Skylar moving, about leaving their old life and finding a strange man in the mountain, Skylar wouldn't have done it. He knew how much Callie wanted to make her mom happy, and he loved her for that.

"You're part of the family now," Rhylee said. "And we're damn happy to have you."

"Actually," Caleb cut in, "there's one more thing I want to show you before the crying, okay?" Both Rhylee and Skylar leveled him with a glance but he just grinned. The nerves were gone. All he felt now was excitement, overwhelming and powerful and full of opportunity. "I hung the first piece on the wall. I hope you don't mind."

He led her over to a standing wall close to one of the picture windows, where a framed miniature hung off the side, inconspicuous and quiet, until she stepped closer. And gasped.

It was an illustration of the mountaintop where she had accepted his binds for the second time, where they had confessed their love to each other and promised forever, where the next chapter of this amazing story had begun. And on that mountain top, a scruffy cowboy was down on his knees, holding out a small box and looking up at a woman in a white dress like she was the center of his world.

And she was.

When she turned around to face him, Caleb was already on his knees, holding out a matching box to the one in the illustration and looking to Skylar the way he had looked at her for the last eight months, two weeks and three days.

"Sunshine?" he began, but before he could get another word out, she tackled him.

"Yes." Her voice was thick with emotion and Caleb laughed.

"You didn't let me finish."

She was crying and laughing now and he was too. "Finish, please, finish."

"Will you do me the greatest honor of lighting up my world for the rest of our lives?" She held back and he grinned. "You can say yes now."

She tackled him to the ground and kissed him square on the mouth in front of their friends and family.

"Yes, yes, yes." It was the only word that mattered, in between the kisses and the tears. Then their friends were helping them off the ground and he was sliding his ring onto her finger, a small band of gold and light blue stones that reminded him of her, of the sun shining bright in the sky, twinkling gold against blue.

His friends hugged him and wrapped Skylar up in their arms and he found himself flanked by Rhylee and Callie, who, thinking as one, elbowed him in the arm, before Rhylee was hugging him too, then Callie then Skylar, right in the middle. More than half a decade ago, his life had derailed, and he had taken a path he had never expected for himself. Two years ago, his wife had left him, and he'd been wandering the mountains of Montana wondering what the hell to do next.

And now, now his heart was fit to bursting with the love and support and joy of friends and family and the woman he loved most in the world. And when he looked out to the mountains, to the golden sunlight cutting across the purple plains, the future looked bright indeed.

That night, in the privacy of their shared cabin, Caleb showed Skylar exactly how much he planned to cherish her, to care for her, to love her and protect her for the rest of their lives. And, as he brought her to the edge of pleasure a dozen times, as he tormented and tortured her with desperate, aching lust that drove them both crazy, he knew, without a shadow of a doubt, that she was his other half. They had found themselves in the darkened halls of The Ranch, bared their bodies before they had bared their souls, but wrapped in excess pleasure, in the heat of the roaring fire, and the powerful love that had taken them so far apart and brought them back together, there was no question that this was forever.

"I love you," she murmured into his arm, after their night had slowed and the toys had been put away and his satiated fiancé was snuggled close to him in the kind of embrace he had never again expected for himself.

"I love you too, sunshine," he replied, holding her close, pressing their bodies together like he couldn't bear to be apart from her. "I'll always love you."

Truer words had never been spoken.

Want to see more from this author?
Here's a taster for you to enjoy!

Triple Diamond:
The Lovin' is Easy
Gemma Snow

Excerpt

"A *what?*"

Against the din of the ancient window air conditioner chugging into the room, Madison's voice had a tinny, almost petulant sound. But of all the things she had expected from the impromptu meeting with some family estate lawyer she'd never heard of, *this* wasn't it.

"A *ranch*, Ms. Hollis," Mr. Sidney replied, the tone of his voice indicating that he'd picked up on her confusion and ensuing frustration with the afternoon's events and that, frankly, he didn't care. "The Triple Diamond Ranch in Wolf Creek, Montana, to be exact."

Madison rubbed her hands over her face and tried to make sense of everything. Mr. Sidney had contacted her a week prior about a will left to her by some uncle on her mother's side, an uncle she'd never heard of, from a mother who'd been gone some eighteen years now. She took a deep breath, trying a different tack.

"Are you certain this is my uncle"—she glanced at the stack of legal documents two inches thick on the desk before her—"Mason?"

Mr. Sidney peered down at her over the wire rim of his thin glasses—a remarkable feat, given that she had at least two inches on the man, who sat short and boney in the chair across the desk.

"Mr. Mason Westerly King first arranged this inheritance with Sidney and Sidney nearly two decades ago," he replied. "We've had ample time to determine and confirm your identity, Ms. Hollis."

Madison resisted the urge to roll her eyes, but only just. Mr. Sidney's attitude came on the tail of what had already been the week from hell. She sighed, her heavy breath spilling out of her mouth like a deflating hot air balloon. *It's only Wednesday.*

"Mr. Sidney, I'm afraid I still don't quite understand. What am I supposed to do with a ranch"— she gestured with her hand—"I don't know, eight, ten hours away from here?"

He gave a slow blink. "My advice, Ms. Hollis, is to go inspect the ranch yourself. You have all the information on the mineral rights and past financial records. Once you get the lay of the land, you can determine whether you wish to sell or keep the property. But otherwise, after I get your signature on these forms, I'm afraid there's not much else I can help you with."

Madison did scowl that time, but with her head bent over the stack of papers while signing the requisite lines, he couldn't see it. She was perfectly pleased to be done with Mr. Sidney for good, but he was wrong about one major thing. She wasn't going to decide whether or not to keep the ranch—she had decided the very first time he had mentioned the word *inheritance*. No, the second she got out to Montana, she would sell the damn thing and be done with it. Maybe then everything would go back to normal. *Ha. Yeah, right.*

Home of Erotic Romance

Sign up for our newsletter and find out about all our romance book releases, eBook sales and promotions, sneak peeks and FREE romance books!

About the Author

Gemma Snow loves high heat, high adventures and high expectations for her heroes! Her stories are set in the past and present, from the glittering streets of Paris to cowboy-rich Triple Diamond Ranch in Wolf Creek, Montana.

In her free time, she loves to travel, and spent several months living in a fourteenth-century castle in the Netherlands. When not exploring the world, she likes dreaming up stories, eating spicy food, driving fast cars and talking to strangers. She recently moved to Nashville with a cute redheaded cat and a cute redheaded boy.

Gemma loves to hear from readers. You can find her contact information, website details and author profile page at https://www.totallybound.com

CPSIA information can be obtained
at www.ICGtesting.com
Printed in the USA
BVHW031556110521
607040BV00003B/300